Ryan's eye snapped open and stared furiously at the ceiling

His lips peeled back from his teeth, and a roar of shock and horror erupted from his throat. His arms and legs jerked into spasmodic motion, forcing everyone to hold on for grim life.

Mildred withdrew the knife for a moment, turning to look at Dean. Tears coursed down the boy's cheeks. "Hold his head still with all your strength," she demanded.

"Don't move, Dad!" he cried. "We got to save your life."

But it did nothing to calm the anguished man. The next time that the knife touched the yellowed gash, the one-eyed man screamed and kicked out. Doc and Krysty nearly fell off the bed, and J.B. and Michael used every ounce of their strength to keep hold of his arms.

The doctor peered intently at the wound. The core of pus still throbbed, veined with crimson. But the heat of the flensing knife seemed to have cleaned up the area around the edges of the ragged sore.

Ryan, mercifully, had passed out.

"How is he?" Krysty asked.

"Looks cleaner. Don't know if his heart can stand up to my doing it again."

"Do it. Leave a shred of poison and it'll kill him."

Also available in the Deathlands saga:

JAMES AXLER

DEATH LANDS

Twilight Children

A GOLD EAGLE BOOK FROM
WORLDWIDE®

TORONTO • NEW YORK • LONDON
AMSTERDAM • PARIS • SYDNEY • HAMBURG
STOCKHOLM • ATHENS • TOKYO • MILAN
MADRID • WARSAW • BUDAPEST • AUCKLAND

Two of my greatest loves are speculative fiction and rock and roll. Rog Peyton, who runs the Andromeda Bookshop in Birmingham, England, is one of the world's experts on both. For that, and for other good reasons, this is dedicated to him. With my sincere thanks.

First edition June 1994

ISBN 0-373-62521-9

TWILIGHT CHILDREN

Copyright © 1994 by Worldwide Library.

Printed in U.S.A.

The historical, deconstructive and complex-dynamic-based approach to the future looks at an imbalance of the chronologically senior against the junior and predicts proactive hypotheses. Put more simply: one day the small number of kids are likely to try to slaughter the large number of the old.

> —*Hope You All Die Before You Get Old*
> by Dave Lankhford, Runcible Press, 1992

Chapter One

The cold fingers of fog were drifting away, out of Ryan Cawdor's brain.

The one constant thing that someone could safely say about making a matter-transfer jump was that there was *no* constant thing about making a jump. Sometimes there were dreams during the period of unconscious blackness, gibbering nightmares more often than sweet dreams. Sometimes there was no sensation of time passing at all. The mind closed down and then opened up again like a parched flower during a spring rain, with no awareness that anything at all had happened—except the one certainty that the complex machine, dating back nearly a hundred years, to the last days before the nuclear holocaust devastated the Earth, would definitely have taken you somewhere different. It could be a hundred miles away, or it could be ten thousand miles to another of the so-called gateways that had been built and buried in one of the chain of triple-secure military complexes known as redoubts.

The trouble with jumping was that you had no control over the destination. All the instructions had vanished during the nuking and the long winters that followed, and every living person who might once have known was long, long dead.

Most mat-trans jumps left you feeling like someone had sliced the top of your skull off, scrambled the soft tissues inside, then jammed the lid back on. It also churned up your guts like you'd been strapped under a war wag going flat out across forty miles of bad road.

As Ryan lurched back toward waking, he was aware that this particular jump hadn't been too bad.

"Some you lose and some you draw," he muttered.

When he'd locked the sec door on the chamber in the redoubt in Kansas, triggering the mechanism, everyone there had been holding hands, and the armaglass walls had been a virulent shade of cherry red.

Now his hands were free.

Several jumps ago something had gone horrifically wrong, and Ryan and his six companions had all ended in different destinations, only getting back together by a mix of judgment and luck.

Ryan opened his good eye.

The walls in this gateway were a dull, indeterminate shade of gray, closer to black than white.

The metallic disks dotted across the floor and the ceiling had resumed their usual color, and the white mist that often flooded the chamber during a jump had vanished.

Everyone was there.

Krysty Wroth, next to him, lay sprawled against a wall, her brilliantly red, sentient hair packed tight across her shoulders, crowding onto her nape as though it were trying to protect her.

His eleven-year-old son, Dean, was halfway across Krysty's lap, his eyes squeezed shut, moaning softly, looking like he'd be next to recover consciousness.

Nineteen-year-old Michael Brother was doubled over, his knees drawn up in the fetal position, a tiny thread of scarlet blood at the corner of his mouth, as though he might have nipped his tongue during the jump.

J. B. Dix, Ryan's oldest friend and armorer to the group, was also beginning to stir, muttering in his sleep. His normally sallow face was even more pale than usual. Without his glasses, his eyes looked oddly naked and unprotected. His scattergun was at his side, his Uzi clutched to his chest.

Mildred Wyeth was next. The black doctor was breathing very heavily, her mouth sagging open, her left hand gripping J.B.'s right.

The last of the seven friends was Doctor Theophilus Algernon Tanner, who was stretched out next to Ryan, flat on his back, his hands folded across his stomach, holding the gold-plated J. E. B. Stuart Le Mat blaster.

Normally it was Doc who had the biggest problem in using the mat-trans system. Even at the best of times his brain was a touch unreliable, and the pressures of jumping sometimes pushed him a few inches closer to the edge.

On occasion it had even pushed him completely into the abyss of insanity.

Ryan looked at the wrinkled face, the silvery stubble showing through the leathery skin.

It wasn't that surprising that Doc often found life in the last part of the twenty-first century hard to bear.

He'd been born in South Strafford, Vermont, on February 14 in the year of Our Lord, 1868, and was married to Emily Chandler twenty-three years later on June 17. Had two children—Rachel, born in the second year of their marriage, and little Jolyon, born to the happy parents two years later.

In November of 1896 Doc had been in Omaha, Nebraska. In a nanosecond he was transported to a laboratory in a discreet and heavily guarded building somewhere in Virginia, one hundred and two years later.

It was a time of extreme fragility and suspicion in international relations, and the United States of America had poured limitless squillions of dollars into the ultrasecret Totality Project, which explored arcane and esoteric possibilities for future warfare.

One of its subdivisions was Overproject Whisper, which, in its turn, had spawned numerous other research missions. One, Cerberus, involved the transfer of matter from one location to another, which became known as "jumping."

Another research mission was called Operation Chronos and focused on time trawling.

Chronos had some spectacular and hideously disgusting failures. Not many of their targets ever arrived in the year 2000 either physically or mentally whole. Some simply disappeared.

But Doc arrived—mentally scarred, but he arrived and lived.

However, they had picked a bad subject. Doc wouldn't sit quiet under their battery of tests and interrogation, insisting on trying by every means necessary to try to rejoin his wife and family.

In the end, the faceless military scientists got rid of him. They sent him forward in time, to the heart of Deathlands, where he came close to death before being rescued by Ryan Cawdor.

Michael Brother was also one of the tiny number of successfully trawled victims of Chronos, helped into the dubious future by Ryan and the others.

In the late 1900s he'd been taken as a baby into a closed-monastic order near Visalia in the Sierras. He'd spent all of his life as an oblate within the serene community of Nil-Vanity, then was sucked away by Chronos into the late part of the next century.

Mildred was also from the past.

But time trawling wasn't responsible for her being stuck in Deathlands.

Born in 1964, Mildred had become one of the country's leading experts on cryogenics and cryosurgery, the science of medical freezing. Ironically, at the age of thirty-six she'd gone into hospital for routine minor surgery.

Which had gone wrong.

She'd been frozen, deeply unconscious, not long before the missiles darkened the skies of the world and civilization came to a grinding halt.

Not with a whimper, but with a megabang.

During the exploration of one of the concealed redoubts, Ryan and his friends had come across Mildred, sealed away, her life-support system powered by a long-running and reliable nuke generator. And they had brought her back to the land of the living.

"Feel sick, Dad."

"Hang on, Dean. Just try to sit up and keep your head still. It'll pass."

J.B. was also coming around.

His first movement was to fumble his fingers over the stock of the Uzi, then reach down for the Smith & Wesson M-4000 shotgun on the floor.

"Not too bad, as jumps go," he said, his voice sounding hoarse. "You okay, Ryan?"

"Yeah. Wasn't a bad one."

Krysty sighed and opened her emerald eyes, turning to Ryan and giving him a lazy, jump-stoned smile. "Hi, lover. Once again we made it with nothing worse than a nauseous headache."

He stood, reaching a hand down to help her to her feet. The heels of her dark blue Western boots skidded a moment, but Ryan steadied her.

Dean and J.B. were also up, stretching, easing the kinks out of their spines.

Michael was coming around, his eyes blinking fast, his head shaking from side to side. "Hey," he said, "I don't feel too bad. We did jump, didn't we?'' He looked at the sludge-colored walls. ''Oh, yeah. They were red last time, weren't they?''

Only Mildred and Doc were still unconscious.

''Can't feel much.'' Krysty closed her eyes and took a dozen slow, deep breaths. ''No. Air tastes like it generally does. Flat and... There's a kind of bitter, chemical smell to it, though. Least it's not corpses like the last place.''

Mildred sneezed, making them all start. ''Bless me.'' She shook her head, the tiny beads in her plaited hair clicking softly against one another.

''All right?'' the Armorer asked, never a man to use three words when two would do the job.

''Think so.'' She looked inward for a moment. ''Yes. Not too bad. Must be one of the better jumps. I suppose we really have... Walls were that screaming red last time, weren't they? Not sure this gray's much improvement.''

Now everyone was up but Doc, who slept on, oblivious to the six friends gathered around him. Mildred put her index finger against his throat, checking his pulse. ''Slow but not that slow,'' she announced.

J.B. was examining the walls of the gateway chamber. ''You notice this, Ryan?''

''What?''

''Sort of careless built.''

Ryan looked more closely and saw what J.B. meant. The sheets of armaglass didn't quite match up, and some kind of sealant had been pushed into the gaps.

One of the walls was cracked, and two of the ceiling disks were actually hanging loose.

"Yeah. That's the first time I've ever noticed anything like that."

"Last year's loving, bitter, still remains," said a familiar deep, resonant voice.

Ryan turned. "Doc's on his way back out of the darkness," he said.

"There is no memory of her here." Doc's eyes blinked open, staring sightlessly at the ceiling, gradually returning to focus on the walls and the six faces looking down at him. "Upon my soul, my dear friends, I wondered when we seven would meet again. And here we are, but not upon a blasted heath. A bastard wreath. Last teeth." He struggled to sit up, helped by Mildred and J.B. "Have we successfully completed our jump? I see we have, from the change in hue. But I confess that I feel less sickly than is usual at such moments. Perhaps I am finally building a tolerance to such events."

"We all feel better than we normally do after a jump." Ryan looked around. "If we're all okay to go, we can take a look at where we've finished up."

He didn't need to tell them all to draw their blasters.

Coming out of the gateway was one of the potentially triple-red scenarios in Deathlands. But this time was oddly different.

Chapter Two

Normally there was a small anteroom immediately off the actual mat-trans chamber. The size varied a little from redoubt to redoubt, but they were usually somewhere around ten feet square, plainly decorated, mostly unfurnished.

This time it was simply a cave, roughly hewn from bare stones, a dull gray rock lined with narrow seams of shimmering green quartz. The ceiling was less than eight feet high, and the walls were only about six feet apart. Other than a patina of very fine dusty sand, it was empty.

Michael Brother ran his finger down the stone. "Still got the marks of the chisel," he said. "Looks like it was done only yesterday."

"Must've been one of the last redoubts to be built before skydark," J.B. suggested.

Nobody had ever known how many of the massive military fortresses had been constructed during the last years of international tension before nuke-day came and went. When Ryan had ridden with the Trader they'd been lucky enough to come across several.

One in the Apps had contained several mothballed war wags on which the Trader had based his whole operation. Another, one hundred and fifty miles north of the ruins of Boston, had contained enough stored tanks of high-octane gas to keep them in jack for years.

All that was known was that the chain of redoubts had been a part of the Totality Concept and they'd been constructed under conditions of the utmost secrecy. Despite the whining of the pinko conservationists, the government had compulsorily taken over huge sectors of the country, including thousands of square miles of some of the most favored, most beautiful and most isolated national parks.

The irony was that the eventual war was so sudden and apocalyptic that the redoubts proved to have absolutely zero military significance and most showed signs of having been rapidly evacuated in the last few weeks of what remained of civilization and order.

By traveling from gateway to gateway, Ryan and his companions had located many more hidden redoubts, in varying stages of preservation or destruction.

But they'd certainly never come across one that looked like it was still being built.

Not until now.

"Look here, Dad!" Dean had gone ahead, through the crudely carved doorway into what would normally be the control room for the entire mat-trans operation. There would be rows of consoles and banks of comp desks, with dancing gauges and flickering dials and lights. All were powered by a hidden nuke gen, pulsing away in the deeps of the fortress.

"There's something seriously wrong here, lover." Krysty had followed the boy through, pausing and looking around her in disbelief.

"It's just a hut, Dad."

The walls and ceiling of the building were bare rock, with the same thread of emerald quartz running through it. But it was barely a quarter the size of the normal control room. There were comp consoles, but only twenty or so, mounted on makeshift tables, some with broken legs propped on red bricks.

"The air," Mildred said, sniffing. "Not like it usually is, either."

Ryan breathed in, half closing his eye. The woman was right. It didn't have that dusty flatness that recirculated air normally had. This was bitter and sharp, like a vaporized acid-rain storm.

There were loops of multicolored cable draped all over the place, with junction boxes and ends of sprayed bare metal. It was amazing that the gateway was still functioning after the best part of a century—though it crossed Ryan's mind to wonder whether this mat-trans unit might actually have been rebuilt within the past few years. If so, it was a staggering thought and opened all kinds of unsuspected possibilities.

J.B. was walking slowly around, reaching up to touch the rock overhead, examining his fingers. "It's dry. This couldn't have run if it had been damp."

"These portals to the outer world are unlike any that I've ever seen. They resemble nothing more than an ordinary door on a frontier outhouse."

Doc was exaggerating a little. But only a little.

The familiar vanadium-steel sec doors, weighing hundreds of tons and operated by a complex system of gears and counterweights, weren't there.

There was a single wide door, with an ordinary handle like you might put on a garden shed. It was made from wooden planks, some of them warped and crooked, with a length of one-by-four nailed across to hold the thing together. Once upon a time it had been white, but the paint had dried and flaked, like buildings in a desert ghost town.

The strip lights overhead were harsh, and at least a quarter of them had malfunctioned.

"I don't get it." Ryan shook his head. "This isn't like a mat-trans unit. It's like some handyman got a load of bits and pieces that fell off the back of a wag and he just put them all together and found he'd built a gateway. But the damned thing worked. Got us here all right."

"Mebbe we should leave right now. Could be safer." J.B. tapped on the door with the butt of the Uzi. "One-armed baby could knock this down."

"Why not open it?" Dean asked. "Least take a look outside, huh, Dad?"

"I guess..."

The door wasn't even locked.

The boy simply turned the handle and pushed, and it opened, revealing a dark, constricting passage.

"Wait," Ryan snapped. "Don't go rushing into that like a double stupe, Dean. Could be anything out there."

"A most maleficent odor," Doc commented, applying his swallow's-eye kerchief to his protuberant nose. "Like touching your tongue to tarnished brass."

Mildred laughed. "Nice one, Doc. Know what you mean. It isn't that deathly medical smell from the other redoubt in Kansas, but it isn't normal."

Ryan went to the door, pushing past Dean. The place was so small and cramped that there hardly seemed to be enough room for the seven of them.

Once again, the contrast with other complexes they'd visited was stark. Instead of the wide corridors, with antiseptically clean concrete walls and high curved ceilings, this was more like the mouth of a tunnel built by gnomes. There were no lights and not a sign of the usual ob-vid cameras.

The passage was around ten feet at its widest, so low that Ryan felt he had to stoop, oddly aware of the enormous weight of rock and earth hanging over him.

As his eye became accustomed to the gloom outside the control area, Ryan realized that there was a very faint glow visible away to his right.

"I think this place is totally open," he said, holding the SIG-Sauer at the ready. "Doesn't look like artificial light, and the smell of the air is stronger."

Doc's description hung in his mind. The taste was definitely metallic in origin.

One by one they followed him, all stooping, though the ceiling was just high enough for Doc, tallest at six feet three, to stand straight without bumping his head.

"Hi, ho," Mildred sang quietly. "Looks like we're all going off to work."

They didn't have far to go.

The light ahead grew steadily brighter, showing that the whole place had been hacked out of living rocks, also showing that the gateway seemed to be on its own, without the usual surrounding redoubt.

Ryan held up his hand as the rough-floored passage curved sharply to the right, almost in dogleg. "Hold it just a minute. Krysty?"

"Yeah."

"Feel anything?"

"No."

"Nothing? Must be some sort of life around."

Krysty pressed the tips of her fingers to her forehead. While she concentrated hard, Ryan became aware that the fiery sentient hair was curled tight around her head and neck, often a sign of potential danger.

"No." Krysty bit her lip. "Can't pick up anything at all. Not close by, anyway."

He nodded. "Best go see."

The tunnel simply ended in a roughly circular opening, with daylight beyond.

One of the oddities about jumping was that it screwed up time in a way that Ryan had never been able to work out. Sometimes you might jump in the middle of the night and you'd find that you'd arrived at the next redoubt in the middle of the afternoon.

Now his wristchron said that it was eleven minutes after nine in the morning.

"Think we might be near the sea," J.B. said. "Walls are wet and the air seems damp."

Ryan was first out of the passage, finding himself on a ledge of sculpted rock, barely ten feet wide. To his left there was a steep wall of granite, rising into a thick mist. To the right, the ledge became a trail, winding out of sight.

There were no doors and no sign of anything else that might have been a part of a bigger complex.

"Don't get it," Mildred said. "Anyone could just have walked in and smashed up the gateway. Nothing to stop them."

"Maybe it's so completely isolated that there isn't anyone here. Not even a passing mutie." Ryan holstered the SIG-Sauer. "Fireblast!"

"What?" Krysty jumped at his loud exclamation.

"Mebbe this a triple-bad hot spot." He checked the tiny rad counter stitched into the sleeve of his coat.

But it showed only a placid, safe green.

J.B. also checked his, finding the same reading. "No hot spot."

"Where are we?" asked Dean. "Looks like the inside of a stickie's ass."

Everyone fell silent, looking around them.

There seemed to be a mist both above and below them, cutting off visibility. The air was cool and moist, the cliffs jagged and irregular, rising all around them. The more Ryan stared, the stranger it all looked. He couldn't find any trace of life anywhere, not even smears of moss or lichen on the boulders.

He scuffed his boots in the dirt, noticing that even the most ubiquitous plant in Deathlands was absent. The tiny multipetaled daisies, with their delicate yellow-and-white coloring, were found from Alaska to the Gulf.

But not here.

"Yeah, J.B.," he said. "Where are we?"

The Armorer fumbled in his pockets and pulled out the microsextant, squinting around the sky. "No sun," he said. "Still, find where light's brightest." After a couple of minutes he shook his head. "Can't get a reading at all. Might be something wrong with this." He put the miniature instrument back in his coat. "Try the compass and see if... Dark night!"

They all gathered around him, seeing that the needle on the magnetic compass was swinging wildly, from north to south, then revolving in a blur of speed, not settling for a moment at any particular point.

"Anomalies," Doc pronounced. "They are known to exist in certain places where the underlying strata contain high proportions of lodestone. Some kind of considerable electromagnetic disturbance."

Michael had walked to the edge and was peering cautiously over the brink. "Can't make out anything. Though... No. I thought I saw something flying through the fog, way below, but it vanished." He hesitated. "Something real big."

Mildred joined the teenager. "Looks to me like the valley of the shadow of death, doesn't it? The land that time forgot. Ultima Thule. End of all things."

There was a puddle of water by Ryan's boots and he stooped and dipped a finger in it, noticing that there was an oily, rainbow sheen on it. He touched his finger to his lips, immediately spitting the substance out and rubbing his mouth. "Bitter! Tastes like Badwater, down in the heart of Dry Valley."

"Do you think there could have been some kind of chemical pollution here?" Mildred asked. "Not radiation. There was a lot of talk before I got to be ill and got frozen, talk that the Russkies had all sorts of nerve and chemical agents. Nobody knew if it was true. Been some used in the Middle East, in the eighties and nineties. This just looks like some ghastly leakage or spillage of some industrial poison."

"Ow!" Dean slapped at something. "Stung me on the cheek. Look, I got the fucker."

Nobody corrected his language, all of them looking at the bizarre insect that he held, trembling in the palm of his hand.

It was an inch and a half long, its narrow body a dull gold color. There were four sets of filmy gray wings, and its head had six separate eyes, like tiny orbs of polished copper. At the end of its tapering tail there was a sting, grossly out of proportion to its overall length.

"Like a scorpion," J.B. stated, examining it carefully. "Hooked and barbed."

Krysty peered at the boy's face, where a nasty lump was already swelling. "Keep an eye on that, Dean."

"Don't think it had much chance to squirt its poison in before I got it. Hurts like a bastard, though."

He tipped it off his hand onto the shale at his feet and crushed it under his heel.

"The whole atmosphere is redolent of despair." Doc looked around at the misty wasteland. "For once I would like my voice heard on behalf of making a jump again immediately. I have not been an eager apostle for this, but—''

Ryan held up a hand. "Sorry, Doc. But there's something triple-weird here. That gateway looked like it had been thrown together. No redoubt. Open to anyone passing through. Now we can't find any way of even knowing where we are. So, I figure we should explore a little.''

The old man shook his head. "I do see the gist of your thinking, my dear fellow. No doubt the rest of our little party agrees with you.'' He looked at the others. "Well, nobody disagrees with you. Come, then, let us leave this peak in Darien and venture into this slough of despond.''

Ryan felt more uneasy than he had for a very long time. The short hairs at his nape were prickling.

But, apart from the undoubted dreariness of the region, there didn't seem any immediate danger.

"Let's go look," he said.

Chapter Three

"This air's so rotten it makes you feel tired." Krysty was second in their skirmish line, with Dean following close behind her. "It seems like a part of the planet that Gaia must've overlooked."

As usual, the rest of the group was strung out, with J.B. bringing up the rear, the 20-round, 9 mm Uzi held loosely in his hands.

By the time they'd descended about one hundred and fifty feet, they found themselves in one of the swirling banks of fog. It was puzzling the way the banks of cloud kept moving around them, as there wasn't a breath of wind.

The stones were soft and crumbled beneath their feet, making progress unsteady and dangerous. At no point was the man-made track wider than a dozen feet, and there was no way of guessing the deeps that lay to their left. Dean had thrown a fist-size stone over and listened for its fall. But all they heard was what sounded like a human cry of pain, which wasn't repeated.

Once they were within the acrid mist, visibility was down to fifteen or twenty feet.

Ryan told everyone to close up and keep on triple-red alert, knowing from previous experience that muties loved to attack from the heart of fog or darkness.

There was still little or no sign of life around.

But Mildred pointed out that there were little tufts of sickly yellowish sedge growing in some of the cracks between the moldering stones.

The canyons were so deeply blighted that Ryan twice checked his rad counter, tapping it with his forefinger in case it was malfunctioning.

But it remained stubbornly in the safe, green level, showing no inclination to move toward yellow or orange, which meant there was no residual danger from the nuking.

J.B. was thinking along the same lines. "Nearest thing to a hot spot I ever saw," he called, his voice muffled and flattened by the damp fog.

The trail zigzagged sharply, the surface furrowed by rains and broken up by years of frosts. Ryan doubted that any sizable wag could ever have gotten up it. Now it would be totally impassable, except on foot.

There was a sudden swooping sound and all of them ducked, raising their blasters. Ryan stared up into the mist, aware only of something vast flying close by them, bringing with it the stench of rotted meat. The cloud was too thick to make out details, but Ryan had a momentary flash of a long leathery neck and an elongated reptilian head, with several sets of protruding, yellow teeth. It seemed to have a wingspan in excess of thirty feet, but it could have been distorted by the fog.

"What was that?" Krysty was standing upright again, facing the direction that the creature had taken. "Anyone able to see it properly?"

"Like a gator," Dean said, pointing his Browning vaguely into the slate sky.

"Flying alligator?" Mildred was perspiring, despite the dank chill in the air. "Seen most things, but—"

"I confess that I caught only the merest glimpse of the creature," Doc said. "But it bore a more-than-passing resemblance to what the boy said."

There were more pools of the oily water, lying in hollows and crevices, all of it so alkaline and bitter that it was hopelessly undrinkable.

At one of the labrynthine turnings of the track there was the rotted stump of a vast tree, a good five yards in diameter. Since it was one of the first signs of anything approaching normal life, Michael stopped to look at it. He recoiled in disgust, his face screwed up.

"It's a mass of sort of maggots. But they're big as your thumb and like white jelly."

Ryan was having second and third thoughts about the wisdom of carrying on with the recce.

"MY CHRON'S STOPPED."

J.B.'s voice, from a little way behind him, brought Ryan to a halt. He checked his own chron, finding that the numbers had frozen, showing a time only a few minutes after their arrival in the open air.

"Must be that electromagnetic thing that Doc mentioned. Screws up direction and time."

They were in a particularly thick band of mist, and the figure of the old man was only a dimly seen silhouette. "If you relied on a real timepiece instead of those tinny and cheapjack digital bits of frippery, then you might care to know that we've been on this shifting, whispering trail for just over fifty-three minutes."

Doc was holding his silver half-hunter in his right hand, angling it to catch the poor light.

"How come his chron has that kind of pair of needles to tell the time?" asked Dean.

"They are called 'hands,' dear boy," Doc replied. "My pocket watch is a good deal older than I am, which is saying something. It is also a sight more reliable than my body or my brain. And vastly and unarguably to be preferred against those 'wristchrons,' I believe."

He succeeded in making "wristchron" sound like something he'd just discovered on the sole of his boot after a morning stroll through a cow pasture.

Now they could catch the noise of running water, a sullen and deathly sound, less than a hundred feet below.

The height of the unseen peaks around, glimpsed briefly through the shifting banks of cloud, laid a leaden weight on everyone's heart, and there was none of the usual good-natured banter. The rocks underfoot were treacherous and slippery, taking full concentration to avoid a nasty fall.

Ryan began to notice more vegetation, though it was in keeping with the desolate place.

Stunted and mutated, it showed no recognizable signs of being a plant any of them could identify. The dominant color was gray—dark gray, with veins of sulfurous yellow running through it.

Most were bushes, though a stooped tree, crooked and broken, had occasionally found a foothold in among the crevices of the boulders, nourished by the poisonous water.

There was also more life.

Of sorts.

They saw no repeat of the monstrous creature floating low over their heads, though the fog occasionally echoed to bizarre cries, yelps and screams.

Ryan spotted some kind of mutie...*thing*. It wasn't exactly an insect or a lizard or an animal, but it was a vile mix of all three. Though it had six stumpy, clawed legs, they propelled it in a peculiar scuttling, sideways movement. The head, with a fringe of spiky hairs, was narrow and fierce, turning to hiss at the seven intruders into its domain. From snout to the quivering tip of its barbed tail it was less than nine inches, the skin a set of overlapping, mottled scales. The eyes were an opaque crimson, standing out from the skull on stalks that enabled it to glare in every direction at once.

"I'll chill it," Dean said, leveling his heavy blaster, but his father knocked his arm down.

"Next time you do something as triple stupe as that, son, I'll put you on your back in the dirt!" The anger rode high in Ryan's voice, and his good eye stared intently into his son's face. "You hear me?"

"Sure, sure." Dean backed quickly away. "Keep the rad green, Dad. No harm."

"No harm!" Ryan felt the pulse throbbing in the empty socket of his left eye, and he swallowed hard to control the red mist. "Little mutie bastard wasn't doin' us no harm. This is a shit-dangerous and fucking creepy place, Dean. I never saw anywhere like this. None of us did. Chrons don't run. Compass don't work. Sun doesn't fucking shine." The anger still burned in Ryan, but he could feel the blood leaving his temper. "We don't know what's out there, do we?"

"Sorry, Dad."

"Yeah. And I'm sorry I went off at you like a rogue gren launcher, Dean. But you pull the trigger on that Browning, and you could alert any living bastard within five miles that there's outlanders in their territory."

"See that now. Sorry."

"Never apologize, son. It's a sign of weakness." Mildred grinned at Ryan. "Not the best John Wayne impersonation in Deathlands, but the only one I got."

AT LAST THE TRACK BEGAN to level out.

It was lined with a kind of sagebrush, and decorated with gray-white berries that gave off a bitter dust if anyone brushed against them. They saw several more of the six-legged mutie creatures, but nothing that represented an obvious threat.

"There's the river." Krysty pointed to their left. "Gaia! It looks as inviting as everything else around here. Dismal isn't the word."

They stood in a row, all staring in silence at the slow-flowing water. Above them, the acidic layer of fog shifted in impenetrable coils, making it impossible to see anything more than a hundred feet high.

The river was forty to fifty feet wide, with a shelving beach on both sides. The rocks that protruded above the surface were greasy, looking as though they were composed of gray mud. The color of the water was an oily brown, but it was moving so unhurriedly that Ryan blinked, thinking he was a victim of a trick of the admittedly poor light.

"That river..." Doc began hesitantly. "I would swear that it was going past us in slow motion. Or are my tired old eyes deceiving me?"

Michael stepped down, perfectly balanced, over the banks of shingle and knelt at the edge of the river. He reached out slowly and dipped a hand into the water, pulling it hastily out, shaking his fingers and wiping them quickly on his black parka.

"It's warm, it stings and it isn't water!" he shouted to them.

"What is it?"

"Kind of thicker than water. Consistency of very thin honey, or cooking oil."

Before any of them could even open their mouths to shout a warning, something darted from the oily liquid, propelling itself toward the oblivious teenager's throat. There was only a moment for a glimpse, but Ryan had the impression of a large rat with fins and webbed feet, or a furred fish with a body and head like a rodent.

Though he was facing away from the foot-long mutie, Michael's astounding combat reflexes saved him from, at best, a nasty bite.

His right hand punched sideways, hitting the thing in midair, chopping it a few yards along the pebbles. It landed on its back, but wriggled over and propelled itself, not back to the safety of the river, but toward the kneeling man.

Mildred had her ZKR 551 drawn and cocked, and she sighted along the barrel of the Czech target revolver, glancing sideways toward Ryan, waiting for his word to put a .38 round through the malevolent monstrosity.

"No!" Michael called, uncoiling and standing with his legs a little apart, braced and ready for the attack.

They could all hear a faint mewing sound, like a kitten being tortured, coming from the thing's needled mouth.

Michael was wearing his sturdy knee-high hiking boots, and he waited until the mutie was within range of him. He kicked out once, sending the creature spinning along the shingle. He followed it, hesitating only for a second before bringing his heel down on it, crushing the small body into the stones.

He turned away with an expression of disgust.

"Skin must be like paper," he called. "It just burst open and rotted in front of me." He bent down. "Now there's just . . . like a sticky puddle of stinking grunge left."

"How's the time, Doc?"

The silver watch appeared from the fob pocket of his waistcoat. "Not too far off noon, my dear fellow. I was wondering whether it might be possible to find anything to eat in this godforsaken place." He laughed. "I have never seen a place that was so literally forsaken by the Almighty."

J.B. looked around them. "I'd be double surprised if there was a creature here that we could safely eat, Doc. Think about that rat-fish that went for Michael."

"What's that?" Krysty was shading her eyes, looking farther down the valley to where the strange river made a sweeping curve from the left.

There was a cluster of buildings, looking to be wood-framed, like some kind of frontier ville.

It was one of the last things that Ryan had expected to see in this hostile wilderness of acid water and fog and ghastly nuke muties.

"Might be some folks there," he said doubtfully. "Could even be food, Doc."

There were no folks.

But there were other things.

Chapter Four

"Looks like there used to be a real blacktop running along here—" J.B. had dropped to a crouch and was peering at the ground "—before whatever blanked out the whole region."

"That a real ville?" Mildred asked, her right hand resting gently on the Armorer's arm.

"Looks like it." He straightened and wiped his spectacles, easing the scattergun across his shoulders. "We going to go in, Ryan?"

"Guess so. From what we've seen since we left the redoubt—I mean the gateway—I hate to think what kind of human muties might live there."

"Looks graveyard creepy, Dad."

"Looks don't hurt you, Dean."

ONE OF THE SUPPORTING posts had rotted through, leaving the sign hanging slantwise. The paint had faded and weathered away so that it could barely be read: Welcome to Lonesome Gulch. The Famous Ghost Town of the Old West.

"We in the West?" Mildred asked. "This doesn't look like any part of the West that I ever saw."

Ryan shook his head. "Nothing makes much sense, does it? Still, we could find some shelter for the evening, then head back to the gateway and make another jump if there's nothing here worth staying for.''

There was another sign a little farther on for a parking lot, a yellow arrow pointing to the right, where there was a large bare stretch of what might once have been tarmac but was now a meadow of rank grass and spiked weeds.

"There's something called a company store." Krysty pointed. "Says it's the first stop and the last stop on the visit. Get your ticket there for the ghost-town tour."

The weather was as good as it had been since the jump. The mist had lifted, though it still hung below the surrounding peaks, and a few threads of watery sunlight seeped through the leaden clouds.

Beyond the store they could all see a street of ramshackle buildings, some of them without roofs, some with collapsed walls. In the distance there was a rusting railroad engine that looked like it dated back well into the nineteenth century, and a few rotting wagons.

Doc was fascinated. "Upon my soul. This is uncommonly like a return to the days of my youth." He shook his head. "Though I would hazard a guess that this place has been reconstructed for the benefit of the tourist industry."

As they reached the first of the buildings, the store, Doc was proved correct.

Under fly-smeared glass, there was a notice that contained the history of Lonesome Gulch, explaining how a local historical society had been formed in the mid-1900s to save and re-create the vanishing parts of the national heritage. Genuine buildings in various states of disrepair had been collected from all over the region and brought together, "so that our children, and their children's children might still be able to relish the romance and reality of the days of yore."

J.B. pushed the door of the store, ignoring the handwritten card that announced it was closed.

A bell gave a dusty tinkle, then fell off the wall, its bracket rusted through.

"I'll stay out and keep watch," Ryan said, leaning cautiously against the wall, half anticipating that the whole place would crumble into sawdust.

He turned quickly as he thought he saw something moving at the far end of the street, by the old locomotive. It moved in an odd way, part wriggling, part crawling, but he didn't react fast enough to be sure of what it was.

It certainly wasn't anything human.

The rest of them roamed through the shadowy interior of the store, which looked like it had been simply abandoned around the time of skydark.

"Look at this." Michael had found a big display case near the rear of the building. "What are they?" He held up a number of small sacks.

"Tobacco?" Doc suggested.

"No." J.B. untied the whipcord around the top of one of the bags and tipped the contents into his palm. It was fine grains, as black as midnight. "Blasting powder," he said.

"Some candy here." Dean called to his father, standing just outside the front door. "Can I try some?"

Mildred joined him. The candy was in narrow sticks, thinner than a finger, about six inches long, wrapped in crinkling twists of cellophane paper. They were in different sections, each one described in old-fashioned golden lettering.

"Cinnamon and mint. Julep and spearmint. Salt-water taffy. Clove and apple. Banana and coconut. Brings back my childhood, this place. I see what you mean, Doc."

"Can I have some, Dad?"

"Let's look around the town first. Before the light starts to get worse."

"Can I go on my own?"

The boy was unbelievably eager, hopping from one foot to the other. Ryan smiled and ruffled Dean's shock of black hair. "I guess so. But don't go beyond the main street, and yell if you see anything. All right?"

"Sure." The boy ran off.

Ryan called after him. "Yell if you even *think* that you see anything!"

The group split up.

Ryan and Krysty crossed over the main street, stepping down off the uneven planking of the boardwalk. J.B. and Mildred stayed on the same side as the store. Michael and Doc strolled together along the rutted center of the street, pausing to investigate any building that looked particularly interesting to either of them.

"See that," Krysty said, pointing to a torn poster stuck inside one of the windows of the nearest buildings. "They were going to hold a pack-burro race a month or so after the long winters started. Just where in Deathlands are we?"

"Lonesome Gulch. Says this was a typical homestead from the late 1800s. Let's take a look."

It was a sodbuster's shotgun shack, with a single hallway and the rooms opening off to one side, a small parlor, then a bedroom with bunks, and finally a tiny kitchen with an iron stove and hand-pumped sink.

Everything was rotting, the surfaces were all slightly moist, with a microscopic covering of mold.

"I'm amazed this place has stayed here as long as it has," Krysty commented. "All around's got the flat taste of death and decay. Why don't we go, lover?"

"Kind of interesting. Seems to me that the frontier villes in the old, old past weren't all that different to some of the frontier pestholes we see nowadays."

The next building, with a shingled roof that had managed to resist the hostile elements, had once been a combination dentist's and doctor's home. Krysty paused in the entrance, shuddering and putting a hand to her eyes. "Gaia!"

"What?"

"So much pain and misery here," she said, looking at a rusted pair of obstetric stirrups, standing in a corner like instruments of torture.

Ryan was examining some Victorian dental tools in a glass case, brushing away the dust with his fingers, wincing at the shape and size. He recognized some of them from his own infrequent visits to fangcarvers around Deathlands.

Doc stood with Michael a few yards farther up the grassy street, staring up at a building with an odd design of a protractor and a pair of compasses carved near the peak of the gable roof.

"A Masonic lodge," he said wonderingly. "First one of those that I've seen since being trawled to this dreadful future. Who would ever have thought that such a widely powerful organization could so simply vanish from the face of the earth."

Dean whooped to them, leaning out of the cab of the old locomotive. "You used to ride in one of these, Doc?"

"Indeed I did, my boy. Lynchburg to Danville was one of my favorite rides. And Durango up to Silverton, along the Animas. Smoke and cinders is what I remember best."

J.B. and Mildred had stepped into something labeled Carpenter's Shop and Morgue.

The walls were covered with a display of old tools, mostly disfigured with a patina of rust, their wooden handles long rotted away.

There was a coffin on two trestles, its chased brass handles tarnished and hidden under a layer of green verdigris. The lace around the edge of the pillow and the shroud had all yellowed and decayed.

Something rattled against the roof and both of them looked up, J.B.'s finger going to the trigger of the Uzi. But the sound wasn't repeated.

"Wouldn't mind spending some time around this place," the Armorer said.

He stood foursquare, stocky, staring up at an embroidered sampler, dated somewhere in the mid-1800s, and bearing a wobbly sewn signature of Esther Wingate. "Man cometh forth like a flower and is cut down. He fleeth also as a shadow, and continueth not."

"Must be odd for Doc." Mildred ran a finger along the top of the coffin, wrinkling her face in disgust. "Everything feels kind of sticky."

J.B. was looking out of the window at the back of the single-story building, wiping the glass with his sleeve. "Yeah. Whole atmosphere is double freaked. The fog's coming back again, rolling up from the river."

Doc was in the offices of the *Lonesome Gulch Courier,* admiring the heavy printing press, while Michael looked at the crumbling remnants of earlier copies of the newspaper, tacked to the lath-and-plaster walls.

"Says here they had some real heavy snow in January 1895." The teenager turned to Doc. "That before your time, Doc?"

"I was a lad of twelve when the worst storms in the history of the United States struck the Eastern seaboard, in 1880. Four or five hundred people died in the hurricane winds and monstrous falls of snow. I well remember, in Vermont where I was then dwelling, that there were banks of snow measured at fifty feet deep. Parlous times, young fellow."

Michael turned away. "Funny, you know, Doc."

"What?"

"Well, it's like Lonesome Gulch isn't a real place. The old papers talk about a holdup in the bank and a stabbing at the faro tables. Snow, a fire and stuff like that but none of it actually mentions *where* we are."

"Passing strange. But much about this region is a deal more than passing strange, Master Brother. Mistress Sister. Mistless twister. Blaster mother. Damnation! I recollect from my studies such foolish verbal confusion is known as 'aphasia.' An indication of some minor brain damage. Yet, that is clearly not true, is it?" He glowered back to where the teenager stood in the doorway of the print shop. "I said that— What are you looking at?"

Dean was leaning out of the starred glass of the side window of the old locomotive, imagining himself flying along steel rails at breathless speed, then his eyes were caught by something perched on the roof of the stagecoach barn, fifty yards farther up the main drag of Lonesome Gulch.

J.B. froze, turning away from the filthy window. Mildred had drawn her revolver, eyes turned up.

"What was that?" she whispered.

He touched a finger to his lips, catfooting toward the front door, blaster at the ready.

Ryan had opened the case and removed a fearsome pair of chromed forceps with jagged teeth, clicking them in his right hand as he lurched in toward Krysty, shoulder hunched to make him look more frightening.

"Don't worry, my dear," he jeered. "This will hurt you far more than it will..." He stopped, putting the instruments silently on the oilcloth-covered couch.

Krysty had already drawn her Smith & Wesson 640, looking out into the street.

"What?" she mouthed.

Ryan shrugged. They'd both heard something, a disturbance in the air, a noise that might have been a cry. But it hadn't sounded like it came from the throat of any creature either of them had ever known.

And on the roof they could all hear a scraping, scratching, grating, like the points of sharp knives being drawn forcefully over the splintered top of an old table.

Moving with incredible lightness for such a big, powerful man, Ryan eased his way to the doorway and looked out.

"Fireblast!"

Chapter Five

Abe had spent some years of his life as one of the best gunners on War Wag One.

He'd also been wounded more often and more seriously than any man that he'd ever known. Or woman. Trader had been perfectly at ease with having female members of the war wags' crews.

Abe's past life was shrouded in mystery. Over the years he'd told so many different stories to so many different people that he'd honestly lost touch with the truth. But the best times had been riding with the Trader.

It meant that you got showed respect.

There wasn't a pesthole from Portland, Oregon, to Portland, Maine, where they didn't know the Trader, a grizzled man with a heart of granite and eyes of frozen jet. They knew him and they feared him. There wasn't a gaudy owner, slut or hired gun in Deathlands who wasn't aware of the reputation of the Trader with his hacking cough and his battered Armalite.

You were with the Trader, or you were against him. There were just the two options.

Abe had always been with him.

When Trader walked clear out of life, Abe had been the last person to see him, watching the rangy figure as it disappeared into the dark forest long months ago.

Ever since that bleak time, Abe had been consumed by a desperate desire to know what had happened to his old leader. Word all around Deathlands was that Trader was dead, died in some mystic ceremony with an Apache shaman; died when a woman of seventy summers, who'd been his latest lover, slit his throat when she found him in bed with both her daughter and granddaughter; died when he had faced down an eighteen-foot mutie grizzly somewhere in the Shens; died when he got bushed by a hundred screaming, blood-crazed stickies. Trader chilled ninety of them, but the last ten finally overwhelmed him and sent him off on that legendary last train to the coast.

But all the rumors agreed that he was gone.

Abe had started to come around to accepting that it had to be true.

Then the counterrumors began.

Trader was alive and running the biggest whorehouse in the world, somewhere around Hawaii or Cuba or Brazil, depending on which story you heard.

One of the most insidious and powerful rumors suggested that Trader headed an unholy alliance; with the steel-eyed Magus, three-fifty-pound Gert Wolfram and his traveling freakshow, Marsh Folsom, Jordan Teague and his black-clad sec boss from the nightmare ville of Mocsin, Cort Strasser, and planned to take over the whole of Deathlands.

Abe had decided that he couldn't sit around and wait for someone to come along with conclusive proof that Trader was alive or dead.

So he'd struck off alone on his quest.

Now, within rifle range of the old ruined ville of Seattle, on the edge of the mighty Cascades, he had finally succeeded and was riding again with the Trader.

"SUCCESS. WILL STAY around Seattle for three months. Come quick. Abe." That had been the message that Trader had agreed should be sent to Ryan Cawdor and the others.

Most of the packmen and travelers that Abe had spoken to had agreed to take the message. Some asked for a handful of small change in return for the errand. Nobody knew where Ryan would be, but they were simply told what he looked like—tall man, well armed, one-eyed, with a woman whose hair was like spun fire. And they were given descriptions of the rest of the group.

Only one person had argued with Abe, pushing the smaller man around, until Trader walked over from the bar and stood right up in the stranger's face and gave him his thin, dangerous smile and asked if there was a problem.

There wasn't.

THINGS WERE DIFFERENT, in ways that Abe found difficult to quantify or understand. All the years when Trader had ridden the helm of War Wag One, often with at least one more of the huge armored vehicles in the convoy, Abe had been one of dozens of men and women who'd formed the crews of the wags.

He saw Trader then for many of his waking hours and his recollection was of having some good times, long talks and shared experiences with him.

Now he was slowly coming to realize that that was an edited version of the truth.

In fact, hardly anyone ever had long conversations with the Trader, except maybe John Dix and Ryan Cawdor, the three men sitting together around the guarded camp fires at the end of a day's driving or trading or fighting, talking, occasionally laughing.

Abe was now coming to recognize the fact that he'd hardly ever had a long talk with the Trader in his entire life. Maybe never.

Now he spent the whole day and long chunks of the night with his taciturn former leader, and it just wasn't at all like he remembered it.

Trader was content to go for hours on end without saying a word to Abe, sitting in a chair, or with his back against a convenient tree, looking vacantly out across a saloon bar or into the glowing embers at the heart of a dying fire.

A few times he would stir and draw out a reminiscence of some firefight or massacre that they'd shared, relishing the way they'd chilled their enemies, seeming to Abe to disregard their own fatalities and wounded.

The one thing that was like what Abe remembered was Trader's bleak toughness.

Two weeks after they'd finally met up, they were camping on the western ridge of the Cascades. The weather had been variable, often starting with heavens of sunrise, followed by a gradual thickening of the cloud from the Pacific and then a cold drizzle moving in over the mountains.

Trader had bought a bottle of home brew from a wizened old woman, her eyes almost blind with the pale milk of cataracts. It was so strong that even to flick a few drops from the tips of your fingers into the fire brought a "whoosh" of flame.

"Remember when those stickies stole a wag full of hard liquor like this, Abe?"

"When was that?"

"Must be ten years. In the Apps. Scranton. No, wait, it was down Odessa way, yeah, that was it. Odessa way. We'd camped near a broke freeway bridge."

It rang a vague bell in Abe's memory and he nodded. Already he'd found that the Trader still didn't take kindly to being interrupted or contradicted.

"Yeah," he said.

"Drink was so potent that they started spitting it into their big fire." He shook his head. "Them stickies surely liked a flame and an explosion." He threw his head back and laughed. "Got them both that night. Some of them kind of exploded when we threw them into the burning wood. Damnedest thing I ever saw, Abe."

Yeah, he remembered all right. Remembered now, like it had been that same night.

The stickies—there'd been about fifteen of them in the raiding gang—had made a try for someone from the wags. Who had it been? Cohn. The radio op had been out fishing in a narrow creek, near to sunset. Stickies had come after him. Abe closed his eyes for a moment, his right hand stroking at his long, drooping mustache, visualizing the wounds when Cohn had been carried back on a canvas stretcher to the defensive circle, in the looming shadows of the two war wags.

The unmistakable wounds were from stickies. They were muties that had developed circular suckers on their palms and fingers, and used them to hold on to their victims. Cohn had the round, raw patches on his arms and one big one on his face, where the layers of skin had been ripped away, leaving the bloody cicatrix, like a massive, burst blister.

Trader had been annoyed.

That's like saying that the midday sun could sometimes be fairly warm.

They'd gone after the stickies, raiding their camp while they were drinking their stolen moonshine, and chilled them all—fifteen muties, eight men, four women and three children. Most were blasted down from hiding. Trader had never been one to take chances.

"Man takes a chance when he doesn't have to can't wait to get into his grave," he used to say.

Survivors were doused in the potent liquor, then burned to death.

The charred remains had been left where they'd fallen, after running, burning and screaming.

Abe remembered.

"YOU'RE MILES AWAY."

Trader's harsh voice rasped through the evening gloom, making Abe jump.

"Remembering."

"What?"

"Old times past."

"Not worth forgetting." Trader grinned.

Abe sat up and peered into the depths of his enameled coffee mug, finding, as he'd suspected, that it was almost empty. He tossed the bitter dregs into the dirt and stood to pour himself a top-up from the dark blue pot that hissed and bubbled in the heart of their fire.

"Hold it!" Trader's voice a whisper that barely rippled the evening air.

Abe cursed himself under his breath, half turning, seeing the glint of metal by his bedroll. His stainless-steel Colt Python, the big .357, was as much use there as if it were at the bottom of a Dubuque shithouse.

"Other side of the clearing."

Abe looked where the Armalite pointed, expecting to see a mutie rattler, ten feet long. Or a giant cougar, fangs bared, crouched to pounce and crunch and rend him open from groin to breastbone.

It was a gray squirrel, a dainty little creature, quite oblivious to the two men watching it, holding a small pine nut between its front paws and picking at it with quick, delicate movements.

Abe turned back, seeing that the Trader was cautiously raising the Armalite to his shoulder, squinting along the barrel, steadying it on the tiny squirrel.

"Waste of a bullet, Trader," Abe said, conscious of how high and reedy his voice suddenly seemed to sound.

"How's that?"

"You used to tell us that a bullet wasted today could be a life wasted tomorrow."

Trader's short, barking laugh was loud enough to disturb the creature, sending it scampering away into the lake of tranquil darkness under the trees.

To his relief, Abe heard the soft click of the safety going back on. Fingers trembling, he helped himself to the hot coffee sub, sitting down again across from Trader.

"You were right, Abe, but I wouldn't cross me too often." A long pause. "Ten weeks for Ryan to get up here. Ten weeks isn't that long."

Chapter Six

Despite being only eleven years old, Dean Cawdor had been most places in Deathlands and seen most things.

But he'd never seen anything like the thing that now sat perched on the back of the rusting locomotive tender, staring at him from golden eyes. There was another on the roof of the stagecoach barn, another squatting up on the splintered gable of the Masonic lodge.

And another.

And another.

The boy slowly drew his heavy blaster, unsure whether it would be a good idea to start shooting or not, not yet certain whether any of the others had spotted the threat.

Then he saw his father, holding the SIG-Sauer in his right hand, peering out of the doorway of another of the tumbledown old buildings, heard him say "Fire-blast!" and knew that meant that he had also seen the sinister creatures that had appeared from out of the shrouding mists.

"I chill it, Dad?" he called, as loud as he dared, his voice bringing the other five into sight, all of them looking up at the apparitions.

Ryan waved his hand low, indicating a negative to the boy's request.

But the mutie thing on the tender still hadn't moved, its eyes boring into Dean with as much passion as a melt-washed boulder of Sierra granite.

J.B. waved a clenched fist to Ryan, gesturing toward the general store, at the far end of the street of the re-created ghost town.

Ryan nodded. The Armorer's tactical skill hadn't deserted them. The alien creatures might not be hostile, but you didn't take a chance on something like that. It was better to gather in what seemed the strongest of the buildings.

He checked that the rest of the companions knew where they were going to go, hefted his blaster and made sure that his rifle was secure across his shoulders.

None of the weird things had moved at all, though five more had arrived, circling lazily from the belt of the fog, settling on other roofs.

"Now!" Ryan shouted.

They moved together at the signal, running along the furrowed main street, up onto the splintered, damp boardwalk to the store.

Michael was there first, followed closely by Dean and Ryan. All of them stood by the open door, ready to give the others covering fire against the threat of the creatures.

"Inside," J.B. said, ushering Mildred, Krysty and Doc into the shadowy interior.

"They aren't moving, Dad."

The things all watched the flurry of movement with a calm, disinterested stare, the protuberant yellow eyes not seeming to register what was happening.

"In," Ryan ordered, gesturing to Michael and Dean with the SIG-Sauer.

He stood and waited.

During the last quarter of a minute a dozen more of the muties had flown in, all finding places to perch on the roofs, all along the strip of buildings. They wheeled down onto Lonesome Gulch in almost total silence, the only sound the beating of their strong-pinioned wings.

Ryan studied them, trying to weigh up what kind of threat they might present, assuming that they were any sort of danger at all. The more he looked, the more it seemed a fair assumption that the things could be bad news.

He guessed that their genetic mutation, triggered by the nuking of a hundred years or so ago, had begun with them being some kind of bird.

They had a wingspan of about five feet. But from what he could see from the doorway, it looked to Ryan as though they didn't have normal avian feathers. There was a metallic, leathery appearance to them, like the wings of robotic bats, with sharp claws spaced out along the leading edge.

The jaws were elongated, like an alligator's, with two very prominent, curved teeth and then a myriad of tiny ones. The golden eyes protruded from sockets of bones, and there was a ruff of crimson spikes around the throat that could have been either feather or bone. None of the things was close enough for Ryan to be able to know for certain.

"They doing anything?"

J.B. had reappeared at Ryan's shoulder, holding the Uzi. He peered out into the street.

"No. What's it look like to defend?"

"Shutters inside, but they got the worm. Wouldn't want to trust them to keep out a spitball. Others are putting them up now. They got ob slits in them."

"Fog's coming lower again."

Now there were about fifty of the bird creatures. Every now and again one of those farthest away would flap into the air and make an ungainly landing on a closer roof.

"We hold out here until night." Ryan glanced at his chron, cursing under his breath at its uselessness. "Can't be that long now. Move out then and head for the redoubt. You know, the gateway. Unless those ugly sons of bitches can see in the dark."

Behind them there was the clatter of wood and iron as the old shutters were eased into position, with the groaning of rusted hinges. Krysty called out to Ryan.

"More of those birds out front, near where that parking lot used to be."

"How many?"

"Ten or a dozen."

"What are they doing?"

"Watching. Don't like this one, lover. Could be we ought to head out of here, soon as we can."

"They're getting restless," J.B. said. "Only trouble in trying to reach the mat-trans unit in the dark is that we don't have a working compass, and those fogs can be a bastard." He rested the blaster against his hip and took off his wire-rimmed spectacles, polishing them on a kerchief. "Thought of getting lost in this place isn't—"

"Here they come," Ryan snapped, interrupting the Armorer. He pushed inside, slammed the door behind him and slid across a stout bolt.

The mist had grown suddenly thicker, sinking from the barren peaks around onto the small ville as though it were a hostile, sentient entity itself.

Simultaneously all of the mutie birds began to cry out, opening their beaks wide, the arrays of teeth glittering in the odd, pallid light. The noise wasn't like the call of any bird any of them had ever heard. It had a deep, penetrating quality that struck at the hearts of the listeners.

To Ryan it conjured a picture of a slack-jawed, gibbering shape in a mold-stained shroud, calling to its fellows from an echoing catacomb.

To Doc it was the cold wind that blew between the long-dead stars.

Everyone of the seven friends who listened to that dreadful chorus heard it differently. But all of them found it a frightful sound.

AT THE PRECISE MOMENT that they began to shriek, the things rose from the roofs and flapped toward the store.

Dean had been watching through the narrow slit in one of the shutters that overlooked the street, and he yelled out a running commentary.

"They're all in the air and the fog's badder than... coming in toward—" He ducked away, though there was no immediate impact, then peered out again. "They're circling, Dad. Hundreds of them!"

Ryan looked around the store, all of his experience and combat sense working overtime. The room was around thirty feet long by twenty wide, with several windows, all of them now covered with the interior shutters. The front entrance was glass, but it had a thick wire inner door.

"Get something against that, Michael," he ordered. "Things that big could break through the screen. Help him, Doc."

"What with?"

"Countertop."

"There's an upstairs, Ryan."

He turned on his heel and stared through the gloom at Mildred, who was pointing along a narrow passage that ran back from near the cash register and the display cabinet holding the sacks of blasting powder.

"Fireblast!" He sprinted along the corridor toward the steep, narrow staircase, dropping his rifle as he ran to give himself greater speed and mobility.

He heard the crash of glass ahead and above him before he'd even set his foot on the steps.

"J.B.!" he yelled, reaching the landing and glancing to left and right. He saw that there was a single gable room at the far end, the door standing a little ajar.

The noise from that dark chamber was almost indescribable. More glass shattered, and the chorus of menacing cries from the lizard birds rose.

There hadn't been many times in Ryan Cawdor's life when he'd been consciously frightened of anything. Yet that shadowy landing, with the half-open door at its end, containing those hideous creatures, made him hesitate for a moment.

But common sense carried him on.

If the things escaped from that upstairs room, then there was nothing to be done to prevent them flooding down into the main part of the store. And the dying wasn't likely to take very long.

Behind him Ryan could hear J.B.'s boots pounding on the rickety wooden steps.

At the farther end, a reptilian head appeared in the gap, unwinking ocher eyes burning through the gloom into Ryan, who snapped a shot at it, missing by inches, gouging a spray of plaster from the wall.

The thing was out, its huge wings cramped by the narrow passage, beak open, shrieking at the human intruder.

Ryan batted at it with the barrel of the blaster, hitting it a glancing blow across the chest, barely dodging a scything jab from the fanged beak.

"Chill it!" he shouted to the Armorer, who was almost at his heels. "I'll close the door."

He grabbed at the dark metal handle, shaped like the head of a buffalo, and tugged at it. But another of the muties had found the gap and was blocking it, head protruding, hissing its ferocious anger, the great pinions flailing at the wood.

Ryan held the door in his left hand, the SIG-Sauer in his right. He reacted like lightning, dropping the gun at his feet and drawing the panga from its greased sheath.

The blade hissed through the dusty air, striking the mutie bird just below the point where its angular skull articulated with his snakelike neck. Ryan had expected the honed steel to slice clear through, but the panga angled off, barely nicking the overlapping scales.

The narrow head struck again at him, the point of the beak ripping at his sleeve, nearly making him let go of the door handle. Behind it Ryan could hear a bedlam of noise, aware of dozens of bodies flinging themselves against the battered wood.

There was also a disturbance downstairs, with shouting and a couple of shots fired, but he was too busy with his own problem to pay it any heed.

At his back there came the sudden flat spitting sound of the Uzi and the shrieking sound ended abruptly.

"Need a hand, Ryan?"

"No room. Fucker's got a skin like sec steel."

Two more desperate hacking blows had more success, opening a gouge in the thing's throat, sending drops of amber blood pattering, hot and acid, onto Ryan's wrist.

He took a chance and eased the door open a few inches, punching with the haft of the panga at the wounded creature, pushing it back into the attic room. He slammed the door shut triumphantly and heard the lock click home. Until that moment it had never occurred to Ryan that there might not be any sort of catch on the door, or that it could easily have rusted away during the endless years after the long winters.

He spun around, stooping with an easy grace to retrieve his fallen SIG-Sauer, seeing that J.B. was standing at the top of the stairs, Uzi at the ready. The dead mutie bird was lying still on the dusty floor, one wing broken off, its head lolling on its muscular neck.

"Door won't hold them long." J.B. smiled at Ryan, his teeth white in the gloom. "Never figured on ending as a bird's dinner."

As RYAN RAN BACK down the stairs into the main part of the old store, he was figuring that J.B. was probably right. It looked as though it were only going to be a matter of time.

It was like being at the still center of a spinning world. Outside there was a cacophony of shrieking noise, orchestrated by the constant thudding of wings and beaks battering at the walls and shutters.

The other five were standing close together by the candy counter, guns drawn, waiting for the moment when the defences were breached and the mutie creatures poured in to chill them.

"Any ideas?" Ryan shouted.

"Yeah," his eleven-year-old son replied.

Chapter Seven

It was so noisy that Ryan wasn't even sure that he'd heard his son correctly.

"What?" he shouted.

"Can I have some candy, then I'll tell you?"

For a moment Ryan nearly slapped the boy hard enough across the face to send him staggering into the middle of next week. That he could joke at a time of such imminent peril brought the crimson mist of rage flooding down across his mind. Krysty, at his side, caught the wave of potential violence from Ryan and gripped him by the wrist.

Very hard.

"Tell us, Dean. Then have as much candy as you want." She didn't let go of Ryan while she spoke.

The heavy counter that had been propped against the wire screen over the front entrance to the store was already rocking under the impact of the things.

"There's a root cellar." Dean pointed back toward the stairs. "Under there."

J.B. was closest and he moved with deceptive speed, opening a dark-painted door. "Throw us a pack of self-lights," he called. "If they still work."

Mildred picked up a box of matches and threw them to the Armorer, who vanished from their sight.

But his voice floated up to them, just audible above the sound of the ceaseless attack. "Cellar, all right. Solid. And—" he paused "—reckon we can get out of here. Double doors." There was another moment of silence from the Armorer. "Yeah. They're stiff, and there's something piled on them, but we can shift them. Definitely another way out."

"But those shithead snake-bird things are all the way around us," Mildred protested, staring out of one of the ob slits, pulling back quickly as the wood splintered and a length was smashed in by the attacking muties.

"If only we could find some way of luring them all in here and then destroy them with some fiendishly cunning ruse," Doc said.

Dean was leaning against one of the remaining counters, sucking pensively on a honey-and-mango sugar stick, tossing one of the little souvenir bags of blasting powder in the air with his other hand.

"Careful that doesn't blow us all up," Ryan said. "That's it! J.B., come here. Something you once showed me."

"TRICK THAT TRADER taught me, first week after I joined him."

The sallow-faced Armorer was down on his knees, oblivious to the threat from the mutie birds flocked all around them. Ryan had just snatched a glance from one of the ob slits and realized then that time was sliding away from them. The fog had closed in and there seemed to be, literally, hundreds upon hundreds of the vicious brutes.

The temperature had also dropped radically in the past few minutes, so that everyone could see their breath misting around them in the store.

"Damnably chill," Doc muttered. "My Aunt Harriet used to have a saying that it was as cold as the blood in the neck of a dead horse."

Ryan ignored him. The seconds were running out, the sand falling ever faster through the thin glass throat of the timer. And the delicate operation he and J.B. were working on could possibly save all of their lives.

Or destroy them a few minutes more quickly.

He had taken a handful of thin black cigarillos from a sealed pack on the counter, making sure with the self-lights that they still worked and hadn't dried away to powder. He carefully got them all glowing evenly at the same length and bound them upright with a length of thin twine from one of J.B.'s capacious pockets. Then he set them amid a pile of wood shavings that Michael had whittled from the edge of one of the shutters, with a number of crumpled, dry pages from some of the old guides.

The main trigger for the ignition was a number of matches, tilted carefully against the pile of small cigars, so that they would eventually come into contact with the glowing ends.

"Nice a little fire booby as I ever saw," J.B. said admiringly. "All we need now is a trail of the black powder from the source to the main stock of the explosive.''

Dean had slipped up the stairs, running down again almost immediately. "The bastards have almost broken through," he yelled. "One of the top panels is split from top to bottom, and I could see their beaks driving clean through."

Ryan nodded. "Right. Take some self-lights and go down in the cellar. Everyone except me and J.B., now."

To his relief they all obeyed immediately, Krysty brushing the tips of her fingers against his cheek as she left. "Don't be too long, lover," she said.

J.B. had scattered a trail of the glistening black grains, leading to the main store of the powder, which he'd packed tightly into a stout wooden box that had been standing in a corner of the store.

"Nearly ready," he said, checking that the matches were still in place and that the cigars were burning evenly.

"Where did you first get this idea from?" Ryan called, standing with the Armorer's Uzi in his hands.

"Guy in Oregon got paid to spot fires for the local baron. Paid jack on results. More fires he spotted, more jack he got. Took to starting them himself. Showed me how he did it."

Ryan glanced one last time through the nearest ob slit, looking out across the main street.

The fog had thickened, intruding through the cracks around the shutters, tasting cold and bitter, like steel and salt water. Every window in the place had been completely smashed, turned to smithereens of sharp-edged glass, and the bird things kept coming. They vanished out of sight into the veiling mist, then turned and drove into the thick wood hard enough to make it shudder. It seemed like the entire building was trembling under the ferocious assault. Ryan kept his eye a safe distance from the slit, aware of the possibility that one of the reptilian beaks might smash through and pierce his skull.

The muties were attacking in a ceaseless stream. It was like watching them flap toward you in their hundreds, along the dark tunnel.

Even in the thickest of the fog, Ryan noticed that their eyes glowed with a fearsome yellow light. He stared intently out at them . . .

Someone was shaking his shoulder and shouting at him.

"What?"

"You got hypnotized, friend. Let's go." J.B. turned toward the passage that led to the stairs into the root cellar.

"We need them in here for the explosion to work. Kill enough for us to be able to risk a break."

"Dark night!" J.B. pounded his right fist into his left palm. "You're right, Ryan."

"Go. I'll pull down that old counter. Should give them a way in. Might have time to throw open one or two of the shutters as well."

Above them they both heard the startling noise of splintering wood, rising over the other sounds, and the screeches of the creatures grew instantly louder.

"They're in!" J.B. yelled. He ran to knock over the counter, while Ryan unbolted two of the pairs of shutters.

The mutie horrors held off for a vital couple of seconds, suspicious of the sudden access to the old store. J.B. led the way toward the door at the top of the basement steps, held open by a watchful Krysty.

Ryan was less than six feet behind him, still holding the Uzi, the SIG-Sauer in its holster. The Steyr had been taken down to safety by Dean.

Death was all around.

Boiling down the stairs from the second story, the creatures clashed in their blood lust, beaks open, their screams of hatred and rage filling the store. Others had surged in through the shattered front entrance and past the open shutters.

Ryan felt something pluck at his sleeve and there was a sharp fiery pain at the side of his neck, warmth running down inside his collar.

J.B. was through the door. Krysty's face, a taut mask of fear, was framed in the rectangular shadow.

Ryan paused a second, the blaster on full-auto, spraying a circle of bloody doom all around him, seeing the mutie birds falling with shattered wings and broken skulls. Then he was through the door and Krysty slammed it shut, pushing across stout bolts at the bottom and top.

"Fucking close, lover," she said.

Below him was a set of stairs, without a handrail, that led down into an earth-walled cellar, about fifteen feet square. Five faces looked up at him, illuminated by the orange glow of the brief self-lights that everyone but J.B. was holding.

"Best get right down," he said. "Cover your ears and open your mouths."

The door at the top of the stairs was taking a dreadful pounding, but that wasn't what concerned Ryan. The passage was so narrow that no more than a couple of the things could attack the sturdy wood.

It was the bomb they'd set that worried him.

He was worried what would happen if it didn't go off, and what would happen if it did go off.

If it didn't, the creatures would get them, either by breaking down the door or, eventually, by waiting them out.

If it went off as planned, then it should chill or mutilate the majority of the attacking muties, and scare the living hell out of any survivors, giving Ryan and the others a decent chance to break for it and head back for the gateway—providing that the explosion didn't wreck the store so effectively that the cellar roof collapsed and the entire place entombed them.

Working in the near dark, under enormous pressure, with one hundred-year-old black blasting powder, didn't lead to the scientific probability of measured success.

On balance, Ryan hoped that it went off.

One by one the tiny halos of light from the matches were extinguished, leaving the cellar in pitch darkness. Everyone was crouched over on hands and knees, palms pressed to their ears, mouths sagging open against the anticipated shock wave.

All waiting.

Chapter Eight

"It hasn't worked, Dad."

The small voice came from the raven blackness, trying to hide its fear.

"Can't tell yet, Dean." Ryan had only just caught his son speaking, through the muffling hands over his ears. "Not like a chron-timed gren."

The others were aware of the conversation and were moving around in the dirt.

"This brings back such happy memories of playing at Sardines with my English cousins at one Christmas party. One had to squeeze into the smallest, darkest space one could find and wait for the other to try to find you."

Doc sounded totally unworried by their intensely dangerous predicament, chatting as easily as if he were relaxing at a faculty tea party.

"How long do you reckon, J.B.?" Mildred asked from near the double doors to the open air.

"Reckon in the next minute or..."

"Or what, John?"

"Or not at all."

"It's coming," Krysty said, quiet and confident.

"When?"

"Soon, lover. Very soon." She paused long enough for three beats of the heart. "Now."

MANY YEARS EARLIER Ryan had been knocked unconscious by an implode gren going off close to him while he was swimming in a deep reservoir. The feeling was similar when their homemade bomb was ignited in the store above.

There was a massive, muffled impact that a person felt rather than heard. It was like having the brain squeezed by a giant's fist, who was also compressing all of the internal organs of the body. It was sensation, rather than actual pain.

The floor heaved, and Ryan felt chunks of wood and dirt raining over him as he crouched on the packed earth.

J.B. was quickest, holding a dozen spluttering matches in his hand. The air was filled with powdery dust, and they could all catch the bitter stench of the explosive.

Krysty touched a finger to her nose, bringing it away streaked with crimson. Dean had a worm of blood creeping from his nose, and Doc complained that he'd bitten his tongue.

Ryan scrambled to his feet, feeling his head ringing. "Can't hear those mutie birds anymore," he said, aware that his voice sounded extremely distant.

"I can't hear anything," Michael countered, brushing dirt off his clothes.

"No point waiting." Ryan walked to the heavy doors and braced himself under them. "Dean, take the rifle and Uzi. Michael and J.B., lend a hand here."

Doc, Mildred and Krysty struck more matches, giving the men enough light to see what they were doing. For a frozen moment, Ryan thought that they might not be able to shift the ancient doors and was on the verge of asking Krysty to use the power of the Earth Mother, even though he knew what a terrible toll it took out of her when calling on the frightful strength.

"Going," Michael panted.

A hinge groaned in protest, then both doors swung up and back, letting in a flood of cold, bitter fog. Outside the building, the day hadn't yet quite run its course, though it was moving toward evening.

"Ladder?" Ryan felt around him, but there was nothing. "No. Michael, climb out first. Here, I'll give you a leg up. Then help pull everyone out."

The place was deathly still, the fog clamped tight around, cutting visibility to less than five paces.

Behind them there was the dimly seen light of a fire burning, dry wood crackling and the distinct sound of sorely wounded creatures.

As they moved away from the tourist ghost town of Lonesome Gulch, the noises faded behind them.

THE JOURNEY BACK to the gateway through the blighted land wasn't entirely without incident. None of the mutie birds that had besieged the store at the entrance to the ghost town came after them, but the fog grew steadily thicker and more menacing, making it less than easy to find the trail with none of the compasses working at all.

They picked up the old road along the side of the slow-running, sinister river without any problems, taking care to keep as far away as possible from the strange semiliquid flow, avoiding attack from any of its lethal denizens.

Dean complained of being thirsty and walked a little way off the trail, looking for pools of water trapped amid the frost-riven boulders.

The others waited, Ryan calling out to him not to go far from sight.

"All right, Dad. Got some..." Then came the sound of spitting and spluttering from the gray walls of fog.

"Dean?"

"Okay, Dad. Sipped at a rain spill. Tasted just like bullock's piss."

"How do you know, Dean?" Michael asked. "You ever drunk the piss of a bullock?"

Dean reappeared, wiping his mouth, gobbing in the dirt. "Real funny, Michael. Real fucking funny."

"Best not to try to eat or drink anything while we're here," J.B. warned. "Soon be back at the gateway. Make a jump. Then get something."

THE TRACK BEGAN to wind upward, and they eventually reached the rotting stump of the huge tree that they remembered from the walk down from the gateway. The huge albino maggots that had infested it had all mysteriously vanished.

While they stood at the bend in the track, something scuttled out of the mist, almost under Mildred's feet, making her jump back with a gasp of fright.

It was like a string of mottled greenish pebbles strung together with threads of gristle, about four feet long, with no apparent eyes or mouth. Without pausing, it snaked across the path and vanished once more into the coils of mist.

"Proper little valley of the shadow of death, isn't it?" Mildred said to no one in particular.

The rank vegetation became more sparse, eventually thinning out completely, leaving them on the narrow, rutted trail that climbed higher between the granite walls.

The small wound on Ryan's neck was stinging and he touched it, finding that it was leaking a colorless liquid. He brought his finger to his nose and smelled at it. There was the unmistakable odor of corruption.

Krysty saw the gesture and moved to walk alongside him. "Problem?"

"Septic poisoning from that mutie back in the store. Can't wash it until we get clean water."

"Light's not good enough to see it properly." She touched it gently and he winced. "Sorry, didn't mean—"

"Sore," he said.

"Feels hot. Best keep an eye on it."

"I know. I already said that."

"Fine. You don't have to snap at me like that when I'm trying to help you."

"Sorry. Bit ragged at the edge."

"Sure."

THEY REACHED the narrow ledge of hewn rock, with the circular entrance to the small mat-trans unit opening off it.

Doc was panting hard, his face pale in the silvery evening light. Now they were well above the mist, and it was like looking down onto a gently moving sea of fresh-picked cotton.

"I shall have no regrets about departing from this place," he said. "My heart is working like a leaking pump, and the breath sours in my throat."

"Want to take a rest, Doc?" Ryan looked at the old man, concerned at how parchment-pale he looked.

"No. No. My thanks, dear fellow, but the sooner we get the next jump over, the better I shall be pleased." He straightened, taking some of his weight on the elegant sword stick. "Let us leave this peak above Darien," he said.

It took only moments for them to walk along the cramped tunnel and into the makeshift control room.

The battered wooden door swung slowly back on its hinges, squeaking softly. Great tangles of multicolored wire hung from the broken rectangles of chipboard ceiling. One of the overhead neon lights was buzzing and crackling erratically, its glow reflected in the vein of green quartz that seamed the bare rock above. The consoles, on their rickety tables, were cheeping and muttering to themselves and to each other.

Krysty ran a finger over the top of one of the comps, her red hair darkened by the blue screen. "I can't believe that this place has existed so long in this condition."

Mildred stood, with her hands on her hips. "Like Michael said, when we jumped here, some of the stone still has marks of the chisel. Fresh as yesterday's sunrise."

J.B. nodded. "With the acid rain and all those muties, you'd have likely thought something would have broken in here, fifty years ago." He took off his glasses and began to wipe them clean from the smearing mist.

Dean had gone back out into the corridor, but suddenly reappeared. "Think there's something coming, Dad."

"What?"

"Can't tell. Just a noise like wet clothes being dragged over a cold stone floor."

"What?"

"Real big load."

Ryan glanced out into the rocky passage, seeing nothing but darkness and a few stray fingers of white mist that were feeling their way into the complex. He listened in the stillness, but he couldn't hear anything.

"I heard it, Dad."

"Believe you, Dean." He closed the flimsy door, aware that it wouldn't do much to deter even a sickly kitten.

J.B. had carefully perched his spectacles back on the bridge of his bony nose. He glanced at Ryan. "We go?"

"Reckon so."

The granite vault of the anteroom was starkly empty, and the door of the gateway chamber still stood ajar, as they'd left it only a few hours earlier.

Ahead of them, the dark gray armaglass walls of the unit were a patchwork of green and yellow lichen.

"Like getting into a toad's belly," Krysty said with a shudder of disgust.

Ryan shepherded them in, one at a time, though nobody was keen to squat on the cold floor. Like the whole of the region, there was something fundamentally unclean and unhealthy about the ill-lit gateway.

Doc leaned uncertainly against the far wall, finally sitting down, his knee joints creaking loudly, checking that the Le Mat was snug in its holster. "Come, then, my friends, and let's away. To seek the fortunes of a gentler day."

"That real Shakespeare, Doc?" Mildred asked, kneeling at his side. "Or just one of your make-ups?"

He smiled at her, his wonderfully perfect teeth gleaming in the gloom. "The truth, my sweet Dr. Wyeth, is that I have completely forgotten."

J.B. took his place next to her. Michael and Dean were waiting their turn, with Krysty and Ryan.

"Was..." he said, half turning.

Krysty looked at him. "Yeah. Think I heard it, too, lover. Like Dean said."

It was a heavy, slow, slithering sound. The picture that sprang unbidden into Ryan's mind was of a giant snail, making its inexorable way through the fog toward them, leaving a wide trail of stinking slime.

"Quick." He pushed his son and the teenager into the mat-trans unit, drawing his SIG-Sauer and glancing again behind him. Krysty joined the others, sitting down, her back against the wall, leaving a space for him to complete the circle.

Ryan pulled the door shut behind him, but realized that he hadn't heard the distinctive click that indicated that the lock had triggered the actual mechanism of the jump.

"It didn't..." Krysty began.

"I know it fucking didn't." Ryan opened it and slammed it shut more firmly, aware through the gap in the door of a shadowy bulk gliding across the control area toward him.

Chapter Nine

The sound, like a giant whispering, had grown suddenly much stronger, and Ryan knew that the creature, whatever it was, had entered the control area less than thirty feet away from the hexagonal chamber.

Most of the mat-trans units were firmly built of almost impregnable armaglass, set into the solid concrete of the main redoubt. But this one had shown all the marks of hasty and amateurish workmanship. With the flaws and cracks in the armaglass, it probably wasn't even proof against a decent handgun.

"Did it shut?" Krysty's voice disturbed Ryan because it showed fear. And he knew that Krysty Wroth almost never got frightened.

"Couldn't tell. Noise outside."

"Try it again." Michael stood now, holding his Texas Longhorn Border Special in both hands.

There was something barely visible through the gray walls, the same thing that Ryan had glimpsed in the nanosecond when the door had been open.

"I do believe that...what was the phrase? That all systems are go."

Doc was the calmest of them all, perhaps because he wasn't yet aware of the horror that was approaching the mat-trans unit from the ravaged world beyond.

Ryan glanced down, seeing the metal disks in the floor were beginning to glow through their coating of moss, and the upper half of the chamber was filling with the familiar white mist, quite unlike the acrid fog outside.

"Sit down, Michael." Ryan took his own place alongside Krysty, the SIG-Sauer leveled at the door.

The light beyond the chamber was blocked out, and Ryan tightened his finger on the trigger.

THE BLACKNESS was streaked with dreams that mixed past and present into a bizarre future, where reality and fantasy were inseparable and indistinguishable, where time and place were familiar and strange.

The woman who stood by the bed was someone who Ryan thought he knew. She was tall and blond, skinny, part woman and part child, and wore an obscenely short skirt of soft red material.

"Suede."

With a fringe. Her legs seemed to begin at her shoulders and were encased in scarlet boots with silver spurs, decorated with tiny bells that tinkled as she walked around the room.

"Lori." That seemed to be the right name for her, though he wasn't sure.

Ryan watched her with his good eye, straining to turn his head to follow her movements.

Aware that he was naked and cold, his breath clouding out into the air in front of him.

Naked and cold, tied by the wrists to the corners of the bed, ankles spread to the bottom of the bed.

Not a bed. Just a metal frame, with narrow strips of steel running from side to side, digging into his hips and spine and shoulders.

"Lori?"

The face, the fringe of hair so blond it was almost white. The makeup around her eyes turned them into dark, smudged pits. Her lips were pale and narrow, unsmiling.

Ryan tested the ropes. Not ropes. Steel handcuffs, biting into his wrists. Chains were around his ankles.

"Keep still, Ryan Cawdor. Don't move or you're dead. Dead men don't move. Quint not move. Quint dead."

Ryan turned from her, looking around the room. There was a single overhead light, a naked bulb that swung slowly from side to side.

There was no other furniture, except a small marble table that stood on wrought-iron legs. Some articles rested on the table, but it was just beyond the periphery of Ryan's right eye.

On the walls were a number of tattered old vid posters, a few with the names of ancient, predark movies that Ryan had heard about. He'd even seen speckled copies of some of them, projected on sheets with temperamental gas generators.

The moving light sent a dancing arc of brightness swinging over the posters.

"Chances run out, Ryan."

"What chances?" To his own ears his voice sounded odd, muffled, the words distorted.

"Chances to tell me. Save yourself."

"I don't understand."

The woman laughed, a bleak sound, a thousand miles away from any humor.

"Thought knocking your teeth out, one at a time, might have helped your memory."

Then he felt the pain, flooding through both jaws, and he could taste the bitter iron of his own blood.

"Aw my teef?"

"Speak properly."

He tried again. "You knocked out all of my teeth? You fucking slut."

He felt her hand on him, finger and thumb squeezing gently at the tender skin inside the top of the thigh. She pinched harder, the pain burning, making him arch his back off the bed.

"Hurts, does it? I'll kiss it and make it better."

Her lips, nibbling so softly, moved higher, her hand cupping his balls, forcing him to an erection that could have bent an iron bar.

"Now you're ready to tell me, Ryan."

"What?"

She smiled, showing stained, broken teeth. "You know what, lover."

"I don't." Whatever happened he wouldn't beg. Trader would never beg. No point.

She was stroking him again, bringing him tremblingly close to the brink of ejaculation. Ryan thought that he'd burst if she went on for just ten more seconds.

"Know what I'm going to do?" She moved out of his vision and picked something up from the table.

"No."

"See this." Lori held up a coil of pale yellow tubing, with a greasy exterior, nearly as thick as a child's little finger. "Know what it is?"

Ryan did know, but it had slipped his memory. He shook his head. "Don't remember, Lori."

"Slow fuse."

"Fuse?" It was like the young woman was speaking some alien tongue.

"It's a length of slow fuse. I call it my friendly persuader, Ryan."

"Like for setting off a bomb?"

She smiled radiantly and clapped her hands. "*Very* good."

"What are you going to do with it?"

She was running it through her fingers, caressing it, bringing it to her lips to touch it with her long tongue. "It'll burn anywhere, even without oxygen. Under water. Anywhere. Once it's lit, it'll burn."

"I know."

She smiled and touched his throbbing penis. "Put the fuse anywhere and light it." Her fingers moved up the shaft toward the flat muscular wall of his stomach. "Insert it slowly and carefully, Ryan. You'd be surprised what a long way it'll go, and nothing can put it out. There are so many orifices of the human body that can receive it."

"Please."

Fuck Trader saying that a man shouldn't ever beg for mercy.

"Please don't."

"Just tell me."

"What?"

Lori had lighted the fuse. It was glowing almost white-hot, like a fiery worm, devouring itself, defecating white ash, moving very slowly, a millimeter at a time.

"Tell me everything."

"I can't." The horror was the way her left hand kept him agonizingly erect, despite the appalling thing that she was going to do to him.

"Start at the beginning. Place of birth."

"Front Royale ville in the Shens."

"Parents?"

"Baron Titus and Lady Cynthia Cawdor."

"Brothers and sisters."

"Two brothers. Morgan and...I can't remember the other one's name."

"He blinded you."

"I know."

"His name?"

"Harvey. That was it. Harvey!"

The glowing tip of the burning fuse was an inch away from the tip of his cock.

Lori laughed at him. "Stupe! Think I give a flying fuck about your family? Or about anything you say? I don't, Ryan. Couldn't care less."

"Then . . . why?"

She leaned over him, and he could taste the rotten sweetness of her breath. "Reminds me of a girl I knew out in Las Cruces. One day she went into the desert and found a prairie rattler. Put her hand out to make it bite her. It did. They carried her back dying. Arm black and shining from finger to shoulder. I asked her that same question. Asked her why she did it."

"And?"

"Said that it seemed a good idea at the time."

The young woman threw her head back and laughed, the eldritch screech of amusement turning into the lonesome howl of the midnight coyote.

Ryan felt the mind-toppling agony as she started to slide the burning fuse inside him, aware that his body was straining off the bed, the steel cutting into wrists and ankles.

He screamed and screamed.

"RYAN!"

He tried to punch at her, but the grip on his wrist was too tight.

"Don't!"

"Just a bad jump, lover. Come on."

Lori's voice was Krysty's voice, loud in his ear.

"Fighting like a bastard to get free."

Krysty's voice became J.B.'s voice.

Ryan opened his eye.

He was spread-eagled flat on his back in a gateway chamber. Doc was lying across his legs, with Mildred helping him with the pin-down.

Dean stood looking down at him, his face confused and frightened. Ryan managed a thin smile for his son. "Don't hurry," he said.

"He means for you not to worry, Dean." It was Krysty's voice.

Ryan was finding it difficult to focus, but his vision was filled by her tumbling mane of bright crimson hair, hanging across his face as she concentrated on holding him still. J.B. was on the other side, with Michael across his upper body.

"Treating me like a rabid panther," Ryan managed to say, though his tongue felt hugely swollen and too large for his mouth. "I'm fine now."

"Bad jump?" J.B. asked.

"Yeah. But you can let me go now." He was uncomfortably aware that the front of his dark blue pants was tighter than usual, though the residual erection was slowly subsiding. Ryan hoped that nobody had noticed it.

They all moved away cautiously, allowing him to sit up and lean against the armaglass walls of the chamber, which were a rich cobalt blue.

"Everyone else all right?"

Doc answered for the others. "Unlikely as it may be, my dear Ryan, we all came through this particular jump with colors flying, bands playing, girls scattering flowers and tickertape tumbling."

Dean nodded. "Hot pipe of a jump, Dad."

A little unsteadily, Ryan stood, looking around him. "Was I out long?"

Krysty touched him on the arm. "Couple of minutes. But you were screaming and fighting. Want to tell me about it?"

"No. Not now and not ever, lover. Best get out and see where we are."

"I recognize this color," the Armorer said. "These dark blue walls. Reckon we might've been here before."

"Not me." Mildred ran the flat of her hand over the silk-smooth armaglass. "Lovely color."

It seemed familiar to Ryan, but he couldn't locate it in his memory.

Chapter Ten

"The bayous."

Ryan looked at J.B. "Yeah. You're right. Place we first met up with Jak Lauren."

He recalled the heat that percolated all the way down through the sec doors of vanadium steel into the heart of the mat-trans unit, and the humidity.

Bayou country. The Cajuns. Lafayette. Baron Tourment. The swamps and alligators.

It had been a time of violence, on their previous visit to the place. Oddly, in all the jumps that they'd made, Ryan couldn't recall finishing up in the same redoubt twice. Since they had no real control over the destination of any of their jumps, that had to be a statistical oddity.

Krysty wiped a tiny bead of perspiration from her upper lip. "Course. Ace on the line there, J.B., remembering that. The dark blue armaglass walls."

"Unless there's someplace similar." Ryan found his breathing was slowing back to normal, his nightmare erection finally subsided.

"Don't find heat like this in many parts of Deathlands." J.B. ran a finger round inside the collar of his denim shirt. "We going to take a look outside?"

"Sure." Ryan tried to recall the layout beyond the control room of the gateway. He had a memory of dense, fetid swamps, with giant skeeters and a broken, rotted causeway over the muddy bayou water.

"Could be we might meet up with some of Jak's old friends." Krysty's face had a sheen of perspiration. "Get some good fried pork and beans and plenty of fresh spring water. You could hold the pork and the beans, and I'll just settle for the drink. Another half hour of this and I'll have dehydrated down to a little puddle on the floor."

"Then we'll go take a look."

Outside the chamber they saw the same notice that they'd seen a number of times before: Entry absolutely Forbidden to All but B12 Cleared Personnel. Mat Trans.

The usual massive sec doors were down and closed, the green lever at the side pointed to the floor. Ryan laid his hand on it and glanced at the others.

"Ready?"

Blasters were drawn. J.B. crouched on the floor, gripping the Uzi on full-auto, preparing himself to peer under the lifting doors, in case anyone—or anything—waited outside. It had happened before.

Ryan noticed that Michael looked a little pale and worried, licking his lips, breathing fast.

"All right, Michael?"

"Yes, of course. Just hot and damp, and thirsty as well. What are you waiting for?"

"Nothing."

Ryan pushed the lever upward, hearing the familiar grinding sound behind the thick concrete walls of buried gears, as the huge weight of the sec doors began to move.

He halted it after six or eight inches, giving the Armorer the chance to peek through the gap.

"Nothing."

The door lifted smoothly, halting with a hiss of compressed air.

The corridor outside was about ten feet wide. Pale cream, seamless stone curved to the right. The arched roof about twelve feet high.

Ryan led the way, noting the sec barriers concealed in the ceiling, and the tiny vid cameras, every forty paces, set in the angle between wall and roof.

The passage bent around and around, always to the right, confirming Ryan's memory from the previous visit to that particular redoubt that it was going to complete a full three hundred and sixty degrees.

"Here's the doors," he said. "They open onto the outside, triggered by some kind of remote scope lock. Just walk up to it and it'll open."

"Lori showed us, didn't she?" Krysty glanced toward Doc, who had once been infatuated with the tall blond young woman.

"Pretty, sweet child." He shook his head. "In my sleep I still hear the tinkling of those tiny silver bells on her boots. Such a dear girl."

The room opened off the corridor and was about thirty feet square, with the smudged marks on the blank walls where pictures or posters had been hung, pulled down in the last dying, rad-blighted days before the long winters.

Dean had moved alongside his father, and now ran toward the dull metal of the heavy double doors at the far side of the room. For a moment it looked like he was going to bump into them, but at the last moment they began to slide back.

"Dean!"

"Yeah?"

Ryan beckoned for him to take his place in the skirmish line. "Wait here."

"Thought you'd been here before, Dad. Knew that it was a safe place."

"Because it was safe then, it doesn't mean that it'll still be safe."

Krysty patted the boy on the shoulder. "Probably be fine, Dean. We'll soon know."

The air was much hotter beyond the sliding sec doors, like trying to breathe with a warm cloth over your face.

Ahead of them, through the enormously wide doorway, they could all see a straight, brightly lighted section of corridor, less wide than the one outside the gateway chamber, that stretched two hundred yards toward a blank steel wall with a single ordinary door set in its center.

"There's the open country beyond that," Ryan said. "Redoubt's covered with creepers and thick vegetation. We figured that was what kept it safe and hidden."

"Can I go look, Dad?"

Ryan touched a hand to the small wound on his neck, wincing at the stinging pain and a swelling that felt tender and badly infected. "No!" he snapped. "Fireblast, Dean, will you just stay where you're told?"

"Sorry, Dad."

The one-eyed warrior led the way, the passage seeming to shrink with the noise of everyone's feet. For a moment he nearly turned and snapped at them to be quieter, but managed to control himself. Blowing through his teeth, he decided that his irritation was probably because of the tropical heat.

His recollection of the redoubt from when they first explored it was that it had been spotlessly clean, with hardly a grain of dust. Now he noticed that the floor was smudged with gray mud, carrying the faint marks of boots.

On the wall was the single piece of graffiti that he remembered from before, stenciled neatly in olive-green paint on the right-hand section of concrete, just above shoulder-height, the single word: Goodbye.

Ryan reached the door and paused, drawing in a slow breath. He checked that everyone had their guns drawn and ready, then pushed at the door.

"Opens the other way," J.B. said. "I remember poor old Hennings made that mistake."

Henn had been a tall black guy off War Wag One, with a lacerating sense of humor. But it had done him no good when a musket ball had struck him just above the right eye.

It hadn't been all that far away from where they now stood, inside the outer portal to the redoubt.

Ryan turned the handle and pulled the door toward him, feeling it open easily.

He took a careful step out, expecting to see the lush vegetation of the bayous.

The shock of what he saw was so great that Ryan nearly squeezed the narrow trigger of the SIG-Sauer. Behind him he was vaguely aware of J.B. and Krysty gasping in amazement.

"Upon my soul, what can . . ." Doc started.

Dean, Mildred and Michael were less surprised than the others, never having been to the place before, not having known what to expect there.

There had been young pecan trees and groves of cypresses, their roots dipping into the water, live oaks and graceful elms, all of them covered in delicate shrouds of Spanish moss, like veiled duennas.

"Gone," Ryan whispered.

"Gone," Krysty echoed, standing so close to him that he could feel her breath against his skin.

"There was bottomless mud." Doc sighed. "Water that became watery mud. I disremember, but I believe I have said this before. Shall I say it again? Yes, I will enter the round Zion of . . . My apologies, friends. Water into mud. Bottomless. And now, all vanished away. And only we remain."

The swamps had disappeared.

Now, as far as they could see ahead of them, was a sunbaked desert. Here and there they could see darker patches that might once have been mud wallows, might once have been small pools. But they could never, by any stretch of the most fervid imagination, have been the endless bayous of old Louisiana.

"The trees are gone." J.B. leaned a hand against the side of the door, staring out in utter disbelief.

"It's a different redoubt." Ryan gave a whistle of relief. "Course. That's it."

"But I remember that single melancholy word on the wall," Doc said. "It struck at my heart with its infinite sadness when I first saw it. And it strikes now. No, my dear friends, this is the same redoubt. But everything else has altered beyond all comprehension."

There wasn't even the rotting stump of any vegetation to be seen. It was like an infinitely boring succession of rolling dunes, vanishing away in every direction.

Without any sign of life.

"Nothing crawled or swam or walked upon the earth or flew above it," Mildred intoned. "I thought that the place we jumped from was drear enough, but this is worse."

"I'm thirsty, Dad."

"Stay here a minute. J.B., come with me. Let's take a quick recce."

Out of the shade of the passage the temperature was broiling, well into the high nineties. The sand shimmered, stinking of decay, giving off waves of sultry heat, the horizon shimmering behind a yellowish haze.

The sky was the color of bronze, with high banks of cloud obscuring the sun. The Armorer pulled out his minisextant and took a bearing on where the light seemed brightest, making quick calculations.

"Well? Same place, J.B.?"

"Yeah. About two hundred miles to the west of Norleans. I can't dig this at all, Ryan."

On an impulse, the one-eyed man checked the rad counter fixed to his lapel.

"Shit. Look."

The tiny safety device was showing a dangerously high radiation count, midway between red and orange, slightly closer to the red.

"Hot spot!"

The two men looked at each other, both turning away to scan the horizon. Apart from the nondescript low building immediately behind them, there was no sign of any sort of life.

"Some kind of big rad leak," J.B. suggested. "Mebbe a quake that shifted the land for a hundred miles around. Drained the swamps into the Gulf. Dark night, I don't know!"

Ryan stared again at his rad counter. "It's moving," he said, "farther into the red."

None of them really knew how precise the little buttons were. The Trader had found hundreds of them in a warehouse ten years earlier, somewhere around Taos. The label on the box had talked about them being a measuring agent for roentgens, and it was obvious that green meant safe and red meant danger.

But nobody knew just how dangerous "danger" was.

"Can't stay." J.B. looked back at their five companions, clustered in the doorway. "Another jump so close to the last one isn't going to be a lot of laughs."

"Rad sickness isn't a lot of laughs. Have to go for it again." He called to Krysty and the others. "Triple danger on a rad hot spot. Gotta jump."

"No." Doc looked ill from the heat. "Need to rest awhile."

"Rest awhile here, Doc, and your teeth fall out, your gums bleed and your liver rots. You'll be able to peel off your skin and hang it in a closet." Mildred patted him on the arm. "Lesser of the evils."

They made their way quickly back to the chamber, locking the sec doors behind them as they went. They entered the actual gateway, sitting in a sullen, depressed circle within the cobalt blue walls.

Ryan closed the door and squatted next to Krysty. "Here we go again."

She held his hand as the mist gathered and the familiar brain-curdling sensation began.

Ryan's last sentient thought was that the sore place on his neck was throbbing fit to burst.

Chapter Eleven

Doc Tanner was the first to come around, blinking open his eyes, rubbing at them where the lids seemed to have gotten themselves gummed together. His gnarled hand grasped at the silver lion's-head handle to his sword stick and he coughed, trying to clear a ball of phlegm that had become lodged somewhere at the back of his throat.

"By the Three Kennedys!" he croaked, looking around the chamber, realizing that the armaglass walls had changed color, indicating, at the least, that they were somewhere else. "For better or for worse," he whispered, seeing that the other six were still unconscious. "Richer poorer. Health and sickness. Until death or Operation Chronos do us part."

The rich, deep blue had changed to a light purple.

The silvered disks in the floor and ceiling of the six-sided room had ceased to glow, and all but the last frail tendrils of white mist had disappeared.

"I feel amazingly well," he stated. "Life in the old dog yet. Best wine comes in old bottles. Many a fine tune played on an old fiddle. I don't much like the constant repetition of that word 'old.' Senior. A gray panther. Not a wrinklie. Perdition take that one! Mature."

Doc heard a low moan from the other side of the chamber and looked across to see that Dean was blinking his way toward waking.

"The oldest and the youngest," Doc said. "Perhaps this is an omen of sorts."

The boy's face was as white as a wind-washed bone. His dark eyes glittered in the caverns of his skull, and his mouth opened a little way.

Then he puked.

He retched and coughed, bringing up nothing more substantial than a few threads of yellow bile.

"Steady as she goes, lad."

Doc crawled slowly across to the young boy, wincing as his knees cracked and protested. Dean stopped being sick and looked up at the old man. For a moment his face showed only fear, then he managed a smile.

"Didn't . . . Oh, my fucking head! Didn't recognize you, Doc. Just for a minute I thought. . . Don't. . .don't know what it was I thought."

"Rest easy, Dean. Don't sit up until you feel like it. Triple jumps are triple painful." Doc grinned at his own joke. Unfortunately the boy was being sick again and didn't hear it.

Mildred coughed. She was lying on her right side, both hands thrust between her thighs, like a small child seeking comfort. There was a little crust of blood beneath her nostrils and more showing among the beaded plaits by her left ear.

"Dr. Wyeth?" Doc crooned. "Are you returning to the land of the bagels? Sorry. I mean the land of the angels. Dangling angles.'' He slapped himself on the wrist. "Shut up, you old fool, Theo."

Mildred lifted a hand and touched her forehead, sighing, a sound that slipped into a moan. "I'll never drink again, Mama, I promise you."

"Take it slow," Doc advised her, rubbing his fingers across her temple with surprising gentleness.

A bloodshot eye winked open, blurred and out of focus, and peered at Doc's face looming above her. "I've died and gone to Hades. Only explanation for seeing you, Doc."

"Welcome to... To I know not where."

Dean was sitting up, looking at the others. "Michael and Dad are triple grunge," he said.

Mildred groaned again. "Sorry. I'm too busy deciding whether to die or not, Dean. Give me a couple of minutes to rejoin the living dead."

Krysty's voice sounded as though it were drifting up from the bottom of some horrendous abyss. "Living dead, Mildred. Not sure about the living bit. Gaia! The only good thing about pain is that your memory of it gets distorted and dimmed. If it didn't then I don't think I would ever... ever make another jump. The price is too high."

Her crimson hair was curled so tightly around her head that it looked like a silken bathing cap. As Krysty tried to sit up, she slid sideways, banging her face against the wall.

"Can I offer you some assistance, my dear lady?"

"Don't be kind to me, Doc. Way I feel right now, I could just burst into tears."

The old man was first on his feet, steadying himself with the sword stick. "I believe that John Barrymore Dix will soon be with us again," he observed.

Dean had slithered over on hands and knees, touching his father on the cheek. "Real hot," he said, so quietly that nobody else heard him.

J.B. opened his mouth, and a trickle of dark, veinous blood ribboned between his lips.

Mildred had just managed to drag herself into a sitting position. "Probably bit his tongue, or the inside of his cheek," she said. "I think." A pause. "I hope."

"Dad feels like he's on fire," Dean said, louder this time.

Mildred sighed. "I'm sure he's okay, son."

"Feel his head."

"All right." She edged over until she was beside Ryan and the boy. She put the flat of her hand on the man's forehead and her eyes opened wider. She took her hand off, then replaced it.

"Well?" Dean caught the expression of concern on the doctor's face.

"Yeah. He *is* hot, Dean. Got a real fever there. Soon as we get out of here we should try and do something to bring it down again. Feels a couple of degrees over the hundred."

It snapped Krysty out of her own comatose state. "Must've slipped asleep again," she said, fingering a small bruise that had sprung up on her cheek. "What's wrong with Ryan?"

"Fever," Mildred replied.

"Could be that scratch he got on his neck from those swift and evil muties."

Mildred half rolled Ryan over, noticing to her own private worry that he seemed utterly unresponsive, moving with the inert weight of the dead. She checked his pulse, which was fast, but regular, without any of the flickering erratic speed of a serious illness.

The chamber was brightly lighted, and it was easy to see the wound, see the way that it had altered for the worse within the past couple of hours.

"Well?" Krysty prompted.

"Not too good," Mildred admitted.

The wound was a jagged tear, slightly deeper at its top, narrowing. It was impossible to be sure, but it didn't look too deep. But it was obviously seriously infected. There was a yellow streak through its clawed center, liquid and leaking, and an inflamed red at the core of the wound that seemed to be extending in livid streaks, both up and down the side of the man's throat.

As Mildred touched it, Ryan gave a small gasp of pain, registering it through his darkness.

"Not too good at all," Mildred said.

J.B. sat up with a sudden, incisive gesture, fumbling for his glasses and perching them on his narrow nose. "Ryan looks ill," he said. "And Michael. You checked his breathing?"

Mildred shook her head. "Not yet, John. Ryan hasn't come around, and he's running a triple-high temperature. The wound in his neck's gone bad."

"Not surprised. Anything connected with that filthy place was probably poisoned."

"Except the candy," Dean said. "Anyone want any? I brought a few of those sticks with me."

"Save them." J.B. realized that the boy had been hurt by his curtness. "Save them, Dean. Could be we'll be real grateful you thought about bringing them."

"Sure. Thing I want most is a good drink. A cold and clear pool of Sierra meltwater." Dean licked his dry lips. "Trade it for most anything."

"Air doesn't seem too bad." Doc took several sniffs through his prominent, beaked nose. "Hardly the nectar of the gods, but at least it lacks that ghastly bitter, sort of chlorine odor of those foggy canyons."

"And it's not too hot, either." Mildred straightened. "Better take a look at Michael. I think we have to get Ryan to some water as fast as we can. Cool him down before he burns up. Might be water in some part of the redoubt. Assuming that there is a redoubt around us."

Krysty had been leaning against the wall, eyes closed, concentrating on trying to pick up some "feelings" from the place. The atmosphere was typical of most of the complexes that they'd visited, flat and slightly stale, as if it had been recycled a million times—which it might well have been during the century since skydark, the hidden nuke gens working away toward infinity and a day. Most redoubts still functioned, with light, heat, air-conditioning and

BC

cleaning all working to the comp-controlled program.

"Nothing to report," she finally decided. "Can't pick up any life vibes."

"How's Michael?" Dean asked, standing close to Mildred as she examined the teenager.

"Move back a little. Give me some space." She peeled back his eyelids and looked intently into his eyes. "Pupils dilated. Breathing very slow. Pulse the same. Almost like he's slipped into some kind of concussive, clinical shock."

"Mebbe the third jump was one too many." J.B. had already picked up the Steyr rifle and strapped it over his shoulders, handing the Uzi to Dean.

Mildred sniffed. "Don't know. Hopefully Michael should snap out of it. Probably come around all at once and wonder what on earth could have happened to him. I suppose that it might be a psychosis induced by the mat-trans."

"Delayed reaction to being trawled?" Doc looked worried. "I do trust that none of you are aware of this fact, but I confess that my own mind is not always the efficient reasoning machine that it once was. I blame those white-coated demons for that. And for much besides."

Ryan shuffled his feet, the soles of the combat boots rasping on the metal disks in the gateway's floor. The fingers of his right hand kept clenching and straightening, as if he were trying to grasp something.

"We should move," Mildred said.

"What about Michael, though? We can't just leave him." Krysty looked at the others. "Won't be easy if we have to try and carry them both."

"Can do it, if it's not too far." J.B. looked down at the two unconscious figures. "Ryan weighs in around the two-hundred-pound mark. I'd guess that Michael is probably fifty or sixty pounds lighter."

"I could take more blasters," Dean offered. "Or give a hand with Michael."

"Have to try it." The Armorer stood there for a few moments, locked into a variety of logistical calculations. Which of them should do what.

"I could carry the lad for a way," Doc offered. "I still recall how to implement what we used to call the 'fireman's carry' method."

J.B. nodded approvingly. "Fine. I can take Ryan for a start. Then, mebbe Mildred and Krysty could spell me for a time."

"What about..." Dean started.

"Don't worry. You get to be a walking arsenal for the rest of us. Doc's sword as well as the Uzi. And the rifle. Reckon that's the best we can do."

"Sure."

Ryan moaned again, his head rolling from side to side. His mouth had sagged open and his breathing was ragged. Mildred stared down at him. "Think I might have to try and cauterize that wound. But we need a fire and some decent water for that. The infection seems to be racing through him. Massive dose of antibiotics might be the ticket." Mildred sighed. "Time's wasting. No point in hanging around here."

Doc nodded vigorously, kneeling beside Michael's motionless figure. "Could someone give me a hand to get him up on my shoulders?"

Without a breath of warning, Michael's eyes opened wide, and he grabbed the old man around the throat with ghastly violence.

"Die, fucking Satan!" he screamed. "Die!"

Chapter Twelve

The attack was so sudden and so violent that it took several heartbeats before anyone reacted.

By then Doc was flat on his back in the chamber, Michael kneeling astride him, gripping him around the neck so ferociously that the old man's eyes were protruding from their sockets.

The teenager maintained a constant stream of foul-mouthed abuse, calling Doc the devil and Satan, screeching that he would exorcise him from his mind.

Krysty moved fastest.

She drew the double-action Smith & Wesson 640 from its holster and hit Michael a roundhouse, clubbing blow with the butt, striking him just behind the right ear.

He stiffened and jerked back, his hands flying apart as though he'd just received some astounding religious conversion. Then he groaned once and collapsed forward, slumping on top of the semiconscious Doc.

"Holy shit!" Dean exclaimed. "If I hadn't been holding all these blasters, I'd have aced him."

J.B. reached into one of the pockets of his coat and removed two lengths of thin waxed twine. "Going to tie him up before he comes around and does some more damage.''

''Think it was probably a madness brought on by the jump,'' Mildred said.

Krysty had holstered the Smith & Wesson and kneeled by the shaken old man, who was rubbing at his bruised throat with both hands, struggling to get his breathing back to somewhere close to normal.

''Land of Goshen! The poor lad was possessed. I thought my last moment had come. Who stopped him from impersonating the thuggish stranglers of the goddess Kali?''

''Me. Bopped him with the blaster.''

''Then you have my heartfelt thanks, my dear Krysty. My whole life flashed past me.''

''Did it really, Doc?'' Dean asked eagerly. ''Heard people say that before.''

''Well, if I lay my hand upon my heart, I have to admit that it didn't really, Dean. Just a pounding across the temples and blood filling my eyes.''

J.B. quickly and efficiently knotted the cord around Michael's thumbs, behind his back, also lashing the teenager's ankles together. He straightened. ''There. Might be all right, but I'm not taking a chance.''

Ryan opened his eye and stared around the gateway chamber. ''Pretty color of purple on the walls,'' he said. ''Successful jump, then?'' He started to lift his hand toward the suppurating wound on his neck.

''No, don't touch it.'' Mildred stooped quickly and checked the movement.

"What? Fireblast, but my neck feels . . . I feel triple sick and . . . where are the snows of . . ." His eye closed again, and Ryan slipped back into the darkness.

"Boy, but we're sure all having a load of fun here." Mildred sighed. "One mad and one sick."

"Best move it," J.B. said. "Doc."

"Yes, my dear chap?"

"Can you manage to carry Michael?"

"I shall resist the temptation to drop him on his skull, if that's what you mean. Though, if he commences to struggle, I shall regard that as an adequate excuse."

THE CHAMBER OPENED onto a small room, eight feet square, wtih a small table in one corner and two rows of empty shelves. There was a rectangle of white card pinned to one of the shelves, crumpled and fragile.

"'Paul and Danny, the Vid Men,'" Dean read slowly. "'Best Selection in all N.H.' What's that mean?"

"New Hampshire," Mildred said. "Looks like we've finished up in New England."

Doc had already begun to pant with the effort of carrying the unconscious Michael slung over his shoulder. "Can we keep moving?" he asked. "I fear that once I lay this burden down I shall not be up to taking it up again."

The control room was much like all of the others that they'd seen—rows of desks and rows of screens, all showing shimmering rows of information; endless blocks of coded numerals, relating to all the aspects of running the redoubt; not a sign of any sort of life anywhere.

On the far end of the room were the usual double sec doors of vanadium steel, with the green control lever set to the right-hand side.

J.B. was far stronger than his slim build would suggest, and he didn't seem to be struggling at all under Ryan's weight. "Dean, you operate the lever. Mildred and Krysty, both of you get your blasters ready and crouch down on the floor. You know how to do it. Seen Ryan and I enough times. Dean, just about nine inches. No more. Understand?"

"Sure," Krysty said, Mildred and Dean both nodding their agreement.

Doc was wheezing. "Can I lay down this sleeping beauty for a moment?"

"Sure. Get the Le Mat out and keep watch."

"Wilco, Commander Dix. You mean to watch the door with the ladies?"

"No. Watch Michael."

"He's tied up safely."

"Long as he hasn't got some sort of crazie strength to break free. Just watch him."

"What if he escapes and looks dangerous?"

J.B. eased Ryan on his shoulder. "Shoot him, Doc. Just shoot him."

THE CORRIDOR WAS BARE.

Dean was sent off on a recce to the right, urged to be careful, returning within less than two minutes with the news that the passage ended in a solid wall of stone only a hundred paces or so around the curve.

The overhead strip lights glared down pitilessly, and the miniature sec cameras probed ceaselessly from the junction of wall and ceiling.

Now that they were on a level expanse of smooth concrete, Doc seemed to have a new lease on life, striding out, knees cracking, Michael still unconscious on his shoulders.

There were no side passages or doors in the first quarter mile. The corridor had been dead flat, but it now began to wind slowly upward.

Doc stopped and gently put Michael down on the floor. "I think a small rest is required."

J.B. lowered Ryan beside the bound figure of the teenager.

"Hard time of it," he said, pushing his fedora back on his forehead.

"Think it'll be much farther?" Dean asked, standing and looking worriedly at his father—who opened his eye.

"Father is farthest," he said. "Don't ask so many questions, son. We'll get there when we get there. Shit, this wound on my neck hurts."

Then he closed his eye and was silent.

"Want us to take some of the load?" Krysty asked. "Must be an elevator or some kind of intersection soon."

"I don't know where I am."

The voice was barely recognizable as Michael's, a strange, wizened, whispering voice, like a walled-up crone in a labrynth.

"I don't know who I am."

It was Doc who knelt by the boy, brushing the hair away from the dark troubled eyes. "Your name is Michael, and you are with friends."

"You lie."

The ferocity of the earlier mood seemed to have altered to a withdrawn passivity. The planes of the young man's face were as smooth as a little child's.

"We are friends, truly," Doc encouraged.

"I'm trapped, deep inside my own bowels," Michael insisted. "All blackness."

His eyes were wide open, staring through Doc. Krysty noticed that he was tensing all his muscles, as if he were testing the bonds.

"Watch him, Doc," she warned. "Could be foxing."

"Either I have taken some drug that has made me mad," Michael whispered, "or I'm totally mad. I can't tell which is the truth."

"Neither. You are Michael and we are friends. I'm Doc. There's Krysty and—"

"Imps of evil. Brother Athanasius warned us against such as you. You come disguised with fucking smiles and fucking lies."

"Best get on, Doc," J.B. said. "Want the ladies to take a turn?"

"Perhaps. I might go ahead on point."

"I was doing that," Dean protested. "Why don't you watch the back?"

There was an uncomfortable moment while the boy and the old man stared at each other. J.B. broke the impasse. "You've been on point, Dean. Take turns. Keep alert, Doc."

"Of course." He stuck out his tongue at Dean when the Armorer turned his back, making the lad grin.

Mildred took Michael's shoulders and Krysty his legs, while J.B. carried on with Ryan.

It was slower and clumsier with two of them, as Michael was conscious and kept wriggling, trying to kick out at Krysty, mumbling an endless stream of curses.

After less than a hundred yards Krysty had taken enough and let go of the teenager's legs. "Drop him," she said.

Mildred lowered Michael, while J.B., just ahead of them, turned around and saw what had happened. He put Ryan down again.

"Bitch fucker shit sucker."

"Nice rhyme, Michael," Krysty said. "Now, you got a choice here." She rested her Western boot on his throat, pinning him between the sole and the heel. She leaned a little of her weight down, making his face flush.

"Fuck off," he gasped.

"No. That's the sort of thing you say when you're on top and under control. I'm on top, Michael and you're under control. Better understand that right now." She pressed harder, feeling the cartilage crackle under her foot. "You swear at me again, or if you try to kick me, then I'll break your neck."

He didn't speak, his eyes closed in pain. Mildred was about to interfere when she saw the look of cold anger on Krysty's face and kept silent.

"I mean it, Michael. You hear? Nod if you hear me." There was a slight movement of his head. "Good. Now, when you feel better, you can walk again. Until then, you get carried."

THEY CAME TO AN OPEN AREA, the corridor forking into a letter Y, a sign on the wall between the two options. An arrow pointed to the left, with the single word "Out." To the right was the word "In."

"I think we'll go in," J.B. said.

"HOPE YOU REMEMBER the way out of here, John," Mildred panted.

They had been past seven or eight multiple-choice branchings of the corridors, each sign becoming more specific and detailed: IC Comms, 2IC Ed, Comp Cont, R&R, Tran Pool, Accts, Armory, which interested J.B. a lot.

But the most important one, which they all agreed to follow, was the sign directing them toward Medic.

The farther they went, the more often they had to stop for a rest.

Ryan seemed to have slipped into a sort of coma, occasionally stirring and muttering, but his voice was quiet, the words garbled.

J.B. had carried him for the past fifteen minutes, but even his wiry strength had become depleted.

Once again he laid him down, while Mildred and Dean, who were taking a turn with Michael, also took a break.

"We go into hell," the teenager said quietly, with the total confidence of the totally insane.

"Is the lad recovering his wits, Dr. Wyeth?" Doc asked.

"Not so's you'd notice. He's quietened, but I think that owes more to Krysty scaring the shit out of him than any medical improvement."

They had seen no sign of life.

The air-conditioning hummed deep within the walls, but every breath tasted flat and dull, as though it had been circulating for a hundred years.

They passed a couple of small sections off to the side, and Dean or Krysty slipped in to recce them. But they were all swept totally clean. The evacuation of the redoubt had obviously been carried out with great efficiency.

"Medics along here," Dean called, scouting a little way ahead of the others.

Mildred was sitting down, her back against the curve of the concrete wall, her eyes closed, hands folded together in her lap. "It's going to be just like everything else, isn't it?" she said very quietly.

"Likely," J.B. agreed. "But like Trader used to say, you go the last mile, the last bullet. The last breath. Might find something there that'll help Ryan." Then he added as an afterthought, "And mebbe Michael."

WHEN THEY EVENTUALLY pushed their way through the swinging, airtight double doors at the entrance to the medical section of the military complex, they found it just as abandoned and empty as the rest of the place.

"Oh, Gaia!" Krysty sighed, feeling despair wash up and over her.

Chapter Thirteen

There were nearly eighty beds set out through four wards, each bed bolted to the floor and each with a plastic-covered mattress that had stood the test of time amazingly well. Beside each bed was a small locker and a folding table.

Ryan was laid on one of the beds, with Michael put gently on another one a little farther down the room. J.B. crashed out on a third bed, looking utterly drained by the efforts of the past hour.

Dean sat beside his father, staring anxiously at him. "Looks triple sick, Mildred," he said.

"Can't argue with that, son. Sinking deeper into the fever with that wound. If I can't find some way of dropping his temperature or cleansing the sore, then..."

"Mebbe they left something in the pharmacy," Krysty said. "Let's go look."

Doc was the most chipper of them all, striding up and down like a grenadier, rapping the beat on the floor with his sword stick.

"This is a challenge, and no mistake. To be without our beloved leader, in such parlous straits. If only one could be assured a cheerful outcome."

There was a notice over a door, announcing that it was the pharmacy. Krysty was first there, pushing open the white-painted door, stopping dead.

"Nothing," she announced. "Cupboard's bare."

Mildred looked around the room. There was a pile of neatly folded cotton sheets in one corner, over-looked during the closing of the redoubt. A double sink stood against the far wall, with chromed taps.

"Do you think the water's still on?" she asked, walking over to turn the blue handle.

There was nothing at all for several seconds, then a faint gurgling sound, like an underground river flowing, many miles away.

"Hey," Krysty said. "Something's coming."

"If there's enough water, then there's hope. Drugs'd be best, but water and a sterilized knife, with his strong constitution then . . ." She spun as clear liquid gushed from the tap. Mildred cupped it in her hands and sniffed at it suspiciously, then touched her tongue to it. "Thank you, God," she whispered. "Fresh as could be."

DEAN WAS FIRST TO DRINK, hardly listening to Mildred's warning not to take too much too fast. The rest of them also drank their fill.

J.B. spotted a foam beaker under one of the beds, and he used that to offer water to Michael, who spit it back in his face.

"The brothers told us that outsiders would try to take us over, steal our spirits, rape our souls. Come in like thieves in the night, as they did in Waco, that terrible time. But we are ready. Armed with the breastplate of wisdom and the shining silver sword of righteousness. Get back to Hell, Azrael, and your brazen hordes."

J.B. wiped the drops from his face and neck. "Then I guess you have to stay thirsty, Michael."

Krysty tore off a length from one of the sheets and soaked it in water, squeezing a few drops onto Ryan's dry, cracked lips. But he didn't seem aware of her.

"We should start with him, Krysty," Mildred said. "Longer we wait, the smaller his chances."

"Sure."

"This isn't going to be easy."

J.B. stood with them, looking down at his oldest friend. "Why?"

Mildred sighed. "I know he's spark out, but when I try and burn away the poison, it's going to be agony for a while. And there's no anesthetic."

"I can tie him to the bed."

Mildred considered that. "Danger is that he's so strong that he could tug real hard. Cut his wrists open to the bone. No, I think we have to try and hold him still."

"Who?" Dean asked. "All of us?"

"Yeah. All of you. I'll do the actual cauterization. Dean, you'll have to help me. Wipe away blood and stuff like that. Only leaves three of you to keep him still. If he jerks away or thrashes around, then I could easily end up cutting open the big artery in his neck."

"We have to try," Krysty said.

"Yeah."

IT DIDN'T TAKE LONG to get everything ready for the operation. Under Mildred's supervision they brought in all of the sheets, having soaked some of them in water, ready to try to bring his temperature down. Ryan's own narrow-bladed flensing knife was taken from the sheath in the small of his back and laid to one side. J.B. handed over nearly all of his store of precious self-lights to sterilize the steel and bring it to red heat.

"Ready as we'll be," Mildred announced.

Michael had wriggled over on his left side and was staring at their preparations with a fixed glare.

"The horror..." he whispered.

Krysty lay across Ryan's legs, pinning them down, while Doc and J.B. took an arm each, bracing themselves for the struggle to come.

Mildred took one of the pieces of torn sheet and dabbed very carefully at the hideous cicatrix on the side of the unconscious man's neck. Though her touch was as gentle as a butterfly's wing, Ryan stirred and moaned.

"Infection's gone deep," she said.

"Ready for the self-heats?" Dean asked. His face was as pale as parchment, and he was sweating profusely. Mildred wiped at his forehead.

"Relax," she soothed. "It'll be all right."

"Promise?"

"Sure."

The doctor hoped that the eleven-year-old couldn't detect her own anguished doubts. Ryan was critically ill, the poison from the mutie creature's attack eating into his body, attacking his immune system. A weaker man would already have been dead.

She held out the slim-bladed knife, while Dean readied the self-heats. He'd listened carefully to her orders: to run the flame slowly up and down the steel, sterilizing it for its surgical use, then holding the matches steady beneath the weapon, until Mildred decided it was hot enough for the task in hand.

"Some blood from the wound, Mildred," Doc said.

"Thanks." She wiped at it again.

But this time the pain from the sensitive sore jerked Ryan back for a moment from the deep unconsciousness and he cried out, trying to kick and flail his arms. It was all that Doc, J.B. and Krysty could do to keep him still.

Mildred jumped back, nearly treading on Dean's foot. "Shit! This isn't—"

"I could sort of hold," the boy offered.

"No. Can't do this single-handed."

"Let me go and I'll help."

Everyone looked at Michael, tied and helpless.

"No," Mildred said.

"You won't hold him."

"We will."

The teenager shook his head. "You saw how he reacted, just at the touch of a soft, damp cloth. How'll he be with red-hot steel on the wound?"

There was a long, taut silence in the hospital ward, broken only by another moan from the wounded man. Mildred looked at the others, wanting some kind of guidance.

"John?"

"He's right, Mildred."

"Why am I tied up? I can't remember anything. Just that we were in that old store, and then we jumped..."

"We could use him," Mildred said.

"No," Dean insisted. "Dad'll die if Michael does anything double stupe."

"I fear, young man, that your dear father might not survive if we reject Michael's offer of assistance."

"Untie me. We jumped again, didn't we? Kind of desert. Must've made me... Let me go, please."

Krysty felt a wave of certainty. "Cut him loose, J.B., quickly."

"Sure?"

"Positive."

J.B. let go of Ryan's left wrist and walked quickly to the bed where Michael was bound. He drew his own knife and cut through the thin cords around hands and ankles.

Michael sat up, wincing in pain as the blood flowed back again into his extremities. "Hurts like..." he said. "Give me one minute and I'm with you."

Mildred was still standing, waiting. "Doc, help Krysty with Ryan's legs. J.B., the left hand and Michael can hang on to the right hand. Ready?"

A little unsteady on his feet, the teenager joined them, smiling at Dean. "Ryan'll be fine now," he said.

"You go stupe and I'll blow your head off your shoulders," Dean replied.

"You do that."

"Self-lights, Dean."

There was a flare of yellow and the smell of sulfur in the deserted room. Mildred moved the flensing knife up and down through the heat, watching the steel change color.

"Good," she said. "Now more of the matches, and hold them still, as long as you can without burning your own fingers. All right?"

Dean nodded. "Right."

"Do it. Hang on to Ryan's arms and legs like his life depended on it. Because I think it does."

The steel darkened, turning black, through cadmium, then began to glow the dark red of a winter sunset. It became brighter as Dean struck another batch of the self-lights.

The steel turned golden, then almost like the fiery, white glow of silver in a furnace. Waves of heat came from it, and Mildred moved her fingers on the hilt.

"Now," she whispered.

Chapter Fourteen

It was the worst kind of endless nightmare.

For the rest of her life, Krysty Wroth would never ever forget that quarter of an hour in the long-abandoned heart of the redoubt in the wilds of New Hampshire. Every detail would come back to her unexpectedly, unbidden—the sight, the smell, the sounds, the shocking physical sensations as Mildred applied the red-hot steel blade to the ghastly septic wound at the side of Ryan's neck.

None of it would ever leave Krysty, nor any of the others there.

Ryan remembered virtually nothing of it, which was some sort of mercy. There was a limit to the amount of remembered pain that anyone could bear.

MILDRED BLINKED SWEAT from her eyes as she leaned forward, her knuckles white on the hilt of the slim-bladed knife.

First came the noise, like spots of water flicked into the heart of a fire. It was a whisper of sounds, followed by a shallow, bubbling as the steel bit into the core of the wound.

The smell came next, a foul, burning stench that was the poison being scorched out by the heat of the dagger. Tendrils of smoke drifted up from the charred flesh into Mildred's face.

Even with his deep coma, it only took a couple of heartbeats for Ryan to begin to react against the searing agony. But it seemed like an eternity, so long that it crossed Mildred's mind that the one-eyed man was actually dead.

Then the pain reached him and he exploded.

Ryan's eye snapped wide open and stared furiously at the ceiling, then found Mildred's eyes and focused on them. His lips peeled back from his teeth, and a roar of shock and horror erupted from his throat. His head flailed back and forth, despite all of Mildred's efforts to keep him steady. His arms and legs jerked into spasmodic action, forcing everyone to hang on for grim life.

Mildred withdrew the knife for a moment, turning to look at Dean. Tears coursed down the boy's cheeks, cutting white furrows through the dirt. "Hold his head still," she demanded, "with all your strength."

The boy put down the matches and the torn strips of sheet, moving quickly, without any argument, and locked his fingers tightly in his father's long black curls. He leaned down to hold him as still as possible.

"Don't, Dad!" he cried. "Gotta save your life."

But it did nothing to calm the anguished man. The second time that the knife, cooler now, came into contact with the yellowed gash, Ryan screamed and kicked out. Doc and Krysty were nearly thrown off the bed, both J.B. and Michael using every ounce of their strength to keep hold of his arms.

"Matches!" Mildred yelled at the top of her voice, barely audible over Ryan's ceaseless inarticulate shouting.

She wiped the dulled knife on the sheet, holding it still for Dean to run the small flames beneath it. The foul smell was appalling.

"His head again, Dean."

She peered intently at the wound before touching it with the red-hot steel. The core of pus still throbbed, veined with crimson. But the heat of the flensing knife seemed to have cleaned up the area around the edges of the ragged core.

"Again," she whispered.

The smoke was blinding, the perfume of charred corruption sickening. But Mildred persevered, biting her lip so hard that she drew a tiny trickle of blood. She moved the knife, so that it probed deep into the gash, Her love for Ryan made her want to withdraw the blade and spare him further suffering, but her medical training insisted that she should go on, delving deeper and deeper, until every last molecule of the filthy sickness was totally exorcised by the hot steel.

"Pass out, you tough bastard, Ryan," she muttered, hardly able to believe the man's strength and resilience under the cauterizing knife.

It wasn't until Mildred applied the red-hot blade for a fourth time that Ryan's whole body quivered, his eye rolled back in its socket and he finally slipped away into the kindness of unconsciousness.

"He's dead," Dean gasped.

"No. Get a piece of rag and mop away all the blackened shit and blood from the wound. Wipe as hard and as deep as you can. Only way to save him."

The woman stared into the cleaned wound, seeing the free-flowing blood, scarcely able to credit her good fortune in not harming any major artery. She tested the wound with her finger, finding it a good inch and a half deep at its core, and at least five inches long.

"How is it?" They were the first words that Krysty had spoken during the operation. She had been hanging on to Ryan, trying to keep him still, praying to Gaia for his recovery from the ordeal.

"Looks cleaner. I don't know whether..."

"To shrink from the last step could cost his life, Dr. Wyeth," Doc warned sternly.

"I just don't know if his heart can stand up to my doing it again."

"Do it," Krysty urged. "Doc's right. Leave a shred of poison in the wound, and it'll kill him."

Mildred sighed. "Yeah. Come on, Dean. Just one last time, then we can clean it up and bandage it."

"And pray," Michael added.

IT WAS OVER. J.B. had managed to disconnect most of the lights in the ward so that Ryan could rest in a pool of darkness, lying on his back, a length of clean sheet wrapped around the wound. He was naked, with just a single sheet covering him.

As soon as the suppurating wound had been purged of its filth, his temperature had begun to drop. He was still hot, but Mildred had chosen not to wrap him in wet sheets to bring it down any more quickly.

"Figure his system's had enough of a pounding for any one day," she said.

The rest of them had moved to an adjacent room in the hospital section of the redoubt, sitting quietly. Dean had fallen asleep, drained by witnessing the operation on his father. Michael also dozed on another of the beds.

Krysty sat next to Ryan, watching over him, occasionally laying cool fingers on his forehead and muttering a blessing from the Earth Mother.

Farther down the ward J.B. sat next to Mildred, holding her hand. Doc was facing them.

They talked together quietly, not wanting to disturb any of the others.

"How long before we can move on, Mildred?"

"Don't know, John. Most patients been through what Ryan's gone through today, and they'd be in rest and recuperation for a month. But he's got the finest constitution of any man I ever saw. Could be up and moving, slow and easy, within a couple of days. Have to wait and see."

"What about delayed shock?" Doc asked. "Is that not a possibility?"

"Course. After that... But his pulse is near normal. Little slow. Respiration a little fast. But you have to bear in mind that Ryan's been through an operation that would normally only have been done under a full general anesthetic. It's amazing he's pulled through this far."

"You did brilliantly, love," J.B. said, kissing her on the cheek. "Think mebbe you should lie down and rest awhile? I could sort of—"

"Come and rest with me, John," Mildred said, smiling. "Well, I could be up for that. Let's go into the end ward and get some privacy from prying eyes."

She grinned at Doc, who actually blushed.

"Upon my soul, Dr. Wyeth! Have you no shame?"

"Enough to go into the end ward, Doc."

They stood up. J.B. looked at Dean and Michael, both soundly asleep. "Food's going to get to be a real problem in the next half day or so," he said.

"Seeing that white steel burning away Ryan's neck was the finest suppressor of an appetite I ever saw." Doc shuddered.

RYAN CAME AROUND from the soul-deep blackness in the middle of the night.

Krysty had dozed off on the adjacent bed, lying on her back, her fiery sentient hair curled protectively about her nape.

But as Ryan's eye opened, she stirred, as if someone had whispered her name in the center of a dream, calling her back from a land far away.

She smiled at him. "Hi, there, lover."

"Feel like a war wag drove over me." His arm came out from under the thin cotton sheet, lifting toward his neck.

"Don't touch it, Ryan."

"Seems like something's sucking my brain out through the side of my throat. What happened?"

"Remember the ghost town?"

"Lonesome Gulch? Sure."

"Those mutie bird things?"

"Blew their asses sideways. Yeah. One of them . . . How come it hurts so bad?"

"Got infected."

He struggled to sit up. Krysty swung her long legs off the bed and helped him with an arm behind the shoulders, easing him to a more upright position.

"Fireblast!" In the gloom of the ward, she could see how deathly pale he was and what the injury had taken out of him. "I got no clothes on."

"You had a temperature to put Death Valley in the shade. Mildred saved your life, lover."

"What'd she do?"

"Took your skinning blade and—"

"Where's my blasters?" A note of something close to panic was in his voice.

She sat on the bed, taking care not to jar him. "Easy, lover. SIG-Sauer's under the bed. Rifle's in the other ward along with J.B. and the others."

"Ward?"

"We jumped to an abandoned redoubt that's stripped about as clean as a mutie's conscience. Think it's probably in New England someplace."

"Anyone been outside?"

"Not yet. Listen, don't keep interrupting me, Ryan. Bad jump. Michael went full psycho and tried to chill Doc."

"Who . . ."

"Me. Pistol-whipped him. J.B. tied him up and he finally got quiet. He helped in your operation. We all did."

"Any food in here?"

Krysty shook her head. "No. Doesn't look like it. Have to do something tomorrow."

He nodded, cautiously raising a hand and touching the wad of white material around his throat. There was a dark patch of blood at its center, and he felt it. "Still leaking some, huh?"

"Some."

"I was out of it, then?"

"We carried you. Took turns."

"Close call?"

She kissed him on the cheek, still feeling the blazing remnants of the high fever. "Close."

"Mildred used my knife, you were saying. Heated it, I guess. Burned it out. Must've been a mess of laughs."

"It was."

He closed his eye again. "Can't really remember anything about it. Not the actual business. Sort of smell myself burning, but that's about it."

"You ought to try and sleep."

"Thought that was what I'd been doing."

"Lie down again. And try and keep flat on your back. Save from hurting your neck."

"You'd make a good nurse, Krysty. Thanks, love. Tell the rest of them . . . tell them thanks."

Chapter Fifteen

Ryan woke several times during the long night, jerked abruptly out of sleep by the stabbing pains from his neck. The makeshift bandage kept sticking to the congealing blood, making any rest difficult.

Krysty slept lightly and stirred every time Ryan moved suddenly.

Mildred had explained that the first twelve hours would be crucial in Ryan's recovery. If his temperature started to rise again, it would probably indicate that the infection hadn't been scoured from his system.

"Then what?" Krysty had whispered to the doctor, as they'd stood together in the deserted pharmacy, sharing a cup of water.

"Then I think Ryan'll probably die. There isn't anything else to be done."

MILDRED HAD ALWAYS HAD the ability, common to many doctors, of being able to control her waking and sleeping. She rose roughly every hour during the night, slipping from J.B.'s side, and padded on bare feet through the silent vault of the redoubt, stopping at Ryan's bedside.

She laid her hand on his forehead, smiling down at him as his right eye fluttered open. "So far, so good," she whispered, finding each time that his temperature was no more than a degree or so up on normal.

"Will I make it?" he asked, late in the small hours of the morning.

"Doing good, Ryan. Bleeding looks like it's stopped."

"Will I play the violin again, Doctor?"

"What?"

"Saw some old vid once and a double-sick person said that. I never really understood it. Some kind of predark joke, I guess, Mildred."

"Yeah. Guess it was."

MICHAEL WOKE UP DEAN. "Hey, you asleep?"

"I was. What d'you want?"

The teenager rolled on his side, facing the boy. "You feel hungry?"

"Some."

"You got any of that candy left?"

Dean fumbled in the pocket of his black denim jacket. "Couple of sticks."

"Give me one."

"No."

"Why not? I'm famished and could eat a horse, if there was one lying around."

Dean shook his head. "Can't. Don't reckon there's any other food around this deserted crap hole. These are sweet, so they could keep us going. Give us energy. My mother told me that once."

"They're too small. Can't share them, Dean."

"Watch me."

Michael rolled onto his back again, lying and staring at the high ceiling. "Dean?"

"What?" he asked irritably.

"Was I . . . was I out of it?"

Dean sat up, making the bed creak. "You kept saying that you were trapped up your own ass."

"Yeah. I can kind of remember that. Sort of blurred. Was I yelling a lot?"

"Until Krysty said she'd break your neck if you didn't calm down."

Michael laughed quietly. "I remember that. Must've been on the way to being normal again. My throat's real sore from her boot. I think I was struggling so I'd know I was still alive. If I'd stopped back then, I might have gone far away into that distant land. And never returned again."

"If you hadn't managed to shake off being triple stupe . . ." Dean hesitated.

"What?"

"Well, I don't think Dad would have made it. He was too strong, and the others couldn't like hold him still."

"The smell from that hole in his neck when Mildred stuck the knife in it—"

"Worse than a stickie's fart."

"Worse than Doc's socks."

Dean giggled. "Worse than a dead dog's guts."

"Worse than . . ." Michael paused, trying to think of something sufficiently gross. "Worse than a stickie's fart after eating a rotting fish from out of a dead dog's guts.''

Dean clapped his hands. "Hot pipe, brother!"

"While it was wearing Doc's socks."

Both of them exploded into uncontrollable sniggering, which covered the sound of approaching feet along the ward.

"My apologies, gentlemen." The laughter stopped like turning off a faucet. "I had thought to find a pair of puking, giggling infants, waiting to be filled up with their mother's milk. Now I find that it is Dean, who I believe is already into his twelfth year of life. And the former oblate from the monastery of Nil-Vanity in the hills above Visalia, a young man who must now be close to his twentieth birthday, both creating such a damned noise and making such childishly stupe jests."

Neither of them spoke, lying on their beds, looking at the towering figure of the angry old man.

Doc rapped the floor with the iron ferrule of his stick. "Go back to sleep, both of you, before you get the good spanking you so richly deserve."

"Sorry, Doc," Dean muttered.

"Yeah, sorry," Michael agreed.

"Very well." He strode off, heels clicking, vanishing into the darkness at the far end of the long ward.

"Good spanking..." Dean whispered.

Michael was struggling not to break out laughing again. "Mother's milk!"

"Silly old fuckhead."

"Right on, Dean."

"If I ruled Deathlands, I think I'd have a law that meant all wrinklies get chilled after their fortieth birthday." Dean stifled another giggle. "That'd teach Doc."

THEY ALL SHARED the two slender sticks of candy, using one of Michael's twin daggers to cut them into small segments.

"Any idea what flavor they are, Dean?" J.B. asked, as he looked at the striped sugary fingers.

"One was mango and mint, I think. Something like that. Can't remember the other."

Doc held out a hand. "See if my ancient scent buds still function in identifying sweetmeats." Dean gave him the unwrapped stick. "Let me see..." The old man sniffed at it.

"Don't breathe it all away, Doc," Mildred said. "Leave some for the rest of us." She shook her head, tiny beads rattling softly together. "I can't believe that seven grown men and women are sitting around sharing out two tiny bits of highly colored, flavored and preserved candy."

"Sassafras and moonlight," Doc said, handing the candy back to Michael, ready to be sliced thin.

"What's that?" Ryan asked, leaning on one elbow on his bed.

Mildred had been amazed at the speed of his recovery. His temperature, respiration and pulse were all back to normal, and he seemed to be gathering and renewing strength with every hour that passed.

"Guess that's what living in Deathlands does for you," she'd explained to Krysty. "So much disease that everyone's a lot more resistant to it. I seriously believe that ninety-nine men out of a hundred from my time would have been long dead with that degree of infection."

"Sassafras and moonlight?" Doc replied. "Just a rather fancy way of conveying the fact that I have no idea at all what flavor it's supposed to be."

There was still the argument of how best to slice up two candy sticks of slightly differing lengths and divide them evenly between seven people.

"It's a total length of about fifteen and a quarter inches," Mildred said.

"That's about 2.17 inches each." Doc looked down at his fingers. "Or should that be 2.18?"

"Crush them all up with the hilt of the knife," J.B. suggested. "Be a lot easier to split up a pile of bits into seven roughly equal heaps."

It was the best idea that anyone could come up with, so that's what they did.

"Delicious. Best half ounce of candy I ever ate," Mildred said, licking her lips.

"Not quite as satisfying as a plate of eggs and bacon and hash browns." Doc wiped his mouth on his sleeve. "Jesting apart, what are we to do about obtaining some rather more adequate sustenance for ourselves?"

"Go out and hunt." Ryan was sitting up in his bed, his face pale beneath the stubble.

"Not you."

"Why not, Mildred?"

"As your doctor, I forbid it. You would fall down, stone-dead, and then your relatives could bring a medical malpractice suit against me."

Ryan grinned. "I can't believe I feel so much better."

"Amazing what a little mango-and-mint candy can do for a man." Krysty leaned over the bed and kissed him.

"You shouldn't try to move today." Mildred saw the look in Ryan's eye. "I'm serious, now. Fever like that puts a real strain on your heart."

"Stay here and starve?"

"You stay here. Couple of us remain with you. John can go out with Dean and Michael and bring back food."

Doc drew himself up to his full six feet three inches. "Am I not to be considered for this hunting expedition, madam? Must I stay with the sickly and the female, which some say are one and the same thing?"

"You dumbshit..." Mildred began angrily.

Ryan clapped his hands together. "Hold it, hold it! This doesn't matter."

"Why?"

"Because, Mildred. Grateful as I am to you for pulling me through, I still don't figure on lying on my back. Without food I'll likely get weaker, so I might as well do it now."

"Hot pipe, Dad!" Dean shouted, his voice cracking to a reedy squeak in his excitement.

Michael punched the air. "Thanks to all the gods. We can have some fresh air, food, water and stuff."

"Like we did around Lonesome Gulch," Mildred warned. "Remember how good that was."

"Won't be like that," Dean said confidently.

IT WASN'T LIKE THAT.

After all taking a long drink of the cold water, they set out toward the main entrance of the redoubt. Despite his claims of fitness, Ryan was glad to accept Doc's offer of the loan of the sword stick to help himself along the echoing corridors.

"Main sec doors just ahead," J.B. reported, taking up the point position. "No sign of life. No sign of trouble."

The panel had the same coding as in all of the other redoubts that they'd encountered. Three-five-two to open the massive doors and two-five-three to close them.

"Want to rest a spell, Ryan?" the Armorer asked.

"You're enjoying this, J.B., aren't you? You never forgave me for laughing at you that time you had the little problem over sitting down with your—"

"That's enough. You swore an oath on Trader's life never to mention that."

Ryan grinned. "It was Trader who used to say that he never knew of a promise that couldn't be broken."

Watched by the others, Dean pressed in the number code and the doors began to slide back.

Chapter Sixteen

It was a truly enchanting vista that stretched out before the seven friends.

There was a plateau of bare rock, looking as big as a football field, that had once been graded and still showed the faint etched lines on the tarmac where parking spaces had been allocated for the military. It was bordered by a row of sturdy concrete blocks along the edge, marking a steep drop toward a narrow valley fifteen hundred feet below.

A flock of pure white doves circled far above, cooing to one another in the warm sunshine. Far beneath them they could just see the silver thread of a narrow river, while in the middle distance, partly obscured by a haze, there was the shimmering expanse of a large lake.

"Looks like the land of Paradise," Mildred said. "If you can't recover even more quickly here, Ryan, then you can't recover anywhere."

"I would beg all of us to bear in mind the sorry but undeniable fact that even the Garden of Eden contained its own serpent," Doc warned.

"Miserable old bastard," Mildred snapped. "Can't you ever try to look on the bright side?"

"Turn over every bright side, madam," he replied, with some dignity, "and you find darkness on the other."

Ryan took in deep breaths of the fresh morning air. "Fireblast! I feel better already. Let's go kill a deer. Or two deers."

J.B. had examined the exterior of the sec doors before setting the code to close them again. "Looks like someone's been having a try at getting in," he observed.

They all turned around from the view, seeing where the Armorer was pointing at some clear scorch marks near the bottom of the right-hand door.

"And I think someone had a go with a couple of frag grens," he added.

"Any damage?" Dean asked, running to look for himself. "Doesn't look like it."

"Not all damage shows on the outside," Michael said, staring vacantly into the clear sky.

"Don't go all mystic on us—" Krysty touched him on the arm "—you'll be slipping into that twentieth-century stuff about being no success like failure."

Michael started as if he hadn't even noticed the others there. He smiled broadly. "Guess you're right. Can we go down and take a look around?"

J.B. watched the doors slide shut, with a barely audible hiss of pneumatic power. "Sure, but all keep together. You ready, Ryan?"

"As I'll ever be."

Before they started the steep descent, J.B. checked their location with his minisextant, confirming that they were somewhere in the middle of what had once been New Hampshire.

"That could be Lake Champlain, then," Doc said wonderingly. "My dearest Emily and I sailed and fished upon that many times. To see it again after... Lord, after close on two hundred years. If we can get down there we might find some of the finest piscatorial sport that man ever knew."

"And women, Doc?" Krysty teased.

"But of course. My own darling wife once hooked onto a monster pike not far from here. Thirty pounds if it was an inch. Sadly I failed to gaff it and fell from our boat into the water. Emily was frightfully cross with me."

The trail was steep, cutting in a series of switchbacks down the side of the mountain that concealed the redoubt. About halfway down there had been a minor earth slip that had totally washed away the blacktop for several hundred feet, though it finally reappeared again just before plunging into a dark expanse of conifers.

"Looks like it could be good hunting," Ryan commented, leaning on Doc's sword stick.

"Hope so." J.B. polished his glasses. "Sooner we get down there, sooner we find out."

"WERE THERE ANY BIG VILLES around here, Doc? In the good old days before skydark?"

Dean and Doc were strolling together in the center of the group.

"Place called Burlington, as I remember, not all that far away. Not a big ville like New York or Chicago, but we thought it pretty up and walking good in New England. I was born only a few miles from here, in that direction." He waved a hand vaguely toward the east.

"Where?"

"South Strafford, Vermont. Admirable little place, Dean. Lovely general store. White frame houses. Woods for miles in every direction."

"And people lived there, in homes?"

"Indeed, they did. There were folk in South Strafford, aged eighty and upward, who had never traveled more than twenty miles from their birthplace in their entire lives."

"Truly?" Dean grinned at the old man. "You greasing my wheels, Doc?"

"How's that?"

"Joking me?"

"Ah, I understand. Colorful slang, young fellow. No, I confess I'm not…oiling your wheels, Dean. Life back then was slower and simpler and cleaner and…so very much better."

"Long ago, and far away, Doc," Mildred said quietly.

"Correct, my dear. And... Oh, so very much better than it is today."

Krysty spotted a bald eagle, soaring on an invisible thermal, sending the dove scattering.

"Whole flock's gone," Michael said. "But the eagle didn't get them."

"Not a flock, young man." Doc turned, nearly stumbling in his eagerness to correct the teenager. "The wrong collective noun for doves."

"Flock of sheep?" Mildred tried.

"Alpha plus." Doc beamed. "But one should talk about a dule of doves."

"Dule? You made that up."

"I did not, Dr. Wyeth," Doc said indignantly. "Many of the names are quite unusual and rather picturesque."

"Tell us some." Dean looked back where his father was slowly bringing up the rear of the group. "Doc's going... You all right, Dad?"

"Yeah, thanks. Might have a sit-down when we reach that earth slip. Go on, Doc."

"Ask me some birds or animals, Dean."

The boy considered the question. "Wolves?"

"A route of wolves."

A snort of disbelief came from Mildred. "How about a 'crap' of old men?"

"Ignore her, Dean. Go on."

"Hawks?"

"A cast of hawks."

"Toads?" Krysty said.

"Ah, that's... Yes, I remember me the word. One talks of a knot of toads."

"How about crows, Doc?"

"Crows, J.B.? One of my favorites. A murder of crows."

"Murder?" The Armorer whistled. "All these names from before the long winters."

"All right, smart-ass," Mildred said. "What about larks? And you better watch it, because I know the answer to this one. Go on, Doc. Larks?"

"An exaltation of larks." He bowed mockingly to the woman. "Is that not correct?"

"Well, as it happens, yeah, it's right."

"A deceit of lapwings. A parliament of owls. A pitying of turtledoves. A siege of herons. A shrewdness of apes. Oh, so many fine terms."

"Angels?" queried Michael, who'd been listening in silence to the conversation.

"Angels? Hardly birds or beasts, dear boy."

"Come on, Doc," he urged with an odd intentness. "You know so much, then. What about angels?"

"A choir, would be the collective noun, I think. But I'm not altogether certain, Michael."

The young man spit in the dirt and stalked on ahead of them, kicking loose pebbles out of his path.

"How is it, Ryan?" Mildred leaned across and took his wrist between her thumb and forefinger.

"Been better. Needed this rest."

"Pulse is up some. Temperature? About normal, bearing in mind the exertion. How's the neck feel?"

He lifted a hand and touched the bandage, then pressed a little harder, wincing at the expected stab of pain. "Still real painful, Mildred."

"Bad as it was?"

"No!" he said, louder than he'd intended. "No, it's not. When can I take off the dressing?"

"I'll look at it later today. I brought some strips of those old sheets ready to clean it up."

Immediately below them, the winding blacktop vanished under a mountain of loose earth and rock. It was obvious from the amount of rich vegetation growing over it that the slide had been many years ago.

Ryan reached out from where he was sitting and plucked a tiny flower. "Compare where we are now to that place we finished up with the mutie creatures," he said. "Acid rain and fog and nothing living worth a spoonful of piss. Look." He swept his hand outward. "Beautiful."

"Would the Trader have appreciated this kind of view, Ryan?" Mildred asked.

He smiled. "A view? Hell, the only view that Trader really appreciated was one where he could make some easy jack without having to break sweat."

She picked up half a dozen rounded pebbles and started to toss them in the air, trying to catch them on the back of her hand. "So, this Trader. How come you and John figure the sun used to shine out of his ass?"

"Because he was the best." Ryan hesitated, looking out over the forest toward the lake. "If Abe's right, then mebbe I should say that Trader *is* the best."

"Easy answer. Best at what, killing people?"

"Yeah. For one thing, Trader knew chilling like other men know breathing."

"Damn!" She shook her head slowly. "Coming here, from my time, I've seen amazing things. There's a lot about Deathlands that's better than the end of the twentieth century. But this emphasis on wasting people. Like the man with the biggest blaster becomes the biggest man. Not very politically correct, Ryan.''

''Don't understand you, Mildred.''

''No, I guess not. I tell you, if Trader really might be alive, then I kind of look forward to the chance of meeting him. Kind of scared about it, as well.''

Dean interrupted them, bounding up like a puppy. ''I'm starving hungry, Dad. Can we get moving again?''

Ryan leaned on the sword stick and pulled himself upright. ''Yeah. Right now.''

IT TOOK THEM MORE THAN an hour to descend over the jumble of shifting stones and earth. The footing was treacherous, and twice they set off minor slides.

Ryan found it hard going. He slipped and fell heavily when they were close to the bottom, and rolled helplessly, banging his left shoulder hard on a jagged outcrop of granite, the impact starting the wound to leak blood again.

He opened his eye to find himself lying upside down, with everyone staring down at him worriedly. The expressions of concern suddenly made him start to laugh, and he was unable to stop himself.

It was only after he'd been helped to his feet and dusted off that Ryan realized that Michael was the only one of the six not to come to his assistance. The teenager had been picking his own path down the steep slope, not even turning his head to watch Ryan's accident.

"BET THAT RIVER'S BURSTING with trout and salmon," Krysty said. "Only another quarter mile or so and we can rest by it. Looks easy going now that we're off the mountain."

Ryan looked up behind them, trying to conceal how weak and nauseous he felt. The hillside scraped up away from them, looking almost impossible to climb. From down in the valley, at the bottom of some loose scree, there was no sign at all of the existence of the redoubt.

It was a little warmer, with a fresh breeze now blowing across the valley, ruffling the tops of the nearest pines. The air smelled like nectar.

Doc had stretched out on his back, arms behind his head, looking up at the sky. "I don't know how the rest of you feel, but I have seldom felt so rested and comfortable. Admittedly I shall be even closer to perfection once I have three or four charbroiled trout inside me. The ones that you mentioned, Miss Wroth."

"Not going to catch and cook themselves," J.B. said. "Let's go get them."

Chapter Seventeen

"Fishing is such a different activity to what it was in my days," Doc said, picking at his excellent teeth with a slender bone.

The ashes of the fire glowed, containing within their heart several more small clay packages, each of which held a tender young trout.

"How did you fish predark, Doc?" Dean asked.

"With long rods of bamboo and thin gut lines. Barbed hooks and lures designed to look like the most delicious flies that a fish ever dreamed of."

"Why go to all that trouble?"

"Sport," Doc replied, his eyes crinkling with amusement at the look of bewilderment and disbelief on the boy's face. "Lots of times we'd fight old brother steelhead for a couple of hours or more, and then, once we'd landed the brute, we'd simply slip him back into the water again."

"That's serious stupe!"

"Looking back I must, peradventure, have to agree with you, Dean. But, as I have oft remarked before, that was then and this is now."

The one point that Dean couldn't begin to appreciate, and Doc never mentioned, was the factor of the stocking of rivers and lakes.

Before the meganukes and the long winters, most of America's accessible waters had been overfished. Since then, with comparatively little threat outside of natural predators, the stocks had built up and up.

The fishing party that day had simply each found a quiet stretch of bank and had laid down in the shadows, bellying up to the water and peering intently into the cold depths until the eyes had adjusted to spot the speckled fish.

Then all you had to do was slide a hand into the pool, move the fingers gently back and forth and ease it toward the nearest of the trout, taking care not to disturb or frighten the fish.

Patience was the main virtue you needed.

And the skill to strike at the right moment, cupping your hand under your chosen victim and simply flipping it up and out onto the bank.

Grab it by the tail and jerk its head against the ground, then drop its flapping corpse a few yards from the edge of the water and go back for another fish.

The cooking took a lot longer.

Once they had a second pile of a dozen or more trout ready to gut and bake, Ryan sent Dean and Michael out into the surrounding forest to search for berries or fruit.

Dean came back in twenty minutes with his pockets filled with boysenberries and loganberries, fat and brimming with juice, a fine complement for the next helping of baked trout.

"WHERE'S MICHAEL?" Doc asked, pulling out the silver half-hunter from his fob pocket. "I believe that the boy has been gone for close on an hour now."

"We split up." Dean rubbed his mouth. "Well, we didn't exactly split up."

"How do you mean?" his father asked.

"Michael just went off on his own and he didn't... didn't sort of reply when I spoke to him."

Mildred wiped a thread of dark crimson juice from her chin. "That jump was real bad for the boy."

"Thought he'd gotten over it." J.B. had stood and was looking out across the river and into the trees.

"Thought so, too, love. Could be wrong. Cryosurgery was my field, not psychiatry. Thought there weren't many specialists around that you could have asked about paranoid psychoses arising from a malfunctioned matter-transfer jump."

"Better go look for him," Ryan said. "I'll stay here with Dean. No, he better go as well. Doc, stay here and keep me company."

"Willingly. But do you think..."

"Don't think anything, Doc. Lad's got the fastest reflexes I ever saw. But he could have been coldcocked."

"We'd have heard a shot," Krysty said.

"Yeah."

"Where's everyone going?" Michael was standing in shadow, leaning a hand against a lodgepole pine, the sound of his approach muffled by the rushing river nearby.

"You all right?" Ryan got to his feet, his hand on the butt of the SIG-Sauer.

"As the gentle rain, thanks. We moving on?"

"Coming to look for you, stupe," Dean said. "You find any berries?"

"Don't call me stupe. I don't like it. Understand?"

"Sure. Don't lose... You get any berries?"

"Berries?" They still couldn't see Michael's face, hidden in the darkness at the edge of the forest.

"That was what you and Dean went for." Ryan was beginning to lose his temper, only hanging on with the feeling that something was still not right with Michael.

"Oh, sure. Remember now. Any of those fishes left?"

"Why, you..." All his life Ryan Cawdor had been plagued by a short fuse on his temper. Though it was better than when he'd been in his teens, there were still moments when it began to flare out of control.

"Leave it," Krysty said, sensing the outburst even before it came. "You didn't get any berries, Michael?"

"No. Didn't see any."

"See anything else?" J.B. asked, the high, stretched tone of his voice showing his own anger.

"No." Michael stepped slowly out of the shadows, and everyone could see the dark stains on his face and mouth from the juice of loganberries. But nobody said anything. "Oh, yeah, I found a sort of building."

"Where?"

"And some bullets and stuff."

"Any sign of life? Recent life?"

The young man sniffed. "No, afraid not, J.B., not even a smell of anyone."

"Show us," Ryan said. "Now."

"Sure, sure."

THE MEAL AND MORE good water had restored Ryan to something close to his original health. He still allowed the Armorer to take point, walking with Michael, while he brought up the rear with Krysty. Doc, Mildred and Dean occupied the center of their group. Everyone had a blaster drawn and ready.

The teenager led them along the river, up a gentle slope, past some moss-green boulders and still pools. They moved through a grove of whispering aspens, then cut away from a narrow trail to the right of a feathery waterfall.

"Far?" J.B. asked.

"Closer than the sun and farther than the end of my dick," Michael replied, smiling hugely at his own humor.

The Armorer didn't respond to the attempted joke. "I asked you how far it was, Michael. Stop treating all this like some fucking game."

The unusual flicker of temper from J.B. quieted the boy. "Another five minutes or so. Suppose it might be a quarter hour."

Krysty pointed out that the trail had been used recently. "Feet."

"Wonder when it rained last," the Armorer said, stopping and kneeling by the side of the track.

"Looks like someone without shoes." Ryan steadied himself on the silver lion's-head hilt of the sword stick and peered down at the ground.

"Not clear enough." J.B. straightened. "Don't think they're that recent, but keep on red alert."

THE CACHE OF BONES was heaped off the trail, near the mouth of a shallow cave. Most had been broken and the marrow drawn from them. A few shreds of dried flesh and gristle hung from the ends of some of the longer bones.

Nobody needed to ask what species of animal the remains came from.

Three grinning skulls, with broken teeth, had been piled on top of the grisly cairn.

Grinning human skulls.

Ryan had begun to feel tired climbing the slope of the hill, and they'd stopped a little way past the discovery of the bones.

Dean and Michael had gone to throw dry sticks into the stream that flowed close by, falling fast over a series of small cascades. The other five sat together.

Ryan broke the silence. "I'll say it, if nobody else is going to. We need to watch Michael carefully."

"He seems better right now," Mildred stated, listening to shouts of laughter from the two boys.

"He says we're nearly at this building he saw. I guess he's bringing us the same way he came."

"Couldn't come any other way by the look of it," J.B. interrupted.

"Right. But he never mentioned those bodies. Had to have seen them. Known what they were. Why not tell us about that?"

Krysty touched Ryan on the arm. "The bones had been there for some days, hadn't they?"

"So what. Three skeletons, looking like a herd of buffalo stampeded over them. Never saw bones so splintered. What do you think, Mildred?"

"About Michael, or the bodies?"

"Both."

"I think there were more than three. I know there was only the trio of skulls. But that looked like at least eight or nine femurs for a start. And the same number of scapulas. Could've thrown the rest in the river."

Ryan nodded. "What about Michael?"

"I agree we need to be a bit careful. I don't think there's much chance of him trying to harm any of us."

"You don't just sit there and say...tell us about being 'much chance,' Mildred. That's about as bastard useless and stupe as..." Ryan bit his lip and breathed slowly. "Sorry. Nearly got real angry again. But you reckon he could hurt us?"

Mildred stared at him. "I don't think either you or Michael are on top of life at the moment, Ryan. Try speaking to me like that another day and you'll be shitting bits of broken teeth. You hear me."

"I'm sorry. Really. But we have to know."

"Should we consider some sort of restraint for the poor lad?" Doc asked.

"Tie him up?" Ryan shook his head. "No. Short of chilling him, all we can do is watch and listen." He stood up again. "And be careful."

A PAIR OF FOXES DARTED across the trail a hundred yards farther along, where it was beginning to level out again and move away from the water.

"What's the name for them, Doc?" Michael called, grinning cheerfully back over his shoulder.

"A skulk of foxes, my dear boy. Though I wouldn't have said that Br'er Reynard was all that much at skulking."

"Is it far, Michael?" Ryan leaned a hand against the smooth trunk of a tall, elegant silver birch. The day was getting much warmer.

"Just over the top. Looked like some kind of shelter. An overlook."

"I can see it," J.B. said. "Hold it here and I'll go on ahead. Rest of you cover me."

The trees had thinned out, and the trail had suddenly turned into a stone-lined path. There was a line of beeches to the right, and to the left the ground dropped off steeply toward the distant water. They could all see the outline of a gray stone building, standing alone in a clearing.

"Feel anything, Krysty?"

She paused a moment before answering. "Not close." Seeing him about to speak, she added, "Before you jump on me, I mean not for several miles. But I feel a kind of contact, recently. In the last day or so, I'd guess."

"Good or bad."

"That's easy, lover. Bad."

J.B. HAD VANISHED, crabbing to the right, moving at a fast crouch, with the Uzi in his hand.

The others waited. Ryan had the Steyr, scanning the land all around through the powerful Starlite night scope with the laser image enhancer, his index finger on the trigger.

The other five were fanned out, watching silently in a combat perimeter, Dean with his heavy Browning and Mildred with her Czech ZKR 551. Krysty looked toward the stream, holding the 5-shot Smith & Wesson double-action revolver. Doc sat with his knees drawn up, back against a live oak, the massive J. E. B. Stuart limited edition Le Mat cradled in his lap. He held a fallen leaf, preoccupied in following the delicate tracery with his fingernail.

Michael lay flat on his stomach, following the progress of J.B., his own Texas Longhorn Border Special resting on an abandoned anthill.

"See him?" Ryan whispered.

The teenager replied without even looking toward Ryan. "No. Saw a blue jay fly out of the trees close to that building. Must be him."

Ryan turned and crawled to lie alongside Michael. "You go right up to that place?"

"Yeah. I thought..." The boy's face changed, almost as though someone had pulled a skintight mask down over it. "No, Ryan," he said. "Got close, then figured I should come back and report what I'd found."

"And you had the berries on the way back?"

"Right."

Ryan spotted J.B. at that moment. The Armorer was kneeling behind a stout sycamore, less than twenty yards from the building. He stood up very slowly, then waved with the automatic pistol for the others to join him.

THEY STOOD TOGETHER a few feet from the southern wall of the single-story shelter. Mildred said that it looked to her like it had originally been a kind of very basic overlook for campers or tourists.

"You said you saw bullets," Ryan said to Michael. "Where was that?"

"Other side. By where there's been the big fire and stuff." He pointed.

It crossed Ryan's mind that only a couple of minutes ago the teenager had specifically denied that he'd gone right up to the place.

"Fire?"

"Go look."

As they walked around the front, it was clear that it was a totally basic shelter, with no windows and only an open doorway. To the left there was a fringe of aspens, hiding the view over the valley and the tumbling falls of the river. Back before skydark, Ryan guessed, the trees were probably not there and the building would have given the hiker an uninterrupted vista of staggering beauty.

The ashes of a big fire were heaped up against the wall, the concrete and stone scorched and cracked. And, as Michael had reported, there were dozens of empty shells, the brass discolored by the heat.

"Thirty-eights," the Armorer said, without even having to pick one of them up. "Someone threw them into the fire so's they'd explode."

"And there's the smell of gasoline." Mildred sniffed. "Why set such a big fire way out here?"

"It seems a veritable midsummer madness," Doc commented. "Who on earth would do such a foolish thing?"

Ryan and J.B. looked at each other, the same thought running through their minds, both of them knowing just who might do such a stupe thing.

But before either of them could put that thought into words, they were interrupted by a shout from the back of the damaged building.

"Dad! Come quick!"

Chapter Eighteen

The first body could have been either male or female.

It had been so badly mutilated, then set on fire, that it was almost impossible to tell. If Mildred had been allowed the time and resources she could undoubtedly have deduced the sex of the corpse from a variety of forensic evidence, beginning, of course, with the pelvis.

It had been bound with strands of baling wire, then strung up onto a large iron hook driven into the wall. It was impossible to be sure, but it looked like the feet had been severed before the burning.

All of the skin had been blackened and crisped, though it had split in several places, showing the veined redness of raw flesh beneath.

The skull was roasted, eyes and soft tissues quite destroyed, leaving only the startling whiteness of the teeth, frozen in an eternal rictus.

The air was heavy with the sour scent of gasoline.

"Last night, I'd guess," J.B. said, his voice seeming loud in the stillness.

The second corpse was male. It lay huddled around the corner, knees drawn up to its chest, arms clasped around itself. A dark hole in the side of its head, with dried blood matting the stringy hair, showed how it had finally died. A massive dark patch over the front of its torn cotton shirt spoke of a mortal wound that had left the man dying in agony.

He looked to be about thirty, with a skinny body, and bare feet. His lips had flared back off his teeth, showing that they were filed to needle points.

But it was the soles of his feet, and the palms and the fingers of the hands that everyone looked at, confirming the unvoiced suspicions of both J.B. and Ryan.

They saw a number of small, powerful suckers, mostly closed in death, but plenty strong enough in life to rip skin away from an enemy.

"Stickies," Dean said.

"Yeah," his father agreed.

It explained the empty shells and the surfeit of gas-powered explosions. The one thing that a stickie loved above all else was causing mayhem and murder with fires and detonations, the louder and grander the better.

It also explained the blackened log that had once been a human being.

Ryan reconstructed what had happened.

"Person on his own. Hunting. Passing by. Trapped by some stickies. Two or five or fifty. Doesn't much matter how many there were."

"Could matter to us, Ryan," J.B. said. "Tracks only show about five or six."

Ryan nodded. "Agreed. The norm probably only had time for a few rounds. Gut-shot that chilled the stickie down there. One of the other muties put the bullet through his head. Unusual to show mercy like that."

"And then they had a stickie party, Dad." Dean shuffled his foot through the ashes of their fire.

"Right."

"Had we not best assume extra vigilance if those subhumans are in the region?" Doc had his Le Mat drawn, the hammer set over the single scattergun round. "I knew that this Garden of Eden would have its share of reptiles."

"Nothing to do here," Ryan said. "We got us a choice. Know there's food and good water here. Probably a lot more game in the woods."

"How are you feeling?" Mildred asked.

"I wouldn't want to go five miles with a rabid grizzly, but it's getting better all the time. The wound on my neck still pains me."

She nodded. "Course it does, Ryan. Could easily take three or four days to begin proper healing. I thought about stitching it for you."

Ryan winced. "Glad you didn't. Had a wound stitched once. Never again."

"Where was that?" asked Krysty. "I know all your scars pretty well, lover. Never seen one that looked it had been sewed back together again."

"It was a long time ago, in another place."

"And the wench is dead," Doc said.

"Yeah." Ryan sounded surprised. "How did you know that? I never told anyone about it."

The old man shuffled his feet, embarrassed. "It was a sort of quote from an old play, Ryan. I hadn't intended to touch upon a sore point."

"It was a bastard sore point, Doc. Slut in a gaudy, when I was fifteen. Tried to cut me for a handful of jack. Did it when we was doing—"

"Were doing, not was doing," Krysty corrected, smiling at Ryan's obvious discomfort.

"Sure. We finished doing it and she tried to cut me with a small boot razor."

"Where did she cut you, Dad?" Dean asked eagerly. Michael was standing alongside him and whispered in the younger boy's ear. "Oh, I get it. There. Wow, Dad! Double-empty scene!"

"Well, she only did part of the job. And after it was over the old bitch who ran the gaudy sewed me up. I said I'd put out her eyes if she didn't help me. It was a real deep cut. I was bleeding to death."

"What happened to the whore?" Mildred asked.

"Chilled her. Slit her throat with her own blade." He was suddenly defensive. "Look, I had no choice."

"Sure," Mildred said.

THEY LEFT THE BODIES unburied.

The discovery of stickies in the area had cast a dampener over the pleasant day. There was very little conversation as they all picked their way down the path toward where they'd caught and cooked the trout.

"Better if we have a council, now," Ryan said, as they finally reached their temporary campsite. He was out of breath, unhappy that attacks of dizziness had made him stumble a couple of times up on the hillside.

"Not much to talk about, is there?" Michael had picked up one of the discarded fish heads and was nibbling at the shreds of meat left on it.

"No. Just do we go or do we stay?"

Krysty flopped down beside him. "There aren't any stickie tracks down here. I've seen worse places to spend a few days. You need a rest, lover."

"Mebbe."

"I don't think that any of us would refuse the possibility of a little gentle relaxation. I cast my vote for remaining here. But, what of the rest of you?"

Krysty lifted a hand. "I'm with you, Doc."

"Me, too," Dean said.

"That's already a majority," Ryan stated. "Anyone going to disagree?"

J.B. looked uncertain. "If we'd only made a single jump, then I'd say leave. You remember what the Trader used to say about stickies, Ryan?"

"Yeah. He used to—"

"Company," Krysty said.

Above the sound of the racing stream came the noise of six blasters being drawn and cocked. Only Michael, still nibbling on the trout head, didn't react.

"Ho, the camp!"

Ryan shouted back. "Come in slow and easy."

"No shooting, friend."

"Just come in slow and easy."

Five strangers walked toward them from the general direction of the big lake. None of them appeared to be over twenty, and they all had a squeaky-clean, laundered look to them. All wore matching stone-washed jeans and pale denim shirts and had hunting rifles slung over their shoulders. Every one had blue eyes and long blond hair. There were four men and a woman.

"Hold it. Don't get too close," Ryan warned.

The two groups eyed each other. For some reason, Ryan noticed, they all seemed particularly struck with the appearance of Doc.

The young woman spoke for the arrivals. "Good day to you, outlanders."

Ryan nodded.

They all kept looking at Doc, as if they couldn't believe what they were seeing. Finally, after an uncomfortable pause, the woman spoke again. "How old is the old one?"

Doc answered for himself. "Old enough to know it is regarded as rude to ask a stranger how old he is, young lady. Perhaps if we get to know each other a little better, then I might allow you the indulgence of asking me again."

"He is very old," one of the young men whispered, very audibly. "Old."

The woman gestured to him to keep quiet. "What are you doing in the lands of our ville?"

"Didn't know it belonged to anyone," Ryan replied, not allowing the SIG-Sauer to waver for a moment from her chest. "Didn't see any signs."

"These are hunting lands. Not the planted lands, of course." She smiled at him.

Ryan deliberately didn't return the smile. "What's the name of the ville?"

"You don't know?" She shook her head, her corn-yellow hair moving around her shoulders like a curtain of spun gold. "We come from Quindley. It's about twelve miles north of here, alongside the big water."

"Big water have a name?" J.B. asked.

"Shamplin Lake," she replied.

"Champlain." Doc hissed the name to Mildred, who nodded her understanding.

"You got a name?" Krysty asked.

"We all have given names. You look like you could be near to thirty."

"What's this about our ages?" Ryan asked.

"Nothing, nothing. You asked my name. I'm called Dorothy. These brothers are Isaac, Ray, Bob and Frank. Not truly brothers, except in the eyes of Moses."

"That your baron?" J.B. said.

"No. We have no baron." One of the young men tugged at her arm and whispered in her ear. Dorothy nodded. "Of course." He said something, more urgently. "Yes, yes, Isaac. But all of that can wait, can't it?"

"What's he want?" Ryan was beginning to relax a little. There didn't seem anything about these callow young folk to threaten them.

"He says to ask whether you have seen his brother. That is, his real brother. Jolyon went missing on a hunting trip. Left the ville yesterday morning."

"Haven't seen anyone for days," Ryan replied.

"What about the things we saw up the hill?" It was the first time that Michael had spoken since the arrival of the strangers.

"Up the hill?" Isaac queried.

Ryan had already made the guess that the charred log that hung from the ruined building above them could once have been the lost Jolyon. But the Trader always used to say that you should take care that you never got involved with anything unless you didn't have a choice.

"Yeah." Michael was all ready to go on, but Ryan stepped in to stop him.

"You had trouble with stickies around here?" he asked.

"Why?" Dorothy glanced involuntarily behind her, toward the dark shadows of the forest. "You seen..."

Isaac was quicker. "Stickies got my brother? Got Jolyon? And you oldies know about it?"

"Oldies!" Mildred exclaimed, unheard by anyone else.

"Moses *told* us not to ever trust oldies," Isaac shouted, grabbing Dorothy by the shoulders, shaking her like a terrier with a rat. His face had gone as white as fresh-drawn milk, and his eyes burned.

"If it's your brother up on the hill, then I'm afraid that he's dead. There's a single chilled stickie up there, too." The young man had let go of the blond woman and turned to stare at Ryan. "Way it looks, they likely jumped him. But, listen. It might not be your brother."

"Got to be, outlander. Any blasters with him?"

J.B. spoke. "There were shells from a .38."

One of the other men spoke. He had a slight stammer. "Jolyon had his W-Winchester repro. The Navy Arms S-Sixty-six. And plenty of ammo."

"Navy Arms Sixty-six was chambered for a .38," the Armorer said. "The stickies had one of their whizbang fires with the spare shells."

"Dead stickie?" Dorothy asked.

"Gut-shot." Ryan felt the burst of tension easing again. "If it was your brother, Isaac, then he took him out first. Then they got him."

The young woman made a positive decision. "Frank, you and Ray wait here with these people. Me, Isaac and Bob'll go... Up by the old shelter, you mean?" Ryan nodded. "We'll take a look. Then we can maybe all go to Quindley." She looked at Doc, as though she was going to say something, then changed her mind. "You'd be welcome as our guests for a day or so."

"Be good," Ryan said.

"Yeah, thanks." Krysty spoke to Isaac. "Just better warn you that what they did to... to whoever it is... wasn't nice. Wasn't nice at all."

"Stickies never do nice, lady," he replied.

RAY AND FRANK WALKED OFF and sat close together on the bank of the stream, saying nothing either to Ryan or the friends, or to each other.

It was nearly two hours before the woman and two men came back down the hillside. There was no need to ask whether the blackened corpse had been that of the one they called Jolyon. Their shocked, dulled faces gave the answer.

"We've taken him down and spoken a saying over him." Dorothy looked on the verge of tears, her eyes brimming. "Couldn't bury him, but we put him safe from the animals. Friends'll return tomorrow and bring him to Quindley for the proper saying. Now we should all go back there and report to Moses what happened. And to warn of the cursed stickies."

She turned on her heel and led them all off into the trees, toward the distant lake.

Chapter Nineteen

"Place looks like a promo vid for the Department of Agriculture," Mildred commented. "You ever see a better kept ville than this, Ryan?"

They had crossed the narrow river at a narrow wooden bridge, made from fresh-treated timbers and held in place by an ingenious system of bolts and thick-knotted rope. Then they followed the five young people along a clear trail, through the mainly coniferous forest, heading toward the lake.

Feeling stronger by the hour, Ryan had handed the sword stick back to Doc and retaken his place as leader of the group. He walked at the front, keeping them on orange alert because of the threat from stickies.

Gradually the trees began to be thinned out, showing obvious evidence of good land management. They could see the silvery sheen of the water ahead of them and then the woods ended and they were out in the open.

Dorothy stopped and waved her hands over her head, as a signal to armed guards in a tall watchtower set in the middle of the cultivated land.

The others looked around. Ryan saw immediately that Mildred was right.

It was a showpiece.

The fields were tended beautifully, the produce in neat rows. Fences and hedges divided one crop from another, all the way from the edge of the forest to the shore of the lake, which was a body of water that stretched to the far horizon.

There were twenty or thirty men and women working in the fields, all of them looking up and waving at the sight of Dorothy and the four men. One of the women was driving an ancient John Deere tractor.

Even at a quick glance, the range of what the ville grew was impressive. Ryan could see the feathery tops of carrots in the nearest field. There were potatoes, squash, okra, peas, several kinds of beans and even what looked like grapevines.

"Got fruit trees over there," J.B. said, pointing to the right.

"Six kinds of apples, for cooking and eating," Frank stated. "Three sorts of pear. Tried oranges and lemons, but the old blue northers did away with them. Got peaches under glass. Melons. So many melons we regularly have to plow half back into the fields. But nothing's wasted. Like Moses tells us."

Dorothy and Isaac had run on ahead and were obviously passing on the bad news about his brother. Several of the group in the fields started to weep, while others made threatening gestures with the rifles that all of them carried.

"You had trouble with stickies before?" Dean asked the young man called Bob.

"Not often. Used to be some outlanders coming down from old Canada."

"You got good discipline here," J.B. said approvingly. "I'm impressed."

Bob looked at him and shook his head. "What would an oldie like you know about things like that?"

J.B. stared at him, completely without any expression on his sallow face, until the younger man finally dropped his eyes and looked away.

Now Dorothy was walking quickly back toward them, along the main track that wound into the ville. The one thing that Ryan hadn't yet seen was the ville itself. Because of the lay of the land, it wasn't possible to be sure, but the pathway looked like it cut sharply to the left, over a narrow promontory that jutted into the lake.

"The brothers and sisters are deeply moved," she said to the three young men. "Isaac has gone on to tell Moses about the outlanders."

"You got the best-kept ville I ever saw," Ryan said.

"Thanks." She looked at the others, but seemed to concentrate on Dean and Michael. "The rest of you can come into Quindley and eat and stay a night if you want."

"Sounds good." Mildred smiled at the woman, who turned blankly away.

THE VILLE, as Ryan had figured, lay just beyond the piece of land that reached out into the lake. There was another, similar causeway, about fifty paces in length, with the ville on what had once obviously been a small offshore island at its end.

"Good place to defend," Ryan said to J.B., as they followed the young woman through the cultivated fields.

"Long as you don't get attacked by a mess of men in boats," the Armorer replied.

Everyone in the ville looked amazingly healthy. Not one of them seemed to have any physical imperfections at all, and every one of them was younger than the mid-twenties.

The blue shirts and jeans were almost a uniform.

As Ryan and the others walked along, every head turned toward them. The big maroon John Deere coughed into silence, and its driver leaned out to get a better look at the strangers. Once again, there was the odd feeling that Doc was some kind of leper. The young people's faces showed something close to a disbelieving revulsion at him.

"Is there something wrong with me, Dr. Wyeth? Some indiscretion of my attire?" he whispered. "They're all staring at me like I have my dick sticking out. If you'll pardon my French."

"Course I'll pardon it, Doc," she replied. "And it's hanging out, not sticking out."

"Very amusing, madam." He snorted and strode on, ignoring the silent spectators.

A HIGH WALL of sharpened stakes surrounded the perimeter of the ville, right at the edge of the water, so any potential enemy would find no land for a footing. There appeared to be about twenty or thirty buildings, many of them obviously storage barns, with roofs of closely thatched reeds.

"Not many small houses," Michael observed, walking close beside Dorothy.

"We live in dorms," she replied. "Men in one and women in the other, over there." She pointed toward two of the biggest buildings in the ville.

"No privacy?" Krysty asked, overhearing the conversation. "No married couples?"

Dorothy stopped so quickly that Krysty nearly stepped on her heels. "Marriage?" She laughed. "All of us who live here in Quindley have set that oldie idea behind us. Moses pointed out the total stupidity of it."

"Look forward to meeting this Moses," Mildred said. "Sounds like quite a guy."

Dorothy opened her mouth, then hesitated and closed it again. She stood looking down at her feet, as if she were taking counsel from an inner voice.

"I know you are old and an outlander, but you will not speak of Moses like that."

"Listen, kid, I'm getting seriously pissed about all this 'old' shit. I'm still a good few years the right side of forty, so just ice it, will you?"

"Forty!"

"That's when life begins." Mildred laughed, uneasy at the younger woman's expression. "Just how do you treat all the old people you got here in the ville? Your own mothers and fathers, for instance?"

"Moses tells us that..." Dorothy stopped. "No, you're right. It is rude of me to show you how we..."

Again she hesitated. "Food and rest should come before talk."

"I'll go along with that," Doc said. "I confess that I would not be averse to a good long rest."

"Oh, you will have that," Frank stated.

Ryan looked around them. "You got no animals. How's that?"

"We have no need of them, outlander," Ray replied. "Moses teaches us that the exploitation of cattle or horses or any other creature is wrong."

"Vegetarians?" Mildred asked.

"Yes."

Ryan smiled at the young blonde. "Then I guess a juicy steak with all the trimmings is out of the question."

His joke was ignored. Dorothy turned on her heel and continued toward the causeway to the ville.

"Like Uncle Tyas McCann used to say back in Harmony, lover. That went over like a lead balloon."

THE WATER WAS COLD and very clear. The shore shelved steeply, but even halfway toward the entrance gate to Quindley it was easy to see the speckled fish moving sinuously near the weeds on the lake's bottom.

"How deep is it here?" Dean asked.

"On the far side of the ville it drops away to well over a hundred feet," Frank replied.

"And you don't eat no fish?"

"Yes, we do eat no fish." Frank smiled at Dean. "While in our home you will eat no fish, also."

An armed guard on the fortified gates watched suspiciously as Dorothy led the seven outlanders into the ville. Ryan paused a moment before entering, looking back across the water, the immaculately tilled fields, toward the shadowed bank of the sweeping forest.

Every bright young face was turned toward him.

But he also caught a glimpse of something else, right at the edge of the pine trees. It was a blurred flash of white. A face? Maybe an animal. By the time Ryan had focused his eye on it, there was nothing there.

ONCE THEY WERE inside the ville, they were able to see that it was laid out on a sort of grid pattern. The streets were packed earth, laid over interlocked logs, the whole of the place locked together with massive cross-members, made from whole trees. Though it was actually floating, tethered to the land by the causeway, there was no sensation of movement.

J.B. had fallen into step beside Ryan, talking quietly out of the corner of his mouth. "Something's not right here."

"What?"

"You feel anything?"

Ryan nodded. "Something. Can't tell."

"Triple-red watch?"

"Sure."

"GOOD DAY TO YOU." The greeting came from a tall young man. Like everyone else, he was wearing jeans and a shirt, his long blond hair tied back in a ponytail. Dorothy had introduced him as Jehu, the leader of Quindley.

"You're young to be in charge of a ville like this," Ryan stated. "How long you been the baron?"

Jehu smiled. "There speaks the outlander, Ryan Cawdor. We have no baron."

"Leader? Chief? What's in a name, Jehu?"

"Our laws come from Moses. I am his chosen instrument, just for a single year."

"How do you mean?" J.B. asked. "You mean you just run the place for a year, then someone else does it? I heard about villes like that. Specially in the old Bible Belt lands. How long before you hand over?"

Jehu had eyes of deep cornflower blue. Now they looked curiously at the Armorer. "I end as the summer ends. I fall with the fall. How old are you, John Dix?"

"More than thirty and less than forty. How about you?"

"This is my twenty-fifth summer."

"Good age to be," Krysty said. "Doesn't seem that long that I was in my twenty-fifth summer."

"You are past it, truly?" Dorothy asked.

"Truly. Does it matter?"

The woman glanced at Jehu, who imperceptibly shook his head. "No," she said. "It doesn't matter. Not much."

"Michael and Dean here are the only ones under the age of twenty-five," Mildred said. "You keep picking on age and being old. What's so special about being over twenty-five?"

The man answered. "It is possible that you will get to speak with Moses before you—" he hesitated a brief moment "—before you leave us. Ask him."

"Where does Moses live?" Mildred asked.

"He doesn't 'live' in the way you might understand," Jehu replied. "Moses is here and there and everywhere."

"Like a god?" Doc asked.

"Better than a god," Dorothy stated. "A god is someone who doesn't exist. Moses exists."

"Does he have a house with many mansions?" Doc pointed ahead of them, to the only stone-walled building in the ville. It was circular, with a conical roof of fresh thatch. The back wall was directly against the outer defensive stakes.

Jehu nodded. "His spirit dwells there."

"Not his body?" Krysty said. "Don't we get to actually see him?"

Dorothy gave her a pitying smile. "Nobody at all gets to see Moses. Except the boy or girl honored by being chosen as the leader for the year."

"Moses picks them personally?" Michael had moved close to Dorothy.

"Not himself. But at the time they are permitted to let fall the reins of their year, it is Moses who releases them."

Jehu coughed. "Sister, it will soon be time for the ending of work for the day. After prayers, the outlanders can come and sit with us at our meal."

Dorothy hesitated. "Does Moses..."

"Yes, he knows. Moses knows all, sister."

"Blessed be that knowledge." Dorothy crossed herself and lowered her eyes.

"Amen to that."

"Can we wash up?" Krysty asked.

"Of course. There is a building set aside for outlanders who are permitted to stay in Quindley." The young man looked at the seven friends. "But it is a place divided."

"Divided? What do you mean?"

Jehu spread his hands like a market huckster displaying his wares. "Men on one side and women the other. As you will not stay long, the old and young can remain together."

Ryan felt his temper flaring, but Krysty sensed it and gripped him by the wrist. "Only for a night. Two at the outside, lover," she said. "Not a problem. We're guests in their ville, so we play the game by their rules."

"When in Rome, one must do as the Romans do," Doc intoned.

"Trader did a good deal in Rome once," J.B. said. "Bunch of knives."

"In Rome!" Doc exclaimed. "I had not realized that the gentleman was familiar with the Eternal City."

"Halfway between Atlanta and Chattanooga, Doc. That the place you mean?"

"Not quite, my dear John Barrymore. Not quite."

Chapter Twenty

"Bugged?" Ryan looked around the semicircular room. Its longer, flat wall of feather-edged boards was what divided them from the women's half of the thatched building. The floor was tongue-and-groove planks.

J.B. sat on one of the narrow wooden beds, laying his Uzi across his lap. "No," he replied. "Quindley doesn't look much like a hi-tek ville to me. Fact is, it looks the opposite. Like those places with Amish barons. Can only just about bring themselves to use the wheel."

Doc lay on another bed, his hands locked behind his head, staring up at the ceiling. "I was never comfortable with thatch above me. I fear that some great cockatrice will tumble into my snoring mouth while I sleep."

"Once had a mutie rat fall on me, Doc," said Dean, who was roaming around the room, peering at the handmade tables and chairs. "Tried to bite my tongue right out, before I was properly woked up."

"By the Three Kennedys! You poor mite." Doc sat up, his eyes wide with dismay. "What happened?"

"I bit its head off," Dean replied, sitting on the bed nearest to the door.

"It had it coming," Michael was lying down on his side, facing the blank wall.

"Right! Hot pipe, but you should have seen the look on its face when I gobbed it out in the dirt."

Jehu had left them, saying that they had half an hour before the evening food would be served. "Get water through the trap in the floor. Bucket on a rope. We barter for soap. But it's costly, so be sparing with it."

There was a single bar on the central table, in a shell dish. It had the look and consistency of old tallow. So far none of them had bothered to use it.

"What do you make of this place, J.B.?" Ryan asked.

"Like to meet up with this Moses" was the Armorer's elliptical reply.

Ryan nodded. "Know what you mean. All this clean, healthy living. Got to be something wrong."

ON THE OTHER SIDE of the partition, Mildred and Krysty had reached the same conclusion.

They shared a bucket of cold, clear water, struggling to get anything approaching a lather from the cake of soap, having to be content with a greasy scum on their skin. Krysty had considered washing her hair, but changed her mind.

"What do you reckon about this place?" she said, sitting cross-legged on one of the beds with her vivid green eyes closed, concentrating on one of the Earth Mother's meditation techniques for inner power.

Mildred stood staring out of the narrow, barred window, across the expanse of the lake. "Don't know. I really don't know."

"Neat and tidy."

"Healthy."

Krysty ran her fingers through her hair, producing a shower of tiny, fiery sparks. "Clean."

"Too clean?"

"Could be."

Mildred turned from the window. "It's like I once visited Disneyland, over in Los Angeles. It was wonderful and I had a great time there, but...maybe it was just a little *too* squeaky-clean. Same feeling here."

"And they're all so damned young!"

"Still, they've been okay with us, Krysty. Apart from being snotty about how old we all are. All except Dean and Michael, of course."

"The way they look at Doc, it's like he's carrying a living curse."

Mildred sat on her bed, considering the wall between them and the men. "Think we might be able to find a way around that for tonight?"

Krysty laughed. "Can't you and J.B. do without it, just for one night?"

"Yeah. It isn't just the sex, though that's real good. It's being close to someone you...you love. There. Now I've said it. Love. Don't you feel that with Ryan?"

"Sure I do, Mildred. There's been times, when we pass through somewhere real beautiful, that I want to settle down with Ryan and raise kids and all that shit.

Other times, it seems we can only ever keep running and chilling."

"They don't call this place Deathlands for nothing."

"I know. I've seen more corpses in the past couple of years than..."

"Than I've had hot dinners? That's the saying from my time. But I haven't had all that many hot dinners since I woke up here in Deathlands."

"Well, if the meal that they promised us is as good as the stuff looked growing in their fields, we could be in for a real treat."

IT WAS DOROTHY who came calling for them a half hour or so later.

They'd heard a noise—like a kind of trumpet booming out over the ville—that they assumed was a signal for all the workers to come in along the causeway so that Quindley could be secured for the night.

"Light's going," Michael said, standing by the open door and peering out into the evening gloom.

"They don't have a generator," J.B. said. "No 'lectric power."

"Saw a couple of gas tanks, along by the place where this Moses lives," Ryan said.

"My recollection of New England makes me think that it could be somewhat cold in the winter." Doc rubbed his stomach. "I admire the morality of those who eschew meat-eating, but I cannot conceal my carnivorous desires for a good chunk of flesh every now and again. I am wondering just how much longer we will be kept waiting."

"Here comes Dorothy," Michael said from the door.

"How did you get all the blasters your people carry?" J.B. asked, as the young woman led them through the quiet lanes of the ville.

"The blasters?"

"Yeah. Guards on the tower and the ones on the gate, all got good long guns. Brownings, a Mannlicher Model S, chambered for a .375 round. Couple of Marlins. Nice Winchester. Not many handblasters, though."

She stopped and looked at him, her face illuminated by the burning torches set in brackets along the way. "Moses knows the answer about the blasters. I heard there was a store in town, miles off from Quindley. But all this was long ago." She frowned with the effort of memory. "Called Jolly Jack's Sporting Goods. Least, I think that was the name."

"Yeah. They'd sell mainly rifles and scatterguns," the Armorer agreed.

"How long has Quindley been run like this?" Krysty was at Dorothy's shoulder.

"Run like what?"

"Neat and not eating meat and well guarded."

Dorothy smiled. "Since the day before yesterday. That's what Moses says to tell outlanders who keep asking too many prying questions."

"How many people live here?"

She looked at Ryan. "That's the end of questions. We have to go for the meal."

Dean tugged at her sleeve. "Come on. Tell us how many live here."

The young woman smiled. "For you, Dean . . . You aren't spoiled like . . . There are thirty-seven men between fifteen and the top. Forty-six women."

"What's 'the top' mean?" Michael had contrived to be right beside Dorothy again.

"The top is what we in the ville here call the ending time." She shook her head, so that her long blond hair caught the reddish glow of the torches. "But I've spoken too much. Much too much, Michael."

"Where are all the children?" Dean asked.

"Heard her say no more questions," Ryan warned.

"No!" Dorothy spit at him. "He and Michael may ask me anything they wish."

"Well?" Dean had his hands on his hips, grinning triumphantly at his father.

"Young ones below five live in one building. Middle ones from five to fifteen live apart as well."

Ahead of them the large double doors of one of the thatched huts swung open, spilling a lake of golden light across the packed earth.

Jehu stood there, staring out into the darkness of the evening. "Late, Sister Dorothy," he called.

"We're coming."

THE DELICIOUS SMELL of cooking seeped out from the long dining hall. The air was smoky from the lights, and from the ovens that could be glimpsed through a door to the rear of the building.

The inhabitants of the ville were seated at two long tables that ran along the wooden walls, with a shorter table laid crosswise at the head.

Every seat seemed to be filled, though Ryan noticed immediately that males and females were strictly segregated—men to the right and women to the left. Only the smaller top table held a mix of both the sexes.

"All young," he breathed to J.B., as they paused in the entrance to the hall.

"All young," the Armorer agreed.

Jehu had taken his own carved chair at the center of the high table. There were already four or five men and women with him, along with eight empty seats, waiting for Dorothy and for the seven friends.

The place had been filled with noisy conversation as they'd walked toward it, but, at the moment of their entrance, an unearthly silence fell over the room.

"Welcome, outlanders," Jehu called. "Come in and sit and receive the hospitality of Quindley."

"Thank you kindly," Ryan replied, checking automatically what kind of weapons the young people were wearing.

Most had knives sheathed at their belts, but only one or two seemed to be carrying handblasters.

But what was most noticeable was the reactions to their presence in the dining room, revealed on every face at every table—a mixture of curiosity and vague dislike. But, here and there, was the clearest expression of something that went a whole lot further than dislike.

The animosity was voiced before they even walked halfway around the room, behind Dorothy, toward the vacant seats at the top table.

"Not right, Jehu!" a man called out, but it wasn't possible to see who.

"Old outlanders not permitted in Quindley." This time it was one of the women.

"Was Moses asked, Jehu?" This time the speaker had risen to his feet, a slender boy, who looked to be about seventeen, with a squint in his right eye.

"Of course, Donnie. Would I admit strangers without the word of Moses?"

A woman, heavily pregnant, also stood up, pointing with a wooden ladle at Doc. "What of him, Jehu? What of that obscene sight?"

"Madam," Doc said, bridling with anger, "I might be many things, but I would suggest that obscene is not properly one of them."

"Two from seven only would pass the test!" shouted the first person to have spoken, finally rising to his feet to reveal himself to everyone.

His hair was cropped short, and he wore a pale blue bandanna knotted around his forehead. He pointed a bony forefinger directly toward Doc.

Jehu was on his feet, shouting for the teenager to sit down again and keep quiet. "Enough, Jimmy. You shall not go against the command of Moses."

"This is a blasphemy, Jehu!"

"You can argue this in council."

"When?"

"Two nights from now."

"Too late." Jimmy pushed his way from the table and stalked toward the outlanders, his fingers brushing the hilt of his knife.

Ryan, Krysty and J.B. all drew their blasters, covering the lad.

"Not unless we have to," Ryan whispered.

Jehu jumped over the table with a casual, athletic ease, his right hand clutching a narrow, glittering blade. "Moses will make you pay the price, Jimmy!" His voice cracked with the sudden high tension of the moment.

"Fuck that. Fuck Moses and fuck you, oldie!"

He moved so quickly that he took everyone, including Ryan, by surprise. He threw his knife with a deadly, practiced, underhand flick, the polished steel slicing across the hall toward Doc's throat.

Chapter Twenty-One

It was Michael Brother who saved Doc's life.

Ever since they'd met, Ryan had been constantly astounded at the dazzling speed of the teenager's reflexes. But he was still shocked at Michael's incredible reaction to the sudden, murderous attack.

It was almost as though time itself had been slowed, the hurled blade spinning in the air as it hissed toward the helpless old man.

In the background there was a collective gasp of indrawn breath at the certain knowledge that the wings of Death were folding around Doc. Nothing could possibly save him.

Nothing.

As casually as if he were plucking a hovering fly from the still summer air, Michael reached out his right hand. Almost lazily, it seemed. He took the thrown knife by the hilt, when it was less than a yard from Doc's neck.

He held it for a moment, then dropped it by his feet, the steel tinkling on the wooden floor.

"No," he said quietly into the total stillness.

The teenager called Jimmy stared in total disbelief. "You fucking traitor."

"Shall I chill him?" J.B. asked.

Ryan shook his head at the question. "No. Wait." For a few heartbeats, it seemed like everything was balanced on the edge of a razor.

Half the young men and women were up on their feet, most with their own knives drawn. One wrong move now and there would be serious blood-spilling.

It was Jehu who defused the moment.

Moving catfooted, he walked behind the paralyzed Jimmy, placed an arm around his shoulders, almost like an old playmate at the end of a day's sport, and cut his throat.

The honed dagger entered just below the left ear, with the faint crunch of punctured cartilage. Jehu drew it swiftly but firmly across, slicing through the helpless boy's windpipe, opening up the big artery under the right ear.

The bright blood jetted out from the white-lipped wound, splashing up to the heavy rafters that ran across the dining hall.

Jehu pushed the twitching corpse away from him, letting it drop to the crimsoned planks. The heart still labored, but the river had slowed to a trickle. Jimmy's hands were opening and closing, as if he were trying to cling to life.

"He shouted 'traitor' to us all," Jehu said, his voice trembling with the emotion of the killing. "But Jimmy was the real traitor here. A traitor to us all. A traitor to Moses. A traitor to Quindley."

There was a murmur all around the hall that could have been agreement.

Or could have been disagreement.

But not a soul lifted a voice to oppose what had happened or what had been said.

"Blasters away," Ryan advised, holstering the SIG-Sauer. He glanced across at Michael. "Done good."

But the teenager simply stared at him, his eyes blank and incurious.

"I owe you my life, Master Brother," Doc said, wiping at his clammy forehead with the swallow's-eye kerchief. "Better than owing Asculepius a cockerel. It is a debt that I shall always stand ready to honor, whensoever you feel the need to call upon me, Michael, and where—"

"All right, Doc," the teenager muttered. "Only caught the knife, is all. Didn't know the poor kid was going to end up like a butchered steer in the shambles."

Jehu stooped and wiped his blood-slick blade on the dead boy's shirt, carefully avoiding daubing his boots with the spreading pool of crimson.

"Come and eat now, outlanders," he said. "I give you my deep sorrow that our ville was so shamed." He turned and pointed to a couple of the youngest-looking lads at the table to the right. "Remove what was Jimmy, and we will inter him, properly, tomorrow. After the dawning."

"Seem to have lost some of my appetite," Krysty whispered to Ryan.

DESPITE THE HORRIFIC outburst of savage violence, the evening meal carried on almost as though nothing had happened. The body was dragged out, leaving a dark, glistening smear behind it.

Immediately the doors were closed again, and Jehu clapped his hands to order the food brought in. It was carried by several of the younger women, on platters of turned beechwood and hand-thrown pottery.

Large bowls were placed at intervals along all the tables, and everyone helped themselves to the steaming mix of vegetables. Ryan noticed that the cutlery on the top table was matching steel, but the rest of the people were making do with a makeshift collection of plastic and cheap metal.

Ryan was seated on the right hand of Jehu, with Krysty on the other side of the ville's leader. Doc sat next to Ryan, with an empty chair yawning conspicuously at his right. The rest of them were spaced out along the high table, with Dorothy sitting between Dean and Michael, engaging them both in a whispered, intense conversation.

The food was excellent, with a richness and diversity that was more than enough to dispel even Doc's proclaimed reservations about vegetarian eating.

There was delicious creamed carrots, mixed in with nutty, macerated celeriac; buttered leeks, with slices of lightly fried turnips decorating the top of the dish; potatoes in all shapes, sizes and varieties, roasted in their skins, mashed up with tiny shreds of cooked red cabbage; curling heads of kale, with deep-fried wafers of potato piled around them; baked potatoes, slashed open, with melting knobs of trade butter and sea salt.

There were at least a dozen kinds of bread. Some of it with little pieces of apple and pear baked into it; soda bread, with a dozen dishes of jelly; rolls so fresh they almost burned the tongue and melted in the mouth.

There was elderflower wine to drink, with apple juice and cold, pure water.

As soon as some of the dishes began to empty, the young women brought in fresh bowls, until the tables seemed to groan under the weight.

To follow the meal there were custards and a range of fresh fruits, including delicious golden melons.

Ryan hadn't realized just how hungry he'd been and he had to ease his belt out a couple of notches. There was little conversation, with everyone concentrating on the meal, though the one-eyed man was concerned at the way that his son and Michael seemed to be hanging on every word from the blond-haired Dorothy.

Only when the first overwhelming pangs had been satisfied did Ryan embark on a cautious talk with Jehu.

"Real ace-on-the-line meal," he said. "Moses responsible for that, as well?"

Jehu nodded, sipping at a glass of water. "Moses is responsible for everything within the ville of Quindley," he replied. "For every thing and for every person. We are what we are, because of Moses."

"Will we meet him?"

"No." Jehu hesitated. "Unless he chooses to let you speak with him."

Krysty had been listening to the conversation. "Speak with him, or see him?"

"Oh, only speak. Nobody sees Moses. I thought you had been told that."

Ryan glanced around the room, noticing that Doc was still the center of attention, though the young men and women of the ville seemed to be under orders to try not to stare at him—orders that they were finding difficult to obey.

"Jehu?" Ryan said, deciding that it was pointless to ignore the obvious question any longer.

"What is it?"

"Your ville has babies and children?"

"Yes. Of course. Or we would all die out."

"But you have no old people here?"

"Ah... You have observed this?"

"Have to be triple stupe not to. Doesn't seem to be a single man or woman over the age of about thirty or so?"

"Younger," Jehu agreed, cutting himself a slice of one of the honeyed melons.

"Younger?" Krysty repeated. "How much younger?"

"Nobody in Quindley ever lives beyond their twenty-fifth birthing day."

"Twenty-five." Ryan nodded. "Yeah, I can believe that. But what happened to all the older men and women here?"

"They were translated to a different place. So Moses teaches us."

"Dead," Krysty said, the word flat and dull in the air between them.

"Outlanders would say that the oldies have died. We do not always say so."

"Some virus, is it? A sickness?"

Jehu looked puzzled. "A sickness, Krysty?"

It was her turn to look bewildered. "There has to be a reason why there's nobody over the age of twenty-five, Jehu. People don't just die on their twenty-fifth birthday."

"Yes, they do."

Ryan and Krysty sat silent, staring at each other across the front of the ponytailed young man, whose bright blue eyes were gazing out over the crowded room.

Ryan swallowed a mouthful of the light wine. "You telling us what I think you're telling us, Jehu? Nobody old in the whole ville, because you chill them?"

"Of course we do. Oh, I know what you think. The ways of many outland villes are different. We know that. Moses has explained how there is no wisdom beyond our lands. This is why we don't normally allow strangers in. Unless they... But let that pass. Dorothy said you helped with stickies and with finding the body of Jolyon, brother to Isaac. So, in the ways ordained by Moses, we take you in and feed you. Let you rest before going on your journey."

Doc had finally picked up on what was being said and he sat, a forkful of carrot frozen halfway to his mouth. "Are my old ears betraying me, my dear Ryan?" he whispered. "Or did that slip of a child say they killed everyone once they reached the age of twenty-five?"

Ryan let his held breath whistle softly between his teeth. "No, Doc, you heard right all right."

"Then that explains the hostility to me. I must seem like some Methuselah to them."

"Who was Methuselah, Doc?" Ryan asked.

"Oldest man in the Bible. He was..." Doc waved his hand, holding the fork, the food spilling back onto his plate. "By the Three Kennedys, Ryan, but I think that we should not linger long in this place."

Jehu had stood up and was rapping on the oak table with the hilt of his spoon, waiting until the dining hall fell silent. "Brothers and sisters, the meal is done. And, as we follow the path of Moses, we shall now retire to meditate on the day and to rest. Our guests will retire to their quarters." He rapped the spoon again for emphasis. "They are the guests of Quindley and of Moses. They will not be harmed and will be shown respect. Despite most of them being oldies."

Ryan looked around the room as the young leader made his short speech. He saw every face turned toward the top table, most eyes averted from the wrinkled face of Doc, avoiding J.B., Mildred, Krysty and himself.

But many of them, particularly the younger women, were staring at Dean and at Michael with something that seemed to approach a kind of hunger.

Both of them had been tucking into the excellent meal with every show of enjoyment. But they'd also both been listening intently to whatever it was that Dorothy had been saying to them.

And that worried Ryan.

IT WAS A MILD NIGHT, with a sky like black velvet, sprinkled with brilliant stars. Frank and Ray had guided them back to their quarters. Michael and Dean lagged behind, whispering to each other.

Before being shepherded into the divided hut, Ryan and Krysty embraced and kissed, as did J.B. and Mildred. The two young men of Quindley scarcely bothered to conceal their disgust.

"Bad enough having oldies in the ville without triple-sick sexing like this," Frank said.

"You want to be careful, sonny," Mildred snapped. "Or I'll come and kiss you when you aren't looking and you'll get to be old and wrinkled like me. Just like *that*." She snapped her fingers. "So watch your little shit mouth."

ONCE THEY WERE ALONE, Ryan sat on his bed and beckoned his eleven-year-old son to him. "Want to have a word with you, Dean."

"What?"

The torches were beginning to smoke and gutter, and someone had placed an ancient brass oil lamp on the central table, which bathed the room in a gentle, golden glow. But it didn't give enough light for Ryan to be able to see properly what was going on in the boy's face.

"Speak to me, Dean."

"What about?"

He wished that Krysty had been there. With her semimutie powers, she was amazingly sensitive to what people said. And, more importantly, to the way in which they said it. She would have heard things in Dean's voice that Ryan could only begin to try to guess at.

"What did Dorothy say to you and Michael during the meal?"

"Nothing much."

"What? She was talking all the way through."

"Why do you want to know, Dad?"

The small vein was beginning to tick in Ryan's temple, the inexorable sign that he was on the verge of losing his temper. Dean was deliberately concealing something from him. He didn't know what and he didn't know why.

"I ask the questions and you answer them. We're in a strange ville. Real double strange. Anything that you've been told could be a help in working out if there's any sort of danger for any of us. All right?"

"Dad, I'm real tired. Dorothy didn't say nothing about stuff like you just said. Nothing like that. Now, is it all right if I go to bed?"

The boy's whole body language was shouting out a stubborn resistance. Ryan had a momentary temptation to slap him senseless, but he struggled and overcame it, knowing it would do no good, except in terms of relieving some of his own feelings.

"Sure," he said finally, ruffling Dean's hair. "Go to bed, son."

Chapter Twenty-Two

"Good day to you." Jehu stood in the open doorway of their quarters, the bright morning sun turning him into a sharp-edged silhouette.

"Hi, there." Ryan and the others had discussed what they'd found out during the evening meal, before they had all retired to their beds.

The fact that Quindley deliberately butchered anyone who passed their twenty-fifth birthday hadn't really come as that much of a surprise. They had all noticed the extreme youth of everyone in the well-ordered ville.

Doc had been most persuasive for their leaving the place at first light.

"Did they explain why they followed this barbarous practice?" he'd asked.

Ryan hadn't known the answer to that. "We never got around to talking about *why* they did it, Doc. Bad enough that they did it at all."

"They have shown us some courtesy, and the one they call Jehu, aided by young Michael here, most certainly saved my life. But who knows how they might feel tomorrow? I have not encountered such overt hostility since I addressed a meeting of young female students in 1888 and opposed the idea that they should ever be allowed to vote."

"Best not let Mildred hear you admit to that argument, Doc," J.B. warned. "Likely to find you've got your balls nailed to the wall."

Doc had smiled. "Well, the truth is, I was never actually opposed to the idea of universal suffrage. I only did it to annoy my dear Emily and draw attention to myself. And it worked well. She was so delighted to have the chance to persuade a young male chauvinist to her views that we spent many late hours together while she wooed me over to her side."

It was eventually agreed that they would stay in Quindley for at least another day. Ryan's argument for this was that they had vastly superior firepower to anything the young men and women carried. And they were being very well fed and should take advantage of the chance to catch up on some decent meals and sleep on good, clean beds.

Now it was time for them to go again to the dining room and break their fasts.

"Many of us are already out at work, either in the fields or in the woods around," Jehu said. "There go some of the youngest, to help to gather branches and twigs for the fires. We need a good store against the cold of winter." He brushed back his long hair. "Perhaps you might go and watch them, later."

There was a group of fifteen little children, all wearing pale blue shirts and pants, most of them with the same blond hair. As they walked along the gently swaying causeway, several of them turned to look back at the outlanders. One or two of them made a curious gesture, with their index finger and little finger stuck straight out, aimed at Ryan and the others, while the two middle fingers were kept clenched.

"They point at us with the sign to ward off the maleficent powers of the evil eye," Doc said. "It saddens me to see such perverse and heathen foolishness in what should be an earthly paradise."

Jehu heard him and turned around. "If it were not for the word of Moses, then it would be more than fingers pointing at you."

"That a threat?" Ryan asked.

"Make of it what you will."

"If Doc had been chilled last night, then there wouldn't have been a living soul left in your fucking dining room! Make of that what you want."

"Is that a threat, outlander?"

Ryan stepped in close, feeling all of the old strength and power surge through his body. It was good to know that his body had purged itself so quickly of what had come so close to being a terminal illness.

"No, Jehu. It isn't just a threat. It's a promise."

THE TENSION EASED over the breakfast.

There were cereals and fruits, eggs, which also came from the ville's trading with other, smaller communities, and wooden platters of breads and conserves.

The hall was almost empty, with everyone already out in the fields. Dorothy came in halfway through the meal and smiled at Dean and Michael. She sat with them at the end of the table. Ryan caught Krysty's eye and frowned, but there was no point in making any sort of an issue out of it.

"When do you want us out of here?" he asked Jehu.

The young man was taken by surprise by the question, spluttering through a mouthful of wholemeal bread. "Stay as long as…long as you want. Both your two boys are interested in what we do. Why not give them another day or so to really understand what Quindley is all about?"

Dorothy looked up. "Don't forget that Moses will want to speak to the outlanders, Jehu."

Ryan ignored her. "Don't like coming and taking anything for nothing, Jehu. Sure you wouldn't like us to go and do some hunting for you?"

"Meat is poison. But there are vermin in the woods. If you could cut down on their numbers, then we'd be grateful to you." He smiled. "That would be good."

They all looked up as the doors opened and a man stumbled in. He was more ragged than anyone they'd seen, his clothing dirty, his chin unshaved. He was escorted by two of the women, each of them with a handblaster at the waist. All three sat down at the far end of one of the long tables, ignoring the outlanders.

"Who's that?" J.B. asked.

"He is soon to be selected." Jehu finished his mug of water and wiped his mouth. He stood, obviously not wishing to pursue the conversation further.

But the Armorer didn't want to let it lie. "What does 'selected' mean? I've seen prisoners in my time. That's what he is, isn't he, Jehu?"

"No. He can leave if he wishes, on his own terms. But he has known since birthing that he is of the people and belongs to Moses and the people."

Dorothy also stood, an arm resting lightly on Michael's shoulder. "If you stay here with us for another three days, then you'll see for yourself how blood returns to blood here in our ville."

Krysty nodded. "I get it. Poor bastard's got his twenty-fifth birthday coming up. That it?"

The young blond woman nodded. "Yes. That's it. Now—" she rubbed her hands as if she were wiping away a problem "—now, I'm taking Dean and Michael on a tour of the ville. Rest of you oldies can go where you please."

"Watch the wood gatherers," Jehu suggested, "and perhaps cull some of the carrion from the deep forest."

"Sure," Ryan said. "Why not?"

THE FIVE FRIENDS RETURNED first to their quarters, to wash and ready themselves for the day. The sun shone brightly, turning Shamplin Lake into a silvered ocean. A gentle breeze whispered from the north, bringing the fresh scent of pine needles. Out across the water a large fish leaped and turned, the light catching the rainbow gleam of its scales.

Krysty was in the men's part of the room, ignoring a scowl from Frank. "It's really beautiful, lover," she said, beckoning Ryan to the view from the window.

"Yeah. Long as you're under the age of twenty-five."

She turned to the young man who was lounging in the doorway. "I just don't get why, Frank."

"Moses says it's what's needed."

"Why?"

He looked a little puzzled. "You don't ask 'why' to things Moses says."

"You mean you just do his bidding and work hard and then, just when most people would be marrying and having children and settling down, you just offer yourself up. And you miss all the good things."

Frank stared at the red-haired woman as if she was totally deranged. "We have to do it. It's the way. Always was the way here in Quindley."

"No point in arguing," Mildred said. "Just like banging your head up against a brick wall."

"It isn't even thought of." Frank was almost lost for words. "To argue about anything Moses... What he says is what happens. That's all."

"We going to get to meet him?" Ryan asked.

"You don't—"

"Yeah. I remember. Talk to him but not see him. When's that happen?"

"Soon. But if he wants it, then it'll happen. But if Moses decides not, then it won't."

DOROTHY HAD VANISHED with Michael and Dean.

The rest walked over the causeway, in among the cultivated fields and allotments. Jehu himself had come to lead them, his hair untied, streaming about his shoulders, making him look like one of the children in the corn.

Most of the young men and women ignored the outlanders, though there was still some residual resistance to the sight of Doc. But the old man strode along, swinging his sword stick, smiling at everyone.

"A good, *good* morning to you all. May the bird of happiness fly up your nose, children. Tote that bale and lift that barge, or something like that. So that juvenile man river can just keep rolling along."

Not one of them spoke to him, several making the same sign to avert the eye of evil.

Jehu paused. "Could you not talk to them, oldie Doc? It will make trouble. Moses said you could walk around, but he would be unhappy if there was difficulties."

"And if Moses is unhappy, then everyone gets to be unhappy. That it, Jehu?" Mildred grinned. "Apart from there being nobody over twenty-five, I can't say there are many black youngsters in Quindley, either."

The frank and open face clouded over. "It isn't that we are preduded...prejudiced? Is that the word?"

"Sure is," Mildred agreed. "Keep talking, sonny. Tell me how some of your best friends are black."

"No, I have no friends who are black," he replied, straight-faced. "Moses would welcome anyone...if they are young enough. In fact, he makes a point in his teachings to us that we need new blood. There are not enough babies being birthed here in the ville. But it seems that no black-faced people come here. I think there might have been one or two, passing by. But none of them have stayed here. Never."

"Us black folk got more sense, land's sake we do."

"THE LITTLE ONES WILL BE just a way along this path here. We can walk up to the top of the hill and look down on the part of the woods where we always come to collect the broken branches for the fires."

"You got guards out?" J.B. looked around, the Uzi ready in his hand.

"There will be four with them, each carrying a long blaster. Moses ordered a doubling of care when he heard about your finding the stickies." Jehu hawked and spit on the path, rubbing it in with his feet, while making the horned gesture with his fingers. "Satan's spawn," he said.

"You not had trouble with them before?" Ryan was taking deep breaths of the morning air, still conscious that all wasn't completely well with the wound in his neck. But Mildred had put on a fresh, much smaller dressing that morning, reporting that the healing process was almost done.

"We have had small attacks by muties. But they aren't organized, and we retreat to the ville and hold them off from there. But stickies are not well-known."

"They can go around in little groups," Ryan said. "But I've known of camps of dozens, and some of them have been well run. Mebbe you've been lucky."

"Quindley looks after itself." Jehu recited it like it was a great religious truth.

THE SCENT OF BALSAM grew stronger as they walked in single file through a sun-splashed path of the forest, climbing along a well-marked trail.

Krysty and Ryan were bringing up the rear when she suddenly stopped, pressing her fingers to her temple.

"Trouble?" he asked, his hand dropping by a combat reflex down onto the butt of the SIG-Sauer.

"Could be. Just felt a flash of something."

"Close?"

"Fairly close. Doesn't feel like norms. More like muties, but . . ."

"Stickies?"

Krysty shook her head. "No. Gone again. Don't mention it to the others. Could be wrong."

Jehu had stopped at the crest of the hill, sweeping out his hand to indicate the woods and clearings below him, dotted with the diminutive figures of the little children, busy collecting wood for the ville's fires.

"Here is the rich and wonderful plenty that Moses has given us," he said. "This is our reward for treading only in the prints of his feet."

Then the screaming started.

Chapter Twenty-Three

Ryan had the Steyr SSG-70 unslung and to his right shoulder before the first echo of that desperate shrill scream had begun to fade across the whispering tops of the pines. He put his eye to the Starlite night scope, using the power laser image enhancer, searching for the best target, the frightened children filling his field of vision.

"Stickies!" Krysty breathed at his side. "Knew I felt something bad."

Jehu rushed down the far side of the gentle hill, toward the panicked little ones. He carried no blaster and had simply drawn his dagger, the same blade that had opened Jimmy's throat the night before.

"Brave or stupe," J.B. said, standing with the Uzi at his hip, looking down at the scene of confusion.

"Why do you not commence firing at the ranks of the ungodly, John Dix?" Doc asked.

"Out of range."

The nearest child was more than three hundred yards away, but they were all running back and forth, screaming for rescue from the four or five muties that had come lurching suddenly out of the undergrowth.

"Can't we go down and help?" Mildred had the Czech ZKR 551 target revolver cocked in her hand.

Excellent shootist though she was, the range and the rapid movement below made it an almost impossible shot.

"Wait," Ryan said. "Could be an ambush. Could be more of them in the trees."

"I make it five. Two children down already." J.B. shaded his eyes with his hands, peering into the sun. "Think they're after prisoners."

"Suffer the little children," Doc muttered, but Ryan was already concentrating on doing some shooting.

The rifle snapped once, and he had the satisfaction of seeing one of the marauding stickies throw up its hands and tumble into the dirt like a discarded sack of old clothes.

The other four paused at the sound of the shot. On the ridge, Ryan could hear their harsh, guttural yells of alarm and warning. He decided that the likelihood was that it probably wasn't any kind of trap.

"J.B., go down there. Rest of you with him. I'll do what I can up here and then follow on down."

The Armorer didn't need to be told twice. Giving a whoop of delight, Uzi at his hip, he ran down the hillside, pursuing the tall, lean figure of Jehu.

Mildred was at his heels, followed by the lumbering Doc. Krysty hesitated a moment, her snub-nosed Smith & Wesson 640 double-action in her right fist.

"Dean and Michael?" she queried.

Ryan squeezed off a second round, cursing under his breath as he saw the shot gouge a strip of white wood out of a larch, inches from the head of one of the stickies.

"Bastard! Dean? He and Michael went with that Dorothy. Both got blasters. Would have heard shooting if they'd been jumped by muties."

She nodded. "Guess so. See you down there." Krysty turned and ran after the others, her blazing crimson hair streaming behind her like a battle pennant.

Ryan knelt down to make himself steadier, aiming carefully and putting the third bullet through the chest of another of the stickies, seeing through the scope the way that the round punched a hole larger than a man's fist out of the creature's back. The stickie staggered backward, tripping over a cowering child before crashing down in a tangle of limbs.

"Two down," he said.

The three surviving muties had gathered themselves into a vaguely defensive ring. Sunlight glittered on steel, and Ryan saw that they all held crude axes.

Jehu was less than fifty yards away from them, arms pumping, mouth open in a soundless scream, his slim knife in his hand. The dappled sunlight filtering through the branches of the trees splashed on his golden hair as he charged.

One of the little girls, eyes staring in mindless terror, actually ran into the arms of the tallest of the surviving stickies. The suckered fingers grabbed at her arms, tearing circles of skin away, blood speckling her pale blue shirt.

Ryan saw it all through the scope, but it was over too fast for him to do anything to prevent it.

The mutie's hand went to the child's throat and clamped shut. The immensely strong fingers squeezed once, and blood gushed from her open mouth and nostrils, from her ears and from her sky-blue eyes.

Ryan didn't have a chance to prevent the brutish murder, but he had time to avenge it.

The stickie whooped in glee at the easy killing, lifting one crimsoned hand to its face, its forked reptilian tongue snaking out to lap the fresh blood.

The 7.62 mm round smashed into the center of its hoggish nose, tumbling as it entered the space behind the face, shredding the vicious brain as it distorted, eventually exiting just behind the creature's left ear.

Stickies rarely carried blasters. Their perverse delight in all fires and explosions meant that any gun falling into their suckered hands tended to be emptied mindlessly into the sky—or into each other.

Also, they had virtually no idea at all of combat skills. Generally they would attack when they felt like it and stop when they'd either been victorious or were dead.

The two muties left standing might have had a chance of survival if they'd turned and run into the surrounding forest. But, despite the fact that Ryan had obviously been able to pick them off at long range, they made no attempt to escape.

"Fireblast!"

Because of the contours of the hillside, Jehu was now directly in Ryan's line of fire, obscuring the chance to take out the last two muties with a pair of easy shots.

J.B. and Midlred were closing in on the stickies Doc twenty paces behind them, Krysty just overtaking him. But none of them was near enough to interfere in the final scene of the lethal drama.

The Armorer's words came to Ryan. "Brave or stupe?" There was no need at all for the young man to risk his own life by throwing himself against the pair of waiting muties. He could easily have stood off and allowed Ryan, Mildred or J.B. to have safely chilled them.

"For Moses!" The cry rose above the sobbing of the surviving children, most of whom were now sitting or lying on the soft grass between the trees, watching the last moments of the muties' assault on them.

The nearest stickie swung its crude ax at Jehu, but the agile young man dodged under it, cutting upward with his own knife. Ryan was on his feet, walking slowly down the slope, knowing that haste would do nothing to alter the eventual outcome. He heard the mutie yelp in pain, and saw a dark patch of blood appear along the side of its ribs.

The second creature grabbed at the diving figure of the young man, and there was the loud noise of ripping cloth. But Jehu's momentum carried him through and past, snatching a moment to try to stab the mutie.

"Stupe *and* brave," Ryan muttered, pausing in midstride, seeing that the leader of the ville wasn't particularly skilled at knife-fighting.

The Trader used to say that you didn't get to live long in Deathlands if you didn't have courage. But you lived even less long if you didn't also have some brains.

"Brains before balls" had been his shorthand saying, though it had sometimes annoyed the tough women who rode with him on the war wags.

Jehu had the balls all right, getting up in a fighter's crouch, facing the two gibbering stickies. But his small knife was no weapon against their hatchets.

"Mildred!" Ryan yelled. "Do them."

For someone who had won a silver medal in the free pistol-shooting at the last ever Olympic Games in Miami in 1996, it was like picking off carp in a bathtub.

The doctor fired two careful shots, the Smith & Wesson .38s easily finding their targets.

One stickie hurled his ax spinning high in the air as he went down, with a bullet through his left eye, the blade sticking among the upper branches of a Douglas fir. His comrade was hit in the side of the head, just above the right ear, the big round exiting through his left cheek, an inch below his eye.

After the flat crack of the revolver, the morning seemed almost silent.

The weeping little ones had fallen away to a quick sobbing. One small boy moaned in pain and shock, a long strip of skin torn away from ankle to thigh, blood soaking into the soft carpet of pine needles beneath him. Jehu had dropped to his knees, his eyes closed, his lips moving.

"Nice shooting, Mildred," J.B. said, his eyes glinting behind his glasses as he continued to scan the darkness beneath the surrounding trees in case there were more stickies on the loose.

Ryan continued down the slope to rejoin his friends. Krysty and Doc were trying to comfort the terrified children. Mildred Wyeth had walked over to check that all of the muties were dead. Not that Ryan had any doubts on that score. He knew killing shots when he saw them.

"All done?" he called.

"Yeah." Mildred looked around the clearing. "We going to leave them here? The kids should be taken back to the ville as soon as possible. There's four of them dead. The one with the wounded leg needs treatment."

"Jehu?" Ryan had nearly reached the kneeling young man, who seemed to be oblivious to what had happened around him. "You all right?"

"Blessed Moses forgive us for our sins."

Ryan laid a hand on Jehu's shoulder, shaking him gently. "Come on. It's over."

But the blue eyes stayed closed, the droning voice not ceasing. "Let us welcome the shadow of death in this dark valley. It is a sign that we have not worked hard enough and have walked from the path of light into the deep midnight. Save us, wonderful Moses, from this place of blood."

Ryan shook him much harder. He'd seen plenty of religious crazies throughout Deathlands and never met one that he'd truly liked.

"Get the fuck up, boy," he said. "You're the leader of this place, and you got some dead children to take home and bury. And there's wounded. Decisions on the stickies." He hauled Jehu to his feet.

"You saved my life. You, an oldie. An outlander. Saved my life."

His voice trembled with shock.

"It was Mildred who took out the last two for you."

"The... the black woman oldie?"

Mildred turned and smiled. "Kind of difficult to come to terms with, is it, boy? Not just an old person. Not even an old woman. But an old black woman. Goin' to take some hard thinking on that, isn't it?"

The children had been herded together, and J.B. had hoisted the injured little boy onto his back. In their horror at the stickies, most of the little ones seemed to have temporarily overcome their revulsion and fear of Doc and were happy to have him standing close by, guarding them.

The woods were returning quickly to normal. A red-capped jay had perched on a broken branch near where the mutie's ax had become jammed. Turquoise flies were gathering to feed on the dark puddles of spilled blood.

Far above them Ryan noticed a jet-black carrion crow, circling slowly, bright eyes staring down at the prospect of some fine feeding.

MILDRED BANDAGED the boy's leg as soon as they got back, covering it with a layer of clean linen, having first washed the raw wound with a bowl of the crystal lake water. As he recovered his nerve, the child became less and less happy about being tended by an outland stranger. All his young life he'd been reared on Moses's teaching that old meant bad and evil.

The bodies were taken away into one of the smaller buildings that backed onto Shamplin Lake, to be mourned by the community. Dorothy appeared out of the crowd, with Dean and Michael following sheepishly at her side.

"You bring death at your shoulder, outlander," she hissed accusingly. "Isaac's sweet brother, then Jimmy and now four of our precious jewels."

"You think we're in league with the bastard stickies? Then you got a sicker warped mind than I thought."

"Dad!" Dean was flushed as he stepped forward. "Shouldn't speak to Dorothy like that."

Ryan's good eye flashed with anger, and he half lifted his fist toward his son. "You don't ever talk out against me... or any of us. Not in front of strangers, Dean. Not ever!"

The boy's head dropped, and he shuffled his feet. "Sorry, Dad, but..." The sentence faltered away into stillness.

Jehu was standing at the back of the group and he pushed through to the front. "Sister Dorothy," he said.

"What?"

He put the tips of his fingers together, making a steeple from them. "Moses would not wish to hear the way you've just been speaking."

"I speak truth. There's been nothing but ill luck and death since they set foot in our lands."

"They didn't bring the stickies. Ryan and Mildred chilled them and saved our little ones from much, much worse."

Dorothy stared at Jehu. "Moses knows this?"

"Of course."

"What did he say?"

"That he would speak to the outlanders himself."

It was the first that Ryan had heard of it. "When will that be, Jehu?"

"Soon."

"Today?"

"Yes. When the word is sent. You should all stay ready and not leave the ville so that you can go as soon as Moses is ready to speak to you."

Ryan bit his lip. "I don't get you people. Never seen a ville like this one. Yesterday you lose one of you to the stickies. Next morning out go your children, free as air. You told me there were armed guards on them. So, what happened?"

Jehu looked embarrassed. "They saw some orchids so they picked them as a tribute to Moses. They thought our young ones would be safe."

"Right. Now you know there are stickies in the forest. Look out the window. There's still people working in the fields."

"But they're close enough to the causeway if the stickies attack." His face brightened. "Anyway, outlander, you forget that you killed them all this morning."

Ryan gripped the young man by the collar of his clean shirt. "Jehu, if I take a boat and catch me a trout in the lake. Catch five trout. Does that mean there aren't any more fish in the whole bastard lake?"

"Course not."

"Course not, shit for brains! And because we chilled a few stickies who weren't expecting to come against well-armed men and women, you think you can sit around and smile and tell yourselves that your fucking Moses is on top of the world and all's bitching well!"

"Don't call him that!"

To Ryan's amazed disbelief, Jehu was actually drawing his dagger, as though he were going to try to slit Ryan's throat, like he had Jimmy the night before. Ryan chopped at his forearm with the side of his hand, the steel rattling on the floor. At the same time he brought his knee up into the young leader's groin. Not hard enough to send him into shock and kill him, but hard enough to put him down and puking on the scrubbed planks.

"Don't you ever do that, Jehu," he said mildly, "or you get to be dead."

When he turned away he saw that Dorothy had gone pale. And that Michael had taken a step toward him, his knuckles white, eyes narrowed in anger.

"Yeah?" Ryan challenged.

Chapter Twenty-Four

"You aren't my father, Ryan Cawdor."

"I know that, Michael." The one-eyed man watched the teenager with every fraction of his concentration. Ryan knew that he was fast enough in close combat, but he also knew that Michael was crucially quicker.

"And I don't have to jump to do every damned thing that you tell me."

"True again. Is there a point to this?"

The youth stepped closer. To the right, and behind Michael, Ryan saw Krysty silently drawing her blaster.

"You know the point!"

"No. Tell me."

"When I was at Nil-Vanity I spent my life being told what to do, Ryan."

"You were a kid then." It trembled on Ryan's lips to tell Michael that he was behaving like a kid now, but he resisted the temptation.

"You and your lot think that being old means never having to say 'sorry' for anything."

"Well done, Brother Michael," Dorothy said, patting him on the back.

"I believe that we would rather hear the organ grinder than his tame monkey," Doc said to the smiling blond woman, instantly wiping away her self-congratulatory grin. "Though, I confess in this case that I am not altogether clear in my mind as to which is which."

"You shut the fuck up, Doc!" Michael snapped. "This is between Ryan and me."

"No." Ryan shook his head. "I think you're wrong when you say that."

"Yeah?"

"Yeah. I think that it's between the young ones of Quindley, with Dorothy here as their mouthpiece, and the five of us." He glanced at Dean. "Or the six of us."

"Bullshit, Ryan." But Michael's anger was slipping away. It was obvious in the set of the jaw and the relaxing of the fists into plain hands. Observing body language was something that the Trader had taught Ryan at an early age, watching not just the eyes and listening to more than the words.

"Look, we never interfere in the way a ville is run. You know that, Michael. Their business. Not mine. Not yours, either. You understand?"

"Sure."

Dorothy wasn't ready to allow the argument to slip away. "Typical oldie lies," she said. "You should listen to Moses, Brother Michael. He can teach you how to see the world clearly. Not through misted oldie eyes."

"When I was a child I saw and spake as a child," Mildred said. "Not sure of the precise words. Something like. Now I'm grown up I put away childish thoughts and desires and I see clearly. Think on that, Michael.''

There was a long silence in the room.

Soon the moment passed.

ABOUT NINETY MINUTES LATER it was Donnie who made a hesitant appearance in the sunlit doorway of their room, his squinting eyes glancing uneasily all around without actually settling on any of them.

Only five of the companions were there. Dean and Michael had left with Dorothy and Jehu and hadn't yet reappeared. Doc dozed on his back, snoring quietly. Krysty leaned on the sill, looking out over the lake. J.B. and Mildred were fieldstripping and cleaning her ZKR 551. Ryan lay on his bed, looking up at a mouse that was picking its delicate path over one of the heavy roof beams.

''Moses will speak to you now,'' Donnie announced.

Ryan swung his legs over the side of the bed and stood, reaching for the Steyr rifle and slinging it across his shoulder. ''Fine,'' he said.

JEHU WAITED FOR THEM outside the only stone-walled building in the ville. A magpie was strutting around and around the conical thatched roof, the bright light making its black feathers glow with a deep purple sheen.

''You should have come more quickly,'' the young man said, looking worried.

''You coming in with us?'' Ryan asked.

"It is permitted. But you must follow the law."

"What's that mean, Jehu?"

"It means that... Well, you'll see for yourselves inside. The temple of Moses is divided—"

"Temple!" Doc snorted.

Jehu carried on, trying unsuccessfully to conceal his irritation at the old man's sniggering. "The temple is divided. The public atrium is where we'll be. There is a wall that closes Moses off from the crude world. He speaks from behind it. But there is a mirror of magic that shows us only our poor faces. Moses watches us from behind it.

They all turned as a blond girl, looking to be about twelve years old, came toward them from the direction of the kitchens, carrying a silver platter.

"Noon food for Moses," Jehu explained, gesturing for the child to go on through. "She will leave it by the locked portal to the inner sanctum, and Moses will take it when there are no mortal eyes to gaze upon his divinity."

Doc turned away, quickly clamping a gnarled hand over his mouth to try to muffle his instant laughter. "Mortal portal," he muttered.

"Cut it out, Doc," Krysty warned.

"My apologies." He bowed to Jehu. "I shall be the utter soul of discretion, young man. It will be an unforgettable experience, to find oneself in the presence of a godhead incarnate. A deity made flesh."

Krysty had looked at the dish carried by the girl. "I thought that you were all vegetarians?"

It was a grilled salmon, taken off the bone, the pale pink meat decorated with parsley, surrounded with creamed potatoes and thin-sliced carrots.

"We eat no flesh of any sort," Jehu agreed. "But Moses is above and beyond any such restrictions. So we either fish or hunt for him or barter for meat."

"Sure enjoys the good life, your Moses, doesn't he?" Mildred commented.

"It is his right. Now come in and...please be respectful inside."

"DARK NIGHT!" J.B. whistled between his teeth at the interior of the circular building.

The rest of them were equally impressed. The buildings that they'd seen in Quindley ville had all been fairly crude and basic, with nothing beyond the simplest furniture.

This was luxury on an almost unimaginable scale. If this was the public, common side of the "temple," then it was impossible to think what the godling's own quarters were like beyond the dividing wall.

A thick carpet of animal furs covered the floor. Directly opposite them was the mirror that Jehu had mentioned. It was set in a frame of precious and semiprecious stones, giving it a rich, almost supernatural appearance.

"There's onyx and chalcedony," Doc said in a reverential whisper. "About ten different kinds of agate. Tiger's eye and jet. Sapphires and rubies. Carved ivory, inlaid with gold."

"Look at the pictures on the walls," Mildred said, turning to Jehu. "Those originals?"

"Don't know what that means," he replied. "Moses sent out for them, years ago. Past history."

The black woman walked around, peering at the paintings. One was of a man working at a gas station on a deserted road by a forest. "Hopper," she said. "And that one's definitely a Wyeth." She stared in disbelief at the strange, haunting picture of a bleached animal skull, set against an arid, pink-and-gray New Mexico landscape. "By God, but I'm sure that's an original Georgia O'Keefe. It's beautiful."

Jehu raised a hand for silence and turned to face the mirror. "We are here, Moses."

There was no reply.

"Mebbe he's not home," Ryan said. "We won't wait."

Jehu's jaw dropped. "You can't leave. Can't."

He spoke more loudly. "The outlanders are Ryan Cawdor, Krysty Wroth, Mildred Wyeth, J. B. Dix and Doc Tanner. Ryan is the father of—"

"The boy, Dean. Yes, I know that, Jehu."

The voice was everything that a god's voice should be, deep and resonant, every word perfectly enunciated, managing to radiate wisdom and knowledge in every rich syllable.

"Wow," Mildred said to Krysty. "A guy with a voice like that could have made a serious fortune doing voice-overs for ads for soap powder or life insurance."

"They are welcome to Quindley. We have heard of your help with the evil mutated creatures that inhabit the wild woods around our sanctum sanctorum. And for that assistance we give you the thanks of Moses."

"You're welcome," Ryan replied, staring intently at his own reflection on the wall facing them, guessing that it was an old-fashioned two-way mirror. The skill of making them had been lost during the long winters, but he'd seen a couple in the top-jack bedrooms of high-class gaudies.

"You know that we have a rule that everyone must willingly sacrifice their lives upon reaching the end of their road at the age of twenty-five?"

"Willingly?" Krysty queried.

"Oh, yes." There was the faint sound of movement behind the mirror, like someone changing position on a chair. "This place is totally safe. Life is wonderful. But only because the supernal ancient ones accept our sacrifices. The balance and harmony must be maintained."

Ryan was aware that the voice was brilliantly sidling into his mind, seeking to convince him of the essential rightness of the man—or god—called Moses.

"Fight it, lover." Krysty's fingers were digging hard into his arm, her voice like a shower of chips of ice on a warm, welcoming fire.

"Yeah," he said, his own voice sounding as though it were drifting to his ears from a dusty corridor in the abandoned west wing of a great mansion.

"How long can they stay with us, Moses?" Jehu stood with his head bowed, hands tangling in front of him like a nest of small pink snakes.

"As long as they wish."

"Even me, O great panjandrum, Moses? Even this disgusting old sack of tripes that befouls the very air of your temple of temples, holy of holies, light of lights, ancient of days, lord of the cherubim and seraphim—"

"Doc," Ryan whispered, "cut it out."

Moses's voice was unchanged. "I recognize an unusual mind, Dr. Tanner. If you are here with us for long enough, perhaps you and I can find some idle moments to discuss questions moral and physical."

"Philosophical and diagnostic," Doc replied.

"Elementary and alimentary."

Doc laughed, genuinely amused. "I admit, Moses . . . where were you when the light went out, by the way? I admit it is a rare delight to speak with someone capable of stringing together words that consist of more than a single syllable."

"How old are you?" Krysty's question brought a silence into the ornate room. "Gone deaf, Moses? I asked you how old you were? Simple enough question."

"The question is simple, Krysty."

Ryan felt he was listening to an exceedingly wise and benevolent uncle, gently reproaching a callow and whining little girl.

"So, why not answer it?"

"I am old enough to have created and succored this ville of Quindley, without fear or favor. And that will be answer enough, Krysty."

She sniffed, but kept silent.

"That will be all, Jehu."

"Yes, Moses."

"Assure all my people that the outlanders mean no harm. Even one so unbelievably antiquated as Dr. Tanner is to be treated with respect."

"You are truly all heart, Moses," Doc replied.

"Now you may leave me. I have seen all I need to see. Take care of them, Jehu."

Ryan took a step toward the mirror. "How about the stickies? You just going to let that go?"

"Nothing needs doing, does it, Ryan? You are the man of action. I can tell that."

"I'd go and send out a search party. Recce the woods. Up and down the coast of the lake. You got enough rifles, Moses. Look for tracks. Could be a whole bunch of muties within a mile of here. Find them and chill them."

Just for a moment it seemed that the voice had lost its overweening self-confidence. There was a hesitation. "I shall think on that. Now, you can all go."

NEITHER DEAN NOR MICHAEL reappeared until it was nearly time for lunch. And when they eventually arrived it was obvious that they'd had a major falling-out.

Ryan could hear them arguing almost before they reached the causeway, their raised, angry voices clearly audible as they strode through the floating ville.

"Why should I?" Dean shouted.

"You heard what Dorothy said."

"So what?"

"So what, yourself. Just because you got One-Eye for a father, doesn't mean you can stir it up between us."

Now they were nearly at the building that housed the outlanders' quarters. "Well, fuck you, Michael."

"And fuck you, too, kid."

"Don't call me that."

Ryan stood up from his bed and walked to the doorway, seeing that his son and the teenager were facing each other a few feet away. Both had hands on the butts of their blasters.

"First person even thinks about drawing down on a friend gets thrown in the lake," Ryan said quietly, making both boys jump guiltily. "What's the trouble?"

"Nothing." They spoke simultaneously, neither of them meeting his eye.

"Well, that's good. Way I heard it I might have thought there was some problem. Since there isn't, you can both come in, wash up and get ready to eat. All right?" Neither of them answered. "All right?" There was an edge to his voice that they recognized.

"Yeah," Michael said.

"Sure," Dean added.

Chapter Twenty-Five

"I'm not sure, Dorothy."

"We keep close to the edge of the lake and then, if the stickies appear, we can swim for it. You are able to swim, aren't you, Michael?"

"Yes. But not very far."

She smiled at him, tucking her hand into the crook of his arm. "Course you can. Anyway, stickies can't swim."

"Who says?"

"Moses."

Michael kicked at the loose pebbles that covered the long expanse of beach. "How's he know that?"

"Stupe!" she said affectionately. "Moses knows everything. Really everything."

"Why didn't he know that the stickies were going to attack the children and chill some of them? If he knew, then he could have prevented it."

Dorothy stopped dead and let go of his arm, turning away to stare silently out over the mirrored surface of Shamplin Lake. She shrugged her shoulders, easing the cord strap of the rifle she carried.

For fifty beats of the heart, neither of them spoke.

"It's true," he insisted.

"No."

"Why not?"

"Because it's all part of the big pattern. Moses says he knows everything, but he often can't tell us because it would spoil the big pattern."

"What?"

Dorothy turned, and he saw unshed tears glistening in the corners of her blue eyes. "Like when there was a sickness in the ville, when I was only about ten summers old. Blackwater fever, Moses called it. Nearly a third of us died, wasted away, shitting black blood. Moses knew it was coming."

Michael shook his head. "I heard all that when I was an oblate in the sanctuary. 'God moves in a mysterious way, His wonders to perform.' Heard it. 'It's God's will, children.' God's will that those mutie bastards butchered the little ones this morning. How can you believe that, Dorothy?"

"Come and sit down with me," she said, wiping her eyes, managing a smile. "Just in among the trees."

"Stickies?"

"Not this close to the ville. Anyway, we'll hear them coming, won't we?"

She placed one hand on his arm, the other hand on the side of his neck, leaning toward him so that Michael could catch the scent of her body. Dorothy lifted her face, eyes closing, her soft red lips parting to show the gleam of white teeth.

The late-afternoon sun was sinking out over the water, sending a great slash of crimson from the western horizon. Michael kissed the young woman, feeling his instant arousal as her tongue flicked out between his lips, pushing it way past his teeth. He put his arms around her and clasped her tightly. Dorothy's right hand dropped from his arm and eased itself between them, across his stomach, feeling lower.

"Mmm." She broke away and smiled at him. "We should definitely go and sit down for a bit."

SHE WORE NO UNDERCLOTHES, and the teenager found her warm and ready for him. The moment he had wriggled out of his clothes, she cupped him in her hand and guided him into her, gasping at the moment of penetration.

"Slowly, slowly," she whispered.

Michael could feel her flexing the inner muscles of her body around him, sucking him deeper. "God, Dorothy... I'm... I'm going to—"

"No, you aren't. Not yet. Not until I'm ready, as well." Her sharp teeth nipped him on the side of the throat, bringing a small cry of delighted pain.

She moved against him, her hips coming off the soft turf, her arms spread above her head. There was a flurry of sound in the undergrowth and Michael checked himself, straining to look over his shoulder. He felt himself beginning to shrink as his mind was flooded with a picture of a giant stickie grabbing him by the genitals with its rending, suckered hands.

"It's okay," Dorothy promised. "Only a squirrel. Don't stop now, or I'll have you put in one of the stand-ups."

"What's a—"

"Shh. Show you later. There's two close by here. Show you . . . later."

LATER MEANT THE SUN slipping halfway down over the edge of the lake, bringing elongated shadows and a chill to the air among the trees.

Michael lay flat on his back, Dorothy lying sprawled on top of him. He felt totally drained, hardly responding when she ran the tip of her tongue into the corner of his mouth. She reached for him, and he winced at the stickiness as she unpeeled his cock from his stomach.

"Don't think I can do it again," he said.

"Maybe not now. But there's tomorrow, Michael, and tomorrow and lots more tomorrows. Right now it feels like you couldn't even raise a smile."

"Did it four times in . . . well, it can't be anything over the hour," he replied, not quite managing the difficult task of mixing pride and modesty.

Dorothy smiled into his face. "You have lovely hair," she said. "Black and strong. And such dark eyes. Hardly anyone around Quindley has dark eyes."

"I noticed. Hey, shouldn't we be getting back to the ville? Be dark soon. They'll think the stickies got us."

She knelt on the grass and pulled on her pants, easing them up over her hips. "That was real nice, Michael."

"Yeah. Good for me, too. Real good."

"You had lots of women, Michael?"

He fastened his belt, checking that the Texas Longhorn Border Special was snug in its holster. "Lot of women? Why, sure I have. Me and Ryan and the others all get our pick, wherever we go. Hardly a ville in Deathlands that I haven't got a lover."

Dorothy kissed him on the cheek. "You're cute, you know. I guess that Krysty and the other woman must have had lovers as well, have they?"

"Sure."

"I'll ask them both about it when we get back to the ville. Be interested to hear how they talk about picking all these male lovers."

Michael swallowed hard. "No, Dorothy. That wouldn't... We have a kind of rule that we don't speak to others about our private life."

She smiled. "I believe you, Michael."

There was a cool breeze blowing, and they both felt a few spots of rain.

"Dean got pissed at me for wanting to be alone with you," Michael said.

"Could that be trouble?"

He shook his head. "Don't think so."

"Will he go and tell the one-eyed man what we've been talking about?"

"No. Don't think so."

"Will he agree?"

Michael sighed. "He's real bright and tough as a diamond. But he loves his father."

"I can never begin to understand that. To feel great affection for someone as old as that."

"Do you feel affection for me, Dorothy?"

"Course. Wouldn't have done the loving with you if I didn't. Never mind what..." She stopped.

Michael didn't notice the hesitation. "How long before you get to be twenty-five, Dorothy?"

"Long enough," she replied. "Hey, I promised to show the stand-ups. Two of them are just along here. Unless the stickies found them, of course."

THEY WERE WITHIN fifty yards of the top of the lake's shore, set among the shadowed fringe of sturdy beech trees, two stone columns, each about eight feet tall and less than five feet across.

"Come on," Dorothy said.

As they drew closer, Michael saw that there was a tiny barred window about five feet from the ground.

"They look like tiny prisons for... Shit a brick! There's someone in that... in both of them. My God, Dorothy, what have they done?"

"The old one is an outlander. He was caught ten days ago. Tried to rape little Eleanor. She told us so."

Michael stepped nearer, peering in with a ghoulish fascination. Now he could see there was a rusted iron door with a large lock set into the front of each stone pillar.

"How do they sit down?"

She laughed delightedly. "They don't. That's why they're called 'stand-ups,' you goose!"

"Who feeds them?"

"Nobody."

"Then they die."

"Eventually."

Dorothy joined him, putting her arm through his, smiling contentedly at the grizzled face that stared out through the bars. Though the light was fading, the teenager could see that the man's eyes were sunken and dulled. His mouth sagged open, but all that came out was a dry, gobbling sound, like an enraged turkey.

"What language does he speak?"

"None at all. We cut out his tongue before he was locked in."

Michael was beginning to feel a little sick. "Is he tied up in there?"

"No. No need. Some of the time when they die and get taken out, we find they've tried to bite open their own wrists or scratched at the blood tubes in the neck."

"Dorothy..." came a croaking plea.

"He can talk!" Michael exclaimed, looking at the second cramped prison.

"Course. It's Heinrich. He was the one you saw in the dining room last night."

"The one who's nearly reached—"

"Twenty-five. Yes." She stood close to the bars. "Stop all that noise, Heinrich. Should have done what Moses told you. Then you could have enjoyed the passing ceremony like most of us do."

"Shoot me, Dorothy, please. Throat hurts and I shit myself and my knees are on fire and my ankles are breaking."

"He's talking stupe, Michael." Dorothy lowered her voice. "Though sometimes Moses tells us to really break their ankles before locking them in."

"Least give me some water."

"Not after what you did. Running away like that. Shames the whole ville."

"Something to drink...in the name of blessed Moses, Dorothy...please..."

She giggled. "I could give him something to drink, Michael. I had three tumblers of water at noon meal and I'm about ready. Think he'd like it?"

"No!" The teenager turned away in disgust. "How can you be so nice to me, and at the same time be so cruel, vicious and sick, Dorothy? It doesn't make sense."

"They deserve it. Both of them. If it wasn't so dark, we could make the loving in front of them. Think how they'd feel, all naked and locked up and helpless... Watching. It'd be excellent, Michael. Part of their punishment."

"No." He suddenly made up his mind and drew the small revolver from its holster.

"What are you doing?"

The young man in the closest of the stand-ups started to beg. "Oh, please, outlander. Please do it."

Michael cocked the .38 and leveled it at the white face in the darkness behind the bars. Dorothy had her hands to her mouth.

"You can't... Blasphemy, Michael! Moses would have you locked up in there. Cut off your lovely strong cock and break your fingers and your ankles and elbows and your knees. It's death to defy him. Bloody death!"

The barrel of the handblaster was steady, Michael's finger tight on the trigger. Everything he knew that was right made him want to fire the gun and put the two wretches out of their prolonged agony, show them mercy.

Dorothy had fallen to her knees, hands lifted as though she were praying. "I beg you, Michael. Moses'll have me chilled, also. Honestly. Think of what we did this afternoon. Think I love you. Think of what we talked about. You and me. And little Dean. All of that'll be for nothing."

"It's not decent, Dorothy, to treat human beings like beasts, no matter what they did or didn't do."

"He raped a little girl." She pointed to the farther stone column. The sun was almost gone, and it was no longer possible to make out the faces of the prisoners. "And Heinrich knew the laws. Lived here all his life. Knew it. Took part when the older ones gave their selves up for the good of the ville. For all our futures. And he ran from that when it was his turn. Yellow-gutted coward."

Michael slowly lowered the blaster, easing the hammer down.

"All right," he said, his mouth so dry he could hardly hear himself speak.

But for most of the way back to the firelit safety of Quindley he heard the screams behind him.

Chapter Twenty-Six

"Abe?"

"Yeah, Trader?"

"Remember that time we got stuck in the middle of the freeway bridge?"

"No. Can't say I do."

The older man shook his head impatiently. "Your brain's fucked, Abe, you know that?"

"Where was this bridge, Trader?"

"Somewhere in the Rockies. We only had War Wag One, doing some dealing around the old Phantom Canyon Highway. Up toward... What the fuck was the place called? Kind of a ghost town. Had a big fire during the long winters."

"Leadville?" Abe offered hesitantly. One of the changes that he'd noticed in Trader was that he seemed even more short-tempered than he used to be.

"No. I know Leadville. Had a theater. Local gaudy used it to put on special shows." Trader laughed and wiped the back of his hand across his mouth. "Not that special. Limit to the combinations, ain't there, Abe?"

The little ex-gunner wasn't altogether sure what his former leader meant, but he nodded enthusiastically. Their camp fire was burning brightly and Trader had used his trusty, battered Armalite that afternoon to take out a small black bear. They'd roasted some of the tender parts, like the tongue and paws, and were both well filled.

"You get a slut with a man. A man with two sluts. Three sluts or four. Seen shows in the outskirts of some of the Eastern city-tombs. Men with men." Trader spit into the smoldering embers. "Turns your stomach, that kind of thing."

"Yeah," Abe agreed. "Never had no time for benders and ass bandits."

"Me, neither." He hesitated. "What the fuck was I talking about, Abe?"

"Shows in Leadville."

"Sure. Sluts with each other. Like that. See 'em goin' down on each other. Get me a rock-solid boner just thinking about it. Know what I mean?"

"Sure do." The previous day Trader had leaned on the elderly owner of an out-of-the-way general store to the east of old Seattle to give them a bottle of home brew. Now it was almost gone. Liquor didn't do anything to improve Trader's temper.

"Like sluts an' dogs. Once saw a full-grown stallion and a three hundred pound breed slut. Up in the shens. Marsh Folsom could've been there. Ripped her in two." He took a last slug from the bottle, then hurled it into the trees around them, where it shattered. "What was I talking about before you started on about sluts, Abe?"

"Some trouble we once had on a bridge."

"Sure. Victor. That was the name of the ville. Remember Ryan Cawdor saying he thought it was real 'picturesque.' That was the word. Old Ryan still use big long words like that, does he? Does he, Abe?"

"Sometimes." That seemed a safe, middle-of-the-road reply to the question.

"Was I telling you about the time on the bridge, Abe? My fucking memory is getting worse and worse. You noticed that, Abe? Huh?"

"No. I got a mind like a sieve, Trader. Words go in one ear and then they fall clear out the other."

The older man nodded, his grizzled hair almost white in the evening light.

"Yeah. You was always like that, Abe. We was on this old freeway bridge. Some local vigilantes put up a burning barricade against us. Behind us there was some stickies that got hold of some implode grens and they was trying to bring the whole mess down, with us in the middle."

The event didn't ring any bells for Abe. It sounded dramatic enough for him not to have forgotten it. It obviously happened before he started riding with the war wags.

"So what happened?"

"Old J.B. popped off a couple of frags from the gren launcher on the rear turret of War Wag One. Blew them stickies into a fine pink spray."

"You go back?"

"Shit, no!" He pounded one fist into the other. "Day Trader turns back is the day Trader catches the last train for the coast. We drove on. That switch-hit dyke Hunaker was at the controls.''

"I liked Hun," Abe remarked.

"Me, too. Some of the time. Not all of the time. I always said that a man who gets too close to a woman might as well cut off his balls with a bayonet."

Abe smiled, though he wasn't really sure that Trader was joking about it.

Far above them, plunging out of the cold infinity of space, they both saw a piece of military detritus finally tumbling from its hundred-year-old orbit. It was an archaic remnant of the old Totality Concept of the United States, or the Eastern Bloc's equivalent, Project Szvezda, a brilliant streak of pink-purple, flaring across the heavens.

Trader stared up, watching it fall, and shook his head. "This used to be a good country, once," he said quietly. "I think about it in those long waking hours of the early morning. But I don't have the learning. Not like Ryan. Wonder if he's got that message we sent after him. How long did we give him? Three months, was it?"

Success. Will stay around Seattle for three months. Come quick. Abe.

That had been the simple message given out to every traveler and packman they could find hanging around the ruins of the once great city.

Abe remembered the last one, just before they moved out of the ghostly charnel house, into the cleaner air of the Cascades. It had been a skinny, hard-eyed man who carried blasters. He had a small black-and-white pony, with a number of handmades and rebuilds in his saddlebags. He was off on his annual trip to the Northeast the next morning, traveling alone across the windswept solitude of the high plains country, through the Dakotas and south of the Great Lakes into New England.

They'd come across him sitting by a small fire, backed into the corner of a broken wall, in a place the locals called Gasworks Park, with rusting metal pipes and tanks, many of them still showing the faded graffiti of the predark era. One said, inexplicably, Grunge Lives. Neither Abe nor the Trader had ever come across anyone whose name was Grunge.

They had explained to the gun trader that they were trying to get in touch with a group of old friends, that they didn't know where in all Deathlands they might be, but they wanted a message delivered to them.

Lonnie had asked for jack. Trader had worked the action on the Armalite and the gun dealer had agreed that he'd be real happy to do it for nothing.

"Man with one eye. Name of Ryan Cawdor."

"Funny to give a name to an eye," Lonnie commented.

Abe had ignored him. "Woman with hair redder than the best chem sunset you ever saw. Skinny little guy with glasses and battered fedora hat. Called J. B. Dix. And don't say that you think it's funny to give a name to a hat. Black woman with plaited hair. Mildred Wyeth. Two younger ones. Little kid called Dean, aged around eleven or twelve. And a teen called Michael Brother. Oh, yeah. And there's a double-crazie old guy called Doc Tanner. You see them you'll know them."

They'd sat around for most of the night, talking about places they'd been, frontier gaudies and bars that they all knew, shootists and sluts. Some of them chilled. Some alive.

They'd parted company in the morning, with Trader giving Lonnie a final warning. "Deathlands is really a triple-small place, friend. I ever get to hear that you met up with Ryan Cawdor and didn't pass on our message, then I'd make certain sure you knew it was a bad move."

THE LAND WAS RICH IN GAME, and the living for the two men was easy. At one point it looked like they were running low on ammo, and they'd killed a fine eighteen-point deer and hauled it to the local store. The owner was a middle-aged woman with an ugly skin condition, and she hadn't been keen to take the venison in exchange for bullets.

Trader looked around the shop, noticing a glass display case filled with delicate porcelain dolls, all wearing old-fashioned costumes.

"Pretty, those."

"Sure. My pride and joy. Want a look?" She went over and opened the cabinet, taking out an Oriental doll in a silk kimono. The pock-marked woman had handled it as though it were a new-hatched butterfly, smiling down at it. Her face had become transfigured, making her seem almost beautiful.

Trader reached out for it, but she pulled back.

"I'll be real careful," he said, brushing with a long forefinger at the sleek, black hair of the doll. "Truly is a work of art, ma'am."

"Please don't squeeze her too hard or muss up her dress, mister."

"We was talking about some ammo for this," he said, gesturing with the doll toward his own Armalite. "And for the big blaster of my little friend with the mustache. Few .357s and he'll be happy as a hog in muck."

"I don't trade much, mister." Her face showed her worry. "Mostly straight jack deals. That venison sure looks good, but I got no need for it."

"Could be making a mistake, lady."

"How's that?"

For a moment Abe had expected Trader to pluck the head off the Japanese doll and crush it underfoot, or take the butt of the rifle and destroy the entire cabinet.

"Anyone could ride on by and all they want is a haunch of good deer meat. And you'd have to disappoint them and who knows what kind of damage they might do."

"If they started to...if anyone started to do some harm to me or anything in this store, then my three sons would take that plenty ill, mister."

"That so?" Trader stood very still, his head slightly on one side, listening. "I hear the wind through the trees. Stream running fast some place out back. And you got some hungry chickens there, as well. I hear them. Hear them all. Don't hear anything much like three sons, lady."

"They're likely sleeping."

"Mebbe I should go and make sure. Could be they got taken by some choking sickness while we out here passing the time of day." He took three long strides toward the curtained rear of the small building.

"No!"

Trader stopped, still holding the fragile doll with the greatest of care. "No? You sure about this, ma'am? Could be they're out working in the forest. Likely they'd relish a good meal of roast venison when they come back?"

The woman seemed to have aged twenty years in a single minute. "Mister..."

"What?"

"You are a real low-life son of a bitch, ain't you? Pickin' on a lone widow lady."

The Trader had appeared to be genuinely surprised and shocked. He laid the Japanese doll gingerly on the chipped counter that ran across the center of the store. "Now, I never thought to be spoken to like that, ma'am."

She gestured to the shelf to the right of a window that had two panes of glass replaced by waxed paper. "Bullets is there. Take what you want and then get out."

"Thank you kindly. We'll leave the meat out on your porch, if that's agreeable."

"Sure, sure." She was almost crying. "Do what you like, you mean old bastard, and leave me alone."

AWAY TO THE WEST, toward the Cific Ocean, Abe heard a rumble of thunder. The sky had been darkening even before the sun went down, promising a chem storm.

"Best get under cover, Trader," he said.

"Yeah. Wonder if any of those messages got through to Ryan yet?"

"We sent enough. One of them'll reach him, Trader. Bound to find them."

"How long did we say we'd wait up here for him and J.B. and the others? Was it a couple months, Abe?"

"Three months."

"Sure. I remember now." He stood, stretching until his muscles cracked. "Hey," he said, "did I ever tell you about the time we got caught in a trap in War Wag One, up on an old freeway bridge?"

"Yeah." Abe kept his face blank. "Yeah, Trader. You told me about that."

Chapter Twenty-Seven

All seven of them ate their breakfasts together. Michael had come in late and gone immediately to bed, answering with monosyllabic grunts Ryan's questions as to where he'd been and what he'd done.

Now, with a bright sun outside and a fresh wind from the north, he seemed in better spirits.

"Had the black dog at your side last night, Michael," Ryan said.

"Yeah. Sorry. Went walking with Dorothy and we sort of talked a lot and I wanted to think about some of the things that she had said to me."

Ryan cut a slice off a watermelon. "Want to tell us about it yet?"

"Not yet. Needs thinking."

"Lot of skeeters in the woods, were there?" Dean asked innocently.

"Some gnats. Why?"

"Just you got a real nasty bite on the side of your neck, Michael."

The teenager blushed, clapping his hand immediately to the sore-looking red mark. "Oh, yeah," he muttered. "Remember it was a kind of big insect."

"With blond hair and blue eyes," the eleven-year-old sniggered.

JEHU ARRIVED just as they were finishing their food, with half a dozen of the young men and women from the ville, including Dorothy, Isaac and Frank.

"Moses wants some fresh fish for his meals for the next two or three days," the ponytailed leader said. "He suggested that you outlanders might wish to spend a day out in the sun on Shamplin Lake."

"Sounds good." Ryan looked around at the others. "Anyone object?"

"I am notorious for not being one of the best sailors in this heathen land," Doc said ruefully. "But I would relish the fresh air and kick of the wheel and the song of the wind and...something about a jolly fellow rover." He shook his head. "But, let it pass, let it pass."

"What kind of fish we going after?" J.B. asked, as he picked up the Uzi.

"The best," Isaac replied. "Moses won't think about eating anything that isn't perfect and cooked perfect."

"How come he eats fish and tells you to only eat vegetables?" Krysty asked. "I know we talked about this before, but I still don't honestly understand."

Dorothy answered. "Moses isn't like the other men and women. When one of us moves on, Moses takes on himself all the sins and imperfections of the flesh." She recited the last part like a child carefully remembering a lesson. "So, he also has to test himself against all evils."

"What piscine treats— I'm sorry, evils, does your prophet and oracle intend to have offered to him today? Delicate baby carp? Trout, plucked from the bone and rolled between the thighs of young virgins? Eels, smoked to mouth-watering wonder over hickory wood? Or salmon, cosseted for his dining pleasure and served with a macédoine of tiny vegetables, picked at dawn and sliced by blind watchmakers until..." Doc looked around, sensing the bewildered silence that hung about him. "Ah, I see that once again I have made the cardinal error of allowing my mouth to operate before I have properly engaged my brain."

"Rainbow trout, mainly, from Shamplin," Jehu said, breaking the uneasy stillness. "We'll catch several and then select the best for Moses."

"Lake should be well stocked." Mildred looked out across the water. "Can't have been fished much for a hundred years or so. Must be some monsters out there."

"There are huge pike," Isaac replied, licking his lips nervously. "Bigger than a grown man."

"And eels," Dorothy offered. "Every year, as the greening comes to the land and the ice melts, we lose little ones to the works of the deep."

Dean glanced nervously at his father. "Mebbe I'll stay behind here," he said.

"We'll be fine." Ryan looked at Jehu. "When do we go?"

ON THE SEAS, lakes and rivers all around Deathlands, it wasn't that unusual to see gas-powered boats, using the crudely refined gasoline that was one of the chief items in the complex barter chain.

But it was no surprise to find that Quindley relied on old-fashioned human power.

The boat was a clinker-built dory, about fifteen feet long, with enough room for about a dozen people. It was made from narrow strips of varnished oak, and high-sided.

"We could step a mast in her, but the wind is gusting quite strong." Jehu looked away to the far north, where there was a thin bank of blue-gray clouds. "Best we watch the weather that way. Shamplin can be a treacherous mistress when there's northerly squalls about."

He took his place in the stern, holding the tiller. Dorothy went into the bow, where there was a pile of weighted nets. She called to Michael to join her. The rest of them found places on the thwarts, handing along the heavy oars and slipping them into the oarlocks.

Ryan sat with Krysty, J.B. with Mildred and Dean with Doc. Isaac sat at stroke, with Frank on his right. There were two other young ones from the ville, named Nanci and Calvin, who took the last empty places.

The boat was tied up to the side of the main causeway. Most of the little children, about to be escorted into the forest again, stood and stared at the outlanders, as they prepared to take to the water.

"Everyone ready?" Jehu called, turning to the teenage boys who waited to loose the ropes. "Let go front and back. Give us a good push out. Keep the oars out of the lake for a moment. Start when I say."

The boat drifted out onto the rippled water, the wind immediately catching it, making it drift awkwardly sideways, toward the south.

"Oars in. Pull when I say. And pull! Out and in! Out, in, out, in. Good. Not too hard, Doc. Save your energy for later in the morning."

IT WAS SURPRISING what good progress they made. Jehu steered them in a roughly northerly direction, into the prevailing wind, pointing out that it would make their return journey that much easier when they might all be feeling a little tired.

They soon established a good rhythm, following the pace set by Isaac, under Jehu's orders. The oars rose and fell in unison, sending tiny whirlpools spinning through the dark, mirrored water. The wake was straight and true, and the lake bubbled merrily beneath the stem of the dory.

"Someone should sing us a chanty..." Doc said, panting a little at the unusual exercise.

"What's that?" Dorothy asked from behind him.

"Old sea song, my dear child. Helps to keep us all together. Older even than me, some of them. Back to the days of beating around the Horn and reefing t'gallants in the teeth of a raging easterly gale."

"You know any, Doc?" Jehu called.

"It's advertised in Boston, New York and Buffalo,
A hundred jolly sailors, a'whaling for to go,

   Singing, blow ye winds of morning, blow them
to and fro,
   Haul away the running gear and blow, boys,
blow.''

Krysty gave a piercing whistle of appreciation between her teeth. "More, Doc, more."

"I fear that I shall become overdrawn on my already weakened state of breath. However, I know a
verse or two more. Everyone must come in on the
chorus. The bit about 'blow ye winds of morning.' All
right?''

Isaac glanced over his shoulder, grinning at the old
man. "Doin' good, Doc. Helps us along into the sharp
teeth of this chilly wind."

   "I'll sing you of the clipper ships,
   A-speeding in and out,
   They say we'll take a thousand whales
   Before we're three months out.
   Singing blow ye winds of morning, Everyone!
   Blow them to and fro..."

Despite his appearance, Doc was blessed with a
powerful, tuneful voice, and he led them through the
old sea song.

Doc also gave them "Unfortunate Miss Bailey" and
"The Leaving of Liverpool," while Mildred chipped
in with "Shenandoah."

If it hadn't been for the wind, which seemed to be getting stronger every mile into the expedition, it would have been a perfect morning.

A few miles north, the shore came sweeping out in a wide, thickly wooded promontory. Jehu encouraged the oarsmen, telling them the best fishing grounds lay only a short distance beyond the point.

"Then we can rest."

As they pulled steadily past the spit of land, all of them looked at it.

There was no sign of life, just the endless rolling slopes of the hills, almost covered in conifers. No trace at all of the advanced civilization that had once stamped its mark upon the landscape.

"Wouldn't have thought this was once a big tourist area," Mildred commented.

"The planet recovers itself, from even the deepest wounds." Doc held his oar clear of the water and leaned on it for a few moments. "Like the old lost road that ran through the woods, where the rain and the wind had destroyed it so completely that you would never have known that there had been a road. There is a poem on that very subject, but I fear that the bones of it have fled from my memory."

Krysty also took a breather, staring at the land that scrolled slowly past them.

"There's..." she began. "No. I thought I saw someone watching us from the edge of the trees."

"Stickies?" Jehu called.

"Gone now. Might have been."

Everyone stopped rowing and the dory quickly lost way, coming to a gentle halt, then starting to move backward as the wind grasped at it.

"Can't see anything," Michael said from his place in the bow.

"Probably my aged eyes failing," Krysty replied.

"Start rowing again," Isaac shouted. "Wind's getting bad. If it rises any more we should think about turning around for home, Jehu. You reckon?"

"Only another quarter mile," the long-haired young man replied. "Can't go back without some good fish for Moses."

Dean had been trailing his hand in the cool water while they drifted. But he suddenly jerked it out, giving a gasp of shock. "Something touched it," he said.

"Fish?" his father asked.

"Felt big. Sort of rolled under the boat."

"The Emperor Pike," Calvin said.

"Maybe." Jehu leaned over the stern, shading his hand to try to see beneath the broken surface. "Thought I saw something as well, but—"

Without any further warning, something lunged beneath the bottom of the dory and turned it over, tipping everyone into the lake.

Chapter Twenty-Eight

Ryan was taken totally by surprise. The loom of the oar came sharply up beneath his chin and rattled his teeth. The very next moment he was beneath the surface of Shamplin Lake, his mouth open, inhaling the chill water.

He felt something brush against his legs, and he instinctively kicked away. His hand pushed at the creature that had turned them over with such effortless ease, and he felt the roughness of scales. The depths around him sucked and swirled as the huge fish whipped its tail back and forth, propelling itself out of sight. There had been a momentary blurred glimpse of a silvery body, narrow and lean, and a head that tapered like an alligator's. Ryan guessed it was the big pike that they'd talked about. But this one was truly enormous, well over twenty feet long.

With a whoop he broke surface, immediately treading water and looking around to try to get his bearings.

The gleaming underside of the boat was less than ten yards away from him, but the strong wind was already pushing it in a southerly direction. Ryan counted heads.

He checked Dean, his hair pasted to his skull, already kicking out toward the overturned dory. Doc, his sword stick between his strong teeth, was doing the breaststroke beside the boy. J.B. and Mildred were a little farther away, nearer the land. The Armorer had his fedora clutched in his left hand, the Uzi over his shoulder.

Something moved past Ryan, only a few feet below him, something that reminded him of the hideous power of the Great Whites that they'd encountered before.

Calvin appeared close by the boat and turned to grin at Ryan. "Must've—" he began.

Then the giant mutie fish came up directly below him. The tail fin broke the surface almost between Ryan's legs, and he rolled out of the way. The one-eyed man glimpsed the elongated, feral head, with the smiling jaws and the cold, passionless eyes. Rows of jagged teeth clamped shut around Calvin's midriff. Despite the yelling and the splashing, Ryan distinctly heard the splintering of the young man's ribs. Calvin's head jerked back and forth as the pike shook him like a terrier with a rat. Blood gushed from his mouth, and one of his eyes literally burst from its socket with the awesome pressure.

As suddenly as it had appeared, the pike vanished. Calvin's right arm, fist clenched, was the last thing to disappear beneath the bloodied surface of the lake.

The killing had taken less than fifteen seconds.

Ryan trod water, easing the Steyr across his back. He checked that Krysty was also there. She'd reached the boat and was managing to hang on to the planking. Her long red sentient hair gripped her skull so tightly that it looked like a bathing cap of crimson silk.

Jehu was there as well, his ponytail undone, his eyes wide and blank with shock. The other young woman, Nanci, was crying, barely keeping afloat a few yards behind Ryan, farther away from the dubious safety of the wrecked dory.

"Michael!" Dean shouted.

The teenager wasn't in sight, though it was possible he'd come up behind the hull of the boat. Dorothy was also missing. They'd been sitting together in the bow, along with the nets. It crossed Ryan's mind to wonder if they might have gotten tangled in them.

Krysty gave Dean a leg up, so that he was able to perch on the pitching dory, looking all around. "Not there, Dad!" he yelled, his voice cracking.

Ryan lifted himself as high as he could, but from his position the wavelets were too high and choppy for him to be able to see more than a few yards. For a moment he thought that he saw something, a looping, glistening coil, covered in iridescent scales thicker than a man's waist, breaking the surface and then vanishing again. He remembered that Dorothy had mentioned there were mutie eels in the lake.

Fighting not to betray too much of his fear, Ryan began to kick his way toward the boat.

"Everyone try and climb on!" he shouted.

"What about Michael?" Dean was rocking from side to side, his arms outstretched like a tightrope walker.

"Can't do a thing."

"We can turn the boat, if we all get together." Jehu had made a valiant effort to pull himself together. "Safer in than out with Emperor Pike looking for noon meal."

"There's an eel, Ryan, closing in behind you!" Krysty was pointing, her green eyes staring in horror.

With a considerable effort of will, Ryan managed to resist the temptation to look behind him. That single, sinuous coil had been enough.

"Go, Nanci!" Jehu had drawn a small skinning knife from his belt, as though he were about to plunge into the water to go to the young woman's rescue.

"No!" Ryan bellowed, now close to the upturned craft.

J.B. had just managed to clamber up the slippery wood and was sitting astride the keel, checking the Uzi, readying it to open fire.

"Duck, Ryan," he called, hardly even raising his voice, calm and in control.

Guessing that he was in the line of fire at the unseen eel, Ryan kicked up his heels and duck-dived, swimming down several feet. He heard the faint impact of bullets above and behind him, conscious, then, of a powerful thrashing turbulence.

The moment his head broke the surface again he looked around, seeing the white, terrified face of Nanci close to him. A few yards away there was a rolling mass of dark gray-green scales and foaming water.

Krysty beckoned them both to get out of the lake to a sort of safety.

There was still no sign of either Michael or the young blond woman.

Ryan had just reached the boat, dragging Nanci behind him with one hand, when he heard a great whoop of exultation from his son above him.

"There he is!"

The turbulence behind him had ceased, and Ryan was able to blink water from his good eye and glimpse the dark head of Michael Brother a good thirty yards to the north. With his sleek black hair, the teenager looked for a moment like a questing seal.

The boy shouted something, but Ryan didn't catch it first time around, his hearing blurred by the wind and the water slapping against the boat. But Michael called out again and, this time, Ryan heard him.

"Trapped in the nets. Help me!"

Without a moment's hesitation, Ryan handed the rifle up to his son and kicked off again. His clothes and heavy combat boots were weighing him down, already making him tired, but there wasn't a moment to be wasted. Dorothy had already been caught and held under water for the best part of a minute, perhaps longer. The passing time was always grossly distorted at moments of extreme action and tension.

Jehu and Krysty were hauling the exhausted Nanci to the temporary haven of the upturned dory as Ryan swam away again from them.

He was aware of the corpse of the enormous eel, floating on the surface off to his left, dark blood trickling from a row of bulletholes from the Armorer's Uzi.

"She's only just below the surface, Ryan!"

Michael was close to panic, frantically beckoning for Ryan to hurry and help him.

"Under you?" The rising wind was ruffling the surface of the lake, making it impossible to see anything below the white-capped waves.

"Yeah."

"Stay on top."

Ryan drew the panga, making sure he had a secure grip on the slippery hilt. He took in a deep breath and released it, took in another, deeper, and dived.

The broken light from above had a dappled effect, but he immediately saw the helpless woman. Dorothy was now unconscious, hanging limply, a tiny stream of bubbles inching from the corner of her open mouth. Her blue eyes were wide open, staring past him with an imbecilic expression of vague surprise. Her arms were spread but her legs were tangled in a pile of netting, keeping her trapped.

Holding the panga in his right hand, Ryan grabbed at the young woman's left leg, just above the knee. He felt his way down, hanging on to her for purchase, and used the honed blade to slice through the outer layers of the nets that were immovably knotted around her feet and ankles.

There was a serious risk that he might cut her badly as he hacked away, working with a desperate, choking speed. There was someone at his side, and he glanced sideways, seeing Michael with one of the twin daggers that he carried. Ryan pointed down, indicating to the teenager to work lower, so that they wouldn't get in each other's way.

A great fold of the clinging nets fell away, but there was still more to cut through. Part of Ryan's brain was a ticking clock. It had to be over a minute and a half. He remembered someone on War Wag Two who'd once gone through the thick ice on an ill-planned fishing expedition. It had taken six minutes to break through and free him. Amazingly he'd still been alive. They'd thawed him out and the medics had done everything they could. He breathed and his heart beat, but after twelve hours he hadn't recovered consciousness and obviously never would. Before they moved on, the next morning, Trader had personally put a bullet through the back of his neck in an act of mercy.

Someone else had joined them, his face and body vanishing behind a wealth of silver bubbles. Ryan carried on with the panga, cutting and cutting, trying to pull away the fronds of the net.

Now he could see that it was Jehu, the young man diving beneath them all, tearing away at the main tangle of nets, towing them a little distance off to remove the risk of all of them becoming entrapped.

Ryan could feel the air becoming exhausted, pressure behind his eye, pain in his lungs and chest. But he knew that time had very nearly run out for the young blonde.

He was cutting blind, slicing, hacking and tearing, aware that he'd almost lost it.

Ryan almost left it too late.

Almost.

There was a sudden steel tightness across his forehead and temples, and a lethal churning blackness. Just for a moment Ryan hallucinated that he was in the middle of a mat-trans jump. Then the last shards of reason cut in and he flailed his way to the surface of the lake.

For several seconds Ryan could do nothing except float helplessly in the good air, kicking feebly, battling to recover. He could hear someone shouting to him, but the wind and his own exhaustion combined to deafen him to the words.

There was a great cry beside him and he saw Jehu, long hair streaked across his pale face, gripping his own knife, sucking in harsh breaths.

"She's dead," he shouted.

Ryan readied himself to dive once more, knowing that it was too late. But Trader had drilled into everyone who rode the war wags that the only possible excuse for giving up was to be actually, certifiably stonedead.

But before he could draw in enough breath for a final effort, Ryan saw Michael's head break the surface, between himself and the overturned boat. And he was holding on to the limp body of Dorothy.

WITH THE SKILLFUL HELP of Jehu, they all managed to heave the heavy boat the right way up, frantically bailing out the swilling water.

The deeply unconscious Dorothy was laid between the thwarts in the wet bottom of the dory and Mildred stooped over her, ready to try to bring her back from the brink of the dark chasm.

Chapter Twenty-Nine

"Moses will be seriously pissed." Jehu sat back in the stern, steering a course southeastward toward Quindley. Fortunately the wind was now behind them, speeding the boat across the slate-gray water.

"Because of Dorothy?" Dean asked, as he sat facing the man.

"No!" Jehu shook his head violently, the damp blond hair clinging to the side of his face. "No, because he won't be getting the fish he ordered."

"Surely her health matters more than whether he gets his trout for his supper." Krysty was on the next thwart, beside Ryan, both of them rowing steadily.

"Why?"

"Because she's a part of his community. Your community as well, Jehu."

Doc and Nanci were one seat nearer the bow. The old man looked tired from the rigors of the ill-fated fishing expedition. "No man is an island, Jehu, entire of itself. We're all linked together, is what that means."

Mildred was kneeling behind him, cradling Dorothy's head in her lap. "Ask not for whom the bells tolls, eh, Doc? Because it might start tolling for you."

"Least it won't toll for Dorothy. You did well there, Mildred." Ryan glanced over his right shoulder, nearly catching a crab with his oar and sending them all into confusion. "She still recovering?"

"So far so good."

As soon as they'd ladled some of the water out of the dory, Mildred had begun mouth-to-mouth resuscitation on the motionless girl, pausing now and again to take a short break and check the slow, fluttering pulse. "Last time I did this sort of thing we had to have on a mask and rubber gloves," she said, explaining that it had been because of the AIDS epidemic of the last years of the twentieth century.

It was a long, slow process, and they were more than halfway back to Quindley before the first encouraging sign of returning life. They had been rowing fairly close to the shore, and Dean spotted a narrow column of gray smoke, whipped into shreds by the strong wind, rising from among the trees.

"Stickies, Dad?"

"Don't know."

At that moment Dorothy had gone into convulsions, kicking and waving her arms, while Mildred laid on top of her, helped by Michael to hold her still. Then she'd vomited copiously, bringing up half the lake, along with strings of bile and the partly digested remains of her breakfast.

Her eyes had opened and she'd stared, bewildered, up at the sky. And began to weep.

"You're fine, girl," Mildred said.

"I'm alive?"

"Sure. Very much so. Good for another eighty years or so... Ah, sorry. Forgot your rules."

"I thought I'd been taken."

"Pike threw the boat over. You went in deep and got trapped in the nets."

"How do I live?"

"Michael saved you, Dorothy. Along with Ryan and Jehu. Cut you free."

"Where's Calvin."

"Pike got him. Sorry."

Michael had knelt in the water at the young woman's side, holding her hand in his. "And Mildred gave you the kiss of life and brought you back from the other side."

"Other side?"

Doc had interrupted at that point. "That dark bourne from which no traveler returns. Apart from the fact that Dr. Wyeth's professional expertise ensured that you were the exception to the ancient rule. You came back, my dear."

"We haven't got the fish that Moses wanted," she replied, studiously avoiding thanking Mildred, or any of them, for saving her life. Then she'd turned her face away and refused to speak until they were home again.

As THEY NEARED THE CAUSEWAY that supported Quindley, they heard the sounds of a trumpet, announcing their return. Many of the young men and women came running in from the nearby fields, exclaiming in shock and horror at the news of Calvin's brutish death. Jehu leaped from the boat the moment they landed, calling out that he had to go and report to Moses immediately. He waved a hand to ackowledge Ryan's warning that he should mention the fact that they might have seen further evidence of stickies.

Dorothy was helped out on rubbery legs, supported on one side by Michael, who went with the young woman into the heart of the ville, leaving the other six to wander back to their own quarters.

An hour later Jehu appeared in their doorway. His face was pale, and he could do nothing to stop his hands from tangling with each other in front of him, a sure sign of his profoundly nervous state. "Moses wants to see you, Ryan. Straight away."

"And the rest of us?" Krysty asked.

"No. Just Ryan."

"You look like your granny just caught your balls in her mangle, son," Doc said, grinning. "Moses come snarling out of his basket in the bulrushes and give you some seriously hard time, did he?"

"He is not pleased with what's happening in the ville since you outlanders came."

"His idea to let us stay," Ryan replied.

"I know, I know." Jehu's voice broke, and he lifted his hands to his face, looking like he was about to burst into tears. "But now... Well, he wants to talk with you, Ryan."

"You tell him about the smoke from the fire?"

"Yes. Moses said he believed that it was only a camp of some beaver hunters, that we shouldn't worry at all about the stickies, that he knew that they'd all gone away and that Calvin had paid the first part of the blood price and all would be well after the rest was settled.''

"What's that mean?" Mildred asked.

"What?"

"Settled. You said that the rest of the 'blood price' would soon be settled.''

"Tonight. There will be a ceremony. Two will be sent on. The outlander and Heinrich.''

"Chilled?" Krysty asked.

"You call it that.'' Jehu shrugged. "Go to Moses now, Ryan. Now.''

THE LUXURIOUS ROOM felt cold, and Ryan was aware that his clothes still held more than a touch of damp. He walked toward the mirror and stared into it, trying to detect some sign of life or movement.

There was a deep, melodious chuckle. "Such curiosity, Ryan Cawdor.''

"Always been my way.''

A silence. Ryan rubbed at the side of his nose, hesitated a moment, then turned and started to stroll out of the stone-walled building.

"And so impatient.'' Again the wise chuckle, making Ryan feel seven years old.

"I don't wait for any man," he replied.

"I believe you, my son. Did you never wait for a word from your father?''

"When I was little.''

"Respect, Ryan Cawdor. That is what I have taught my young people here in Quindley. Respect and order. You would be surprised how eager they are to be told what to do and when to do it. No confusion over having to make choices."

"Right or wrong?" Ryan questioned.

He caught the faint sound of someone clapping, slowly and quietly. "I like you. It's sad that you have brought such gloom and death riding at your saddle horn."

"You know that's shit."

"Do I?"

"Course. Isaac's brother was dead before we got anywhere near your ville. Children died because of bad planning and bad luck. Same with Calvin. Just to feed your face, Moses."

"You speak your mind."

"Damn right!"

"This is because you have more summers."

"Mebbe."

"This is why we do not allow so many summers here in the paradise of Quindley. They lead only to questioning and trouble."

"Paradise! I seen better paradises on flea-bitten beds in stinking frontier gaudies, Moses. This might be paradise for you. You got everything you need. The kids work from when they get born and then, when they might start to get difficult, you simply get them chilled."

Again there was the quiet, deep-chested laugh. "You are the living proof of the great wisdom of the way that this ville operates, Ryan."

"Wise for you."

"Of course. I give them the sense of belonging and of having their lives organized. Without me this ville would be a hole in the ground."

Ryan nodded, becoming bored with the conversation. "That all you wanted to tell me, Moses? How the sun shines out of your ass and when you shit it comes out flat like a ribbon and smells of violets? That all?"

"Someone once said that you shouldn't pay any attention to the man behind the curtain, Ryan Cawdor. You are the first person I've met who has acted on that."

"I'm going."

"Very well. But if you chose to come in with me, we would together wield such power that all of Deathlands could fall to us. One day."

"Old friend of mine used to say that you shouldn't ever plan for tomorrow. Might not come."

"It will not come for Heinrich and for the outlander."

"Heard about them. When?"

"Tonight," Moses replied.

"Might turn in early," Ryan said, yawning. "Been quite a big day already."

"It gets bigger."

"Sure."

"The passing of someone who has resisted being twenty-five is a spectacle worth seeing, Ryan."

"I've seen more chillings than you've eaten fish dinners, Moses."

There came a sigh that seemed to Ryan to be tainted with a strange longing. "I believe you."

"How old are you, Moses?"

Moses laughed, which made Ryan feel, for a moment, as though he'd asked the unseen presence something incredibly stupid. "You must cease wondering about my age. You know the truth that you will never know."

"See you later," Ryan said.

WHEN HE REJOINED the others he found that Michael was back, sitting on the corner bed, arms folded, staring sullenly at Krysty.

"What's wrong?" Ryan asked. "Dorothy hasn't bought the farm, has she?"

Michael shook his head in silence.

"He saw the people they're going to chill tonight," Krysty said quietly.

"When?"

"Day he went into the woods with his special blonde," Dean stated venomously.

"Just shut your flap, kid," Michael spit.

Ryan stepped between them. "You know you should've told us about this."

"No, I don't know that, Ryan. As it happens, I don't fucking know that at all."

"Just what's got into you?" Ryan looked at the others. "Anyone know about this?"

"*Cherchez la femme,*" Doc muttered. "Ancient predark saying. Means that when there's any trouble...all that you have to do is seek out the woman." He glanced at Mildred. "My apologies, my dear. Not very politically correct, I know. But, *c'est la vie.* That's another—"

"I know what it means, Doc," she replied. "And this time I guess you're probably right about Michael's problem."

"Not a problem. Look, all right. I went for a walk, and we saw these two prisoners. That's all. You always told us, Ryan, that we shouldn't mess with the affairs of a ville. Well, I just did like you told me."

The teenager was on the ragged edge. With a shock like cold water in the eyes, Ryan realized something. Michael had been taken into Nil-Vanity as an oblate, an infant who was reared all his life within the strict confines of the withdrawn meditative order. Dorothy was one of the few women that Michael had ever fallen in love with.

"All right," he said. "Let it drop now. But remember where your loyalty lies, Michael."

"Oh, I know that all right, Ryan." He stood up defiantly. "And it doesn't lie with you." He stalked straight out of the door into the heart of the ville.

Chapter Thirty

There was a long discussion between the six friends over the noon meal. Ryan and J.B. were both leaning toward the idea of getting out of the ville before evening came, and the pair of promised sacrifices. Jehu had arrived with the silent serving girls, who carried in trays of food and had explained to them about the doomed outlander rapist that Michael had seen, and about the hapless Heinrich who was to die as an example for the rest of the ville.

The food was less good, as though everyone in Quindley had been shaken by the death of the young man. But Ryan's suspicion was that the depression was linked to the vastly more serious fact that Moses hadn't been allowed to enjoy his anticipated luncheon of fresh-caught fish.

There was cold potatoes, lumpy and dull, scorched on the outside and partly raw on the inside; a mess of peas, gray and heavily salted. At least the bread was good, and the butter tasty. Dean looked at the horn beaker of water that Krysty had poured out for him.

"That come from the lake?"

"Course. They don't seem to have any wells here. No need, I guess."

"Don't somehow fancy it." The boy peered unhappily into the tumbler. "Got the blood of what's-his-name. You know, that Calvin the pike crushed. Don't want to drink it."

Doc brushed some crumbs off his vest. "I confess a certain sympathy with the lad, though I share the opinion of the great W. C. Fields on drinking water. He wouldn't touch it because he said that fish fucked in it."

"Doc!" Mildred exclaimed. "I'm shocked at your language. And you a Harvard man."

"Only a lighthearted jest, madam." The old man appeared to be flustered. "It was not my intention to offend you. Or to offend any lady here present. My apologies."

She grinned. "Only kidding, Doc. Actually this water tastes good enough to me. I wouldn't have dreamed of drinking it back when I was alive before. Most of the lakes, rivers and seas were filthy with all kinds of industrial and chemical contaminants. Fall in some lakes in the United States of America and swallow a couple of mouthfuls and you probably wouldn't make it to the next dawn. They were that bad."

Krysty picked up a bright-skinned pippin and crunched it between her strong white teeth. "We should get back to the subject of leaving or staying." She turned to Ryan. "Look, lover, if you and J.B. think we ought to make tracks, then I guess the rest of us'll go along with that."

The two men looked at each other in silence. Ryan spoke first. "My guess is that we'll probably be leaving young Michael behind here."

"Serve him right." Dean was peeling a ripe pear with his turquoise-hilted knife.

"You and Michael have really fallen out, haven't you?" Ryan looked at his son.

"Yeah. Gone all big-eyed and wet-mouthed over that straw-head slut."

Krysty pushed back her chair, the legs scraping noisily on the wooden floor. "Better watch that mouth, Dean," she said, her voice hard and tight with anger. "Dorothy might be many things, but she's not a slut. You get in the easy habit of bad-talking all women, and you lose all respect for women. You'll be calling Mildred and me sluts next."

"Sorry. But she's trapped Michael into changing. Mebbe she's a witch, Dad."

"No. Michael may have fallen for Dorothy. In love with her. Wouldn't surprise me. Happens, Dean. One day it'll even happen to you."

"No way at all!"

They all laughed. Doc leaned back and pushed away his wooden plate. "When the arrow strikes at the heart, Dean, it will pierce through the strongest defence. And even the bravest and boldest will fall a helpless captive."

"Not me, Doc!" Dean pulled a face of such appalled repugnance that they all laughed again.

Ryan got up and looked casually out of the doorway, making sure that none of the young people of Quindley were close enough to overhear them.

"You think Michael might remain here, Dean? Think about it. That's a serious question."

"What if he does, Ryan?" J.B. asked.

"Then he stays. Time came for Jak Lauren to pull out of the endless moving-on. One day it'll come to all of us." He didn't dare to meet Krysty's eyes. "If Michael decides that his own personal future lies here with Dorothy, then that'll be what happens. It's his decision."

Dean nodded. "I think they sort of want to be together, Dad."

"How about us, Ryan?" Mildred had also stood up. "Must go and take a leak in a minute. Are we going to stay another night or move on while there's light?"

Ryan looked out of the thatched hut, at the range of close-packed wooden buildings. The narrow lanes of the ville were almost deserted, with most of the people out in the fields or the forest around.

"Stickies are out there, somewhere. I'm sure of it. We can make the redoubt in about a half day or so. Wouldn't want to find us stuck in the evening gloom in these woods."

"So we wait until dawn, lover?"

"Yeah, Krysty. Move tomorrow at first light. But keep that to ourselves."

"We telling Michael?" Dean asked.

Ryan considered for a few seconds, finally deciding. "No."

THE TEENAGER still hadn't appeared by the end of the afternoon.

Jehu had come by after the dirty plates had been collected to tell them that the ceremony—that was the word he used—would be beginning an hour after the sun had set over the western edge of the lake.

Then he had gone, saying something they didn't understand about how he had to check that all of the osiers had been properly collected and treated.

"Did he say the 'hoosiers' had been collected and treated?" wondered Doc.

"No, the osiers," Mildred snapped. "Osiers, Doc. Branches of willow trees."

"I am familiar with the term, madam. Just that the young man with the absurd ponytail doesn't open his mouth properly when he speaks. Anyway, why would they be wanting the branches of willow trees?"

Nobody could come up with an answer to that question. So the afternoon wore wearily on.

RYAN AND KRYSTY WALKED out across the causeway onto dry land. Strolling together along the beach, they ignored the curious glances of the young men and women working in the allotments and orchards of the ville.

The sun had dipped partway below the horizon, leaving a golden carpet that stretched toward them across the calm water. The storm had eased away, bringing only a brief shower at around three o'clock, barely enough to lay the dust.

"Where are they going to do this chilling?" Krysty asked, her dazzling hair even more bright in the evening fire.

"Don't know. Have to be close, or Moses won't be able to get to see it. And I can't imagine anything happening in this sick place without his knowing all about it."

"Look."

A hundred yards ahead of them, emerging from the sable shadows at the edge of the pine forest, were Michael and Dorothy, hand in hand.

"Young lovers," Ryan said flatly.

When they saw Ryan and Krysty, the couple hesitated, exchanging a few hurried words. Then they approached.

"Fine sunset," Krysty said.

"Yeah. It is." Michael looked unhappy. "Is...is your neck feeling okay, Ryan?"

"My neck?"

"Yeah. You still got that bit of bandage on it from the mutie creature in the ghost town."

Ryan's wound had healed so well that he'd almost completely forgotten it. Once in the night he had woken with a brief stab of flaring pain, but it had quickly passed. He lifted a hand to touch the place.

"Feels fine, thanks. How are you?"

All four of them were suddenly aware that the question hadn't been a simple, polite one, that Ryan was asking the teenager how he *really* was.

"Better. Think that the last jump, and the ghost town, sort of moved my brain around loose inside my head. You know how it can be, Ryan."

"Sure do."

"But you are feeling better now, aren't you, Michael?" Dorothy asked, not letting go of his hand.

"Sure. Lots."

"That's good." Krysty looked beyond them, along the dark strand, vanishing toward the north. "Can any of you smell smoke at all?"

Ryan paused, concentrating. "Could be. Probably the cooking fires from the ville."

Krysty shook her head. "No. Not wood burning. I'm sure there's gas, as well."

"We didn't see anything in the trees, did we, Dorothy?" Michael said.

"Depends on what you mean by *anything*." She wasn't able to control a suggestive giggle.

Michael blushed and pulled his hand away from hers. "You know what I mean," he snarled, angry at his own obvious embarrassment. "No fires or anything."

"All right, sweetness. Sorry if I upset you. You know I'd do anything not to do that."

She laid a hand on his arm, then stretched up and kissed him softly on the mouth, her blond hair blowing across both their faces.

"You going to the ceremony, Michael?"

"Sure. Everyone'll be there, Ryan. You aren't leaving the ville before that, are you?"

"No. Why do you ask?"

He shuffled his feet in the loose pebbles. "Something I want to talk about before you go."

"Before 'you' go? That sounds different from saying before 'we' go, Michael."

"Yeah."

Krysty watched the teenager carefully. He was looking toward the setting sun, and she saw that his dark eyes were completely veiled, showing no more emotion than a piece of fresh-quarried slate. His mouth was a thin, etched line, and he wouldn't actually look either Ryan or herself full in the face.

At that moment she was certain that Ryan had been right in his guess. Michael and Dorothy wouldn't be separated. Unless something very unexpected happened in the next twenty-four hours, the six of them would be making the next jump without the curly headed teenager.

THEY WALKED a little farther along the coast of the enormous lake, but the sun was sinking fast and they only had their handblasters with them.

"Best get back," Krysty said.

"Sure."

"Lover? What do you think that Michael was talking about? What does he want to say to us?"

"Goodbye."

Chapter Thirty-One

The tiny sliver of a new moon showed in the night sky, hardly enough to cast the weakest shadow.

Far over the lake, to the west, hung a dense bank of cloud, and a few thin tatters of gray-white floated across the silent forest that surrounded the ville.

Within the pools of blackness beneath the larches, firs, pines and aspens, the creatures of the night moved and hunted. Some crawled on their scaled bellies and some flew silently among the stark branches. Many did their work on four legs.

Some did it on two legs.

SUPPER HAD BEEN a hasty and cursory affair: a stew of apples that was so thick you could have cut it into slices, providing you had a sharp enough knife; some sourdough rolls with cherry jelly, and a large bowl of cold boiled potatoes and carrots.

None of them felt all that hungry, though Ryan insisted that everyone eat as much as they could handle. "Might be the last food for some time," he said. "Depending on when we make the jump and where it takes us."

Outside, they had been able to hear the noise of the preparations for the two sacrifices, though Jehu had politely insisted that they shouldn't leave their quarters until they were sent for.

After the brief meeting on the shore of the lake, there had been no further sign of Michael. The tall blond leader of Quindley had told Ryan that the teenager was with Dorothy. "Which means that he is also with us."

"Not an outlander, Jehu?"

"No, Ryan. Michael is neither one thing nor the other. But within a day or so he may have completed his choosing and will speak with Moses."

That was all they knew.

"NOW," JEHU ANNOUNCED.

The ville was in semidarkness, with only an occasional torch burning smokily in wall brackets. They followed the blond figure through the narrow, twisting lanes, until they reached the larger open area directly in front of the conical thatch of Moses's own dwelling.

It seemed that everyone was there, standing in solid blocks: the little children, shepherded by a few of the teenage girls, then the older children, all silent, as though they were overawed by the occasion, and around three sides stood the rest of the young people.

Though there were ripples of movement, Ryan wasn't aware of anyone actually speaking. He looked around, his eye turning to the roof of the temple of Moses. At first, because of the shifting orange glow from the torches, he wasn't entirely sure of what he seemed to be seeing. Then he concentrated, his sight accommodating to the gloom.

There was an opening in the dense thatch of reeds, square, with light glinting off glass. Behind it there was the pale blur of a figure, though it was quite impossible to make out any details. But Ryan realized that Moses was present, watching the proceedings through his own window.

"Over here," Jehu said, pointing to a space in the front row, to the left of the square. "Then you can both see and be seen. Watch and be watched."

"Where's Michael?" Dean asked.

"There." Jehu pointed with one hand toward the mass of people on the opposite side.

Ryan looked as well, thinking he saw the tentative wave of a hand among the crowd, but it wasn't easy to be certain. He half waved back, then thought better of it.

"Wait," Jehu said. "You see that some of us carry our blasters with us. You must not interfere with what must happen. You understand?"

Ryan nodded. "Sure. It's your party."

"And you can cry if you want to," Mildred whispered mysteriously.

"No talking, please." Jehu lifted his right hand over his head in a signal to someone standing on the opposite side of the square.

Immediately there was the sonorous, slow beating of a slack-skinned drum, so deep and resonant that it seemed to echo through the marrow of the bones.

The shuffling stopped, and there was a total silence from the young people, a quiet so intense that everyone heard the far-off, mournful cry of a hunting wolf.

Krysty slipped her hand through the crook of Ryan's arm, and he could feel that she was trembling with the growing tension of the ritual.

Jehu was still by them, his face turned upward, staring with wide eyes at the inconspicuous window in the roof of Moses's stone-built home.

Ryan looked up and saw a tiny flicker of light, no brighter than a firefly. And then they all heard the familiar voice, echoing around the ville.

"Welcome to the time of pleasure, a time for which there is a season. A time to be birthed and a time to take the long road that winds not."

"Sounds to me uncommonly like a nickel-and-dime TV evangelist preacher who has unfortunately swallowed a compendium of quotes."

Jehu turned and hissed angrily at Doc. "You live on borrowed time, oldie! Hold your words!"

Moses was still talking. "Each of you dwells well here in our home of Quindley. Outside is plague and the dark angel of death, escorted by the pale riders. To live outside the ville is only a worse, longer way. Do you want that way, brothers and sisters of the ville?"

There was a great roar of "No!" from all around.

"Five and twenty is the number and five times five shall be the sacred counting."

Mildred was beside Ryan, her voice so quiet that it didn't reach the ears of Jehu. "Four and twenty shall be too little and six and twenty too much and seven and twenty shall be right out,'' she breathed.

"As the day has its measure and the year its turning, so shall each of us have a span allotted. Not a doubtful, troubled time, rife with worry. But a time that we know. We know truly of our coming in and our going out and the grace that lieth with us at exit and entrance."

The crowd was sighing, like the wind through a grove of tall beeches. Ryan felt a deeply uneasy prickling at the base of his spine at the strange, almost hypnotic power of the man who watched over them.

"What is the reward of those who tread the righteous path, brothers and sisters?"

"Light and life" was the chorused reply.

"And what shall be the lot of those who transgress against the word of Moses?"

"Darkness and death!"

Ryan's right hand had slipped down onto the cool butt of his 9 mm SIG-Sauer, without his even being aware of the movement.

"How shall they enter that darkness, brothers and sisters? How?"

This time the shout was deafening. "Through the flame, Moses, through the flame."

"Oh, Gaia!" Ryan whispered. "Look."

Suddenly everything had become very clear—the need for the willow branches, the call for the flames, the path to the endless darkness for those who had gone against the word and laws of Moses.

The drumbeat became even slower, ceremonial and ponderous, like the steps of a giant.

Or the beating of a huge, diseased heart.

The two victims appeared, surrounded by an honor guard of the tallest young women in the ville, all carrying rifles at the high port.

The outlander rapist was first, naked, hands tied behind his back. His head was sunk on his chest, and he shuffled his feet as he walked, not seeming to be aware of where he was or what was happening to him.

Heinrich, the renegade youth who had chosen to try to defy Moses and his laws, followed close behind. He walked with his head up, looking scornfully from side to side, once spitting at someone who whispered something from the crowd.

The eagle eye of Moses missed nothing. "Let us have silence and dignity, brothers and sisters of the ville," he called from his thatched aerie.

Dean pulled at his father's sleeve. "What are those things for, Dad?" He pointed at a pair of large cages, roughly the size and shape of a man, made from tightly bound, narrow strips of willow, being carried by a number of men from the ville, toward two stout wooden stakes that were driven into the ground beneath the watching Moses.

Ryan didn't answer for a moment, though he knew the answer. "You'll see," he whispered.

The older man, whose tongue had been torn from his mouth, kept making choked, gobbling sounds. He stumbled as he was tied first to the stake, then the wicker cage was strapped into place around him. One of the younger women poured some clear liquid all over him and the woven container that held him. The pungent smell drifted across the square.

"Lamp oil," J.B. said.

"They going to burn him, Dad?"

"Yeah. Both of them, Dean."

"Bastards!" The word was spoken loud enough for Jehu to hear him. The blond man turned and glowered at the boy.

"You could've joined us, boy. You know that. And you turned your back."

"Wouldn't join you if you offered me all the jack in Deathlands!"

Ryan patted his son on the back.

Now it was the turn of Heinrich to be imprisoned.

Though he had seemed fairly passive, the sight of the stake and the wicker cage brought on a violent and futile rage. He pulled himself away from the young women guarding him and kicked out at them, buying himself a few moments' breathing space. He stared wildly around him, looking toward the hidden figure of Moses.

"Don't do this to me, friend!" he shrieked, his voice cracking with mortal terror. "Spare me this ordeal. Let me go free and I'll never come back to Quindley again. I swear it. Show me mercy, I beg you."

"Silence him, sisters!" ordered the sonorous voice of the hidden Moses.

"It can't be wrong just to be old!"

The word died away as the nearest woman brought the butt of her rifle around in a crushing blow to Heinrich's groin. He doubled over, flat on his face in the trampled dirt, his cries turning to a feeble, helpless mewing. His whole body convulsed as he vomited.

"I regret that I have no wish to bear witness to this most barbarous performance. I shall return to our quarters with anyone who wishes to accompany me."

"You were warned, oldie!" whispered Jehu, starting to bring the barrel of his own blaster around toward Doc. But he stopped when he found himself staring down the gaping muzzle of Ryan's SIG-Sauer, with J.B.'s Uzi nudging him in the ribs.

Doc smiled. "A little violence is a wonderful thing, is it not?" He raised his voice toward the roof of Moses's temple. "Carry on with your bloody ritual, but you carry on without me!" He turned on his heel and began to walk back toward their quarters, pushing an angry young man out of the way with the iron ferrule of his sword stick.

"Think I'll keep you company, Doc," Mildred called, striding after him.

It crossed Ryan's mind as a vaguely interesting fact that the two members of their group who couldn't face the brutal chilling to come had both arrived in the living charnel house of Deathlands from earlier, perhaps more civilized, predark times. He also wondered what Michael was feeling, across the far side of the square, in the gloom.

"Dad?"

"Yeah?"

"Mind if I go after Doc and Mildred?"

"Course not."

"You staying with Krysty and J.B., Dad?"

"Guess so."

The boy nodded. "See you in a while."

Ryan half turned to watch the slim, lithe figure of his son picking his way through the darkness after Doc and Mildred.

"Best for him not to watch this, lover," Krysty said, taking his arm.

"I guess so." Jehu stood watching them, frozen in an impotent rage at their betrayal of one of the most important of the ville's rituals. "You keep looking at me like that, Jehu, and you'll miss the main event behind you."

"You speaking to me, oldie? You speaking to me?"

"Must be," Ryan replied. "You're the only one here."

Just for a spaced heartbeat he thought the pony-tailed youth was going to go for him, and his finger took up the first pressure on the P-226. But then Jehu managed to regain self-control and ostentatiously spun to watch the ceremony.

Both men were bound inside the cages of thin, strong osier branches.

The scent of the oil was strong in the still night air, filling the nostrils with its rank odor. The drum had stopped its beating, and the watchers were motionless. Ryan listened carefully, and it seemed as though the entire world beyond the fortified walls of the ville was holding its breath.

The calm, gentle voice of Moses drifted down over them all like a layer of warm, silken honey, making the double murder a perfectly reasonable thing to happen.

"For betraying us and all our brothers and sisters, the sentence shall be..."

"Death!" The word wasn't shouted. It was breathed with a religious awe from dozens of throats, making Ryan's hair stand on end.

"Lover?"

"Wait," he whispered.

"Something's wrong," Krysty said.

"Where? The chilling you mean? Course it's—"

"No. Something else." Her head turned wildly from side to side, her brilliantly fiery hair seeming dulled in the smoky dimness of the square.

"What?" He looked around, but there wasn't a sight or sound of a threat.

Not a sight.

Not a sound.

"No sound," he muttered. The forest by the lake was totally quiet, quite bereft of the usual nocturnal range of bird and animal noises.

"Light the fires," Moses shouted, breaking Ryan's intense concentration for a moment.

"No!" The scream from the tortured Heinrich split the blackness.

Two of the smallest children stepped forward, each holding the hand of an older girl, each holding a blazing torch in their other hand.

"Yes, my dears," Moses called from on high.

The wicker baskets caught fire at once, blazing with a truly ferocious intensity, a golden light that shaded into orange and crimson in the shimmering air above the two cages.

"Gaia help their passing and make it fast," Krysty said.

"Breathe in the fire and they're dead in seconds," J.B. observed, the flames reflected off the lens of his glasses, veiling his eyes.

Many of the watchers had fallen to their knees, hands pressed together, faces radiant in the glow of the twin fires.

One of the dying men had begun to scream. Ryan thought it was Heinrich, but he couldn't be sure. Whoever it was kept twisting in his bonds, as the fire consumed.

There was the smell of roasting meat, and, barely audible above the piercing cries, the noise of sporadic gunfire, with a bright blaze beginning near the main gates into Quindley. Yelps and shrieks of hatred and anger emerged from the darkness beyond the causeway.

"Got company," J.B. said. "Sounds like the stickies have come calling."

Chapter Thirty-Two

All the pieces of the jigsaw locked instantly together in Ryan's mind. As he ran toward the causeway, SIG-Sauer ready, J.B. on his right hand and Krysty on his left, his combat memory was ticking off the clues he'd ignored—the figure seen among the trees during the ill-starred fishing expedition; the smoke that they'd glimpsed, dismissed by Moses as being just beaver hunters; the smell of the fire when he and Krysty had bumped into Michael and Dorothy.

But above all, and Ryan cursed himself for having let it pass him by, was the unnatural silence out there among the tall pines, a silence prompted by the lurking, slinking presence of the mutie enemy.

He was aware of the panic and chaos behind. The young people of Quindley screamed and shouted, two or three of them discharging their blasters uselessly into the night sky. Ryan thought he also heard the voice of Moses, struggling to try to make itself heard over the bedlam, and failing.

Still soaring above it all, like a soul in the bottom circle of the inferno, was the endless screaming of Heinrich.

As they drew closer to the main gates of the ville, the noise of voices grew louder and the fire grew brighter.

"Thrown pitch on it and set it alight," J.B. panted. "No bastard guards at all."

"One on top, coming over," Krysty yelled, stopping and drawing a bead on the ragged figure that clung to the large spikes that decorated the wooden doors.

Ryan and the Armorer ran on, hearing the faint snap of her 5-shot Smith & Wesson double-action blaster, seeing the stickie throw his arms wide and topple forward, hanging by his knees to the gate.

The surging mass of Moses's people were on their heels, surrounding and passing Krysty before she could begin to run again.

"Lookout towers, both sides," Ryan shouted, pointing with the SIG-Sauer. "You take left!"

The beechwood ladder was well made, and he ran up it with the agility of a great cat, hardly having to steady himself, reaching the narrow walkway that ran around the inside of the high defensive walls of the ville.

He peered cautiously over the side, toward the causeway below, seeing the stickies' fire reflected in the dark, sullen waters of Shamplin Lake.

On the opposite side of the gates, J.B. also looked down, his Uzi at the ready.

There were black, sticky gobbets of tar stuck to the timbers, burning with a smoking yellow flame. Dancing outside were no more than half a dozen stickies, three of them struggling to raise a crude siege ladder against the wall just beneath Ryan. There was ample light, and he aimed the powerful 9 mm handblaster and fired three times, killing the trio of muties, two of the corpses flailing lifelessly into the cold water on either side of the causeway.

"Something wrong!" J.B. shouted, his clear voice breaking through the hubbub around them.

Ryan was already being jostled by some of the young men and women, Jehu right at his shoulder, all of them shooting wildly down at the surviving stickies.

J.B.'s words jarred Ryan, and he half turned, staring toward the forest, wondering where the rest of the gang was. Stickies had brains with all of the reasoning power of dead sheep, but even they would hesitate to attack a powerful, fortified ville in such small numbers.

Under a hail of lead, the last mutie was down and done for, his body literally shredded to a bloody pulp by the overwhelming firepower.

Immediately Jehu led his people in an ululating chant of victory. He waved his Remington hunting rifle above his head, his expression contorted with a savage delight. "With Moses as our captain, how can we be defeated?" he yelled, his breath hot and feral, directly into Ryan's face.

The noise was gradually subsiding, and Ryan caught J.B.'s eye across the gap between them. The Armorer hadn't fired a single shot from the machine pistol and gestured with it, back toward the heart of the ville. He was looking worried, rather than triumphant, heightening Ryan's concern. Below them, Krysty was looking back over her shoulder.

The crowd was thronged so thickly on the narrow platform that Ryan could hear the supporting timbers creaking. Several of the teenage girls shot at the corpses, making them twitch and jerk. Jehu watched them, laughing delightedly.

Ryan grabbed him by the shoulder. "Get everyone off here," he shouted, "or the whole place could go down."

At first the blank blue eyes didn't register any understanding. Then the danger of their position reached Jehu and he gradually restored a kind of order, telling everyone to get back down again, except for half a dozen men that he nominated as guards. Ryan pushed through and climbed quickly back to street level, where J.B. joined him and Krysty.

The screaming had stopped from the two tortured victims of the sacrificial ceremony, but they could all hear Moses's voice, praising everyone for their bravery and speed of response.

"If he'd had a lookout posted, then none of that would have been necessary," J.B. stated calmly.

Suddenly Michael was with them, Dorothy hanging on his arm. "Moses knew what would happen," said the teenage youth. "He can see the future."

"Yeah," the woman agreed. "It's over and we won! Praise to Moses, we won!"

From the far side of the ville, where it protruded farthest into the huge lake, over toward the living quarters, they all heard the boom of a powerful handblaster, echoing into the night.

"Doc's Le Mat," J.B. said, setting off at a dead run toward the sound.

It was followed by a piercing scream. Scream upon scream. Two shots were fired from another blaster that Ryan recognized as being Mildred's Czech ZKR 551 target revolver, and a single round that he guessed came from his son's Browning Hi-Power.

Jehu had reacted surprisingly quickly, loping alongside Ryan. "What's happening?" he panted.

"Attack at front was a trick," Ryan replied.

The cries for help were shrill, high and thin, the voices of children.

"They've come in from the water and broken in. Taken our little ones."

Ryan sprinted through the darkness at top speed, his arms pumping, Krysty close behind him. "Taken our friends as well," he said.

They passed the open square, where the remains of the two wicker cages were now heaps of glowing ashes, containing what might have been a collection of blackened branches. Had it not been for the smoke-darkened skulls that lay, empty-socketed, among the ruby embers.

Quindley was small enough for them to be able to run from the entrance to their own rooms at the rear in less than fifty pounding heartbeats.

Ryan didn't waste time looking up at the roof of Moses's own shrine, but the voice seeped down as he powered by. "All will be well, brothers and sisters. Listen to me, for I say all will be well."

"Fuck you," Ryan breathed.

But Jehu had skidded to a halt, nearly falling over in the dirt. "We must listen and obey!" he yelled. "Listen and obey the word of Moses."

"Place is fired!" J.B. called. "Near where our rooms are. The back."

Ryan could smell the tang of blazing pitch, smothering the ghastly stench of the burned corpses, and see the orange glint of light between the buildings just ahead of them.

"Wait," Jehu called again.

Now they could see what had happened, read the story of the successful trick that the stickies had managed to play on the ville—a trick that would never have worked on forty-nine settlements out of fifty, with sensible lookouts and sentries constantly alert against just such a sneak attack.

They had come in from the lake, in boats or rafts, and crept in over the back wall while their suicidal companions had given their lives to distract the inhabitants with their feint at the front entrance.

Now the whole of that segment of Quindley was well ablaze, fountains of sparks erupting fifty feet high from the dry wooden walls, floors and roofs.

The outlanders' sleeping and eating quarters were already an inferno of scorching heat, the flames roaring as they consumed everything, chunks of burning timber falling into the waiting water below with a hissing of steam.

"See anything?" Krysty asked, shading her eyes against the ferocious glare, trying to look past the raging fire across the lake.

"Impossible. Guess they came by water and they're leaving the same way."

"No corpses." J.B. looked behind, where the mood of the ville had completely changed. The bravado and delight had vanished, to be replaced by grief and mourning at the loss of all the children who'd been stolen away.

"Could be there. Or mebbe dumped in the lake." Ryan knelt and tried to look inside the nearest burning building, but it was impossible. He straightened again. "Jehu. Get your people to work on putting out those fires, or you're going to lose the whole damned place."

"Moses hasn't given us the order to do anything."

"Wait for an order and you lose your home. Come on, you double stupe!" Krysty looked as though she were about to haul off and slap the young man across the face.

"Yes, yes, I guess . . ." He turned and waved his hands rather helplessly. "Water. Get water and put out the fire."

J.B. clapped his hands loudly to attract attention. "Put water on the nearest buildings first. Can't save those already burning. But you can soak the others and rescue them from the flame spread. Get to it!"

RYAN'S FIRST IMPULSE had been to take one of the rowboats from Quindley and set off immediately in pursuit of the fleeing muties and their prisoners. It was possible that Doc, Dean and Mildred had already been butchered. But it was typical behavior for stickies to spend some time on disposing of their captives, disposal that generally involved a great deal of pain, and as much fire as possible.

Stickies truly loved the brightness of fire.

But Ryan realized that it would be pointless. He had no idea of the numbers of the raiding gang, or how many vessels they had with them.

What he needed to do was set out with as many armed men and women as possible from Quindley, preferably before first light. He could remember where they'd spotted the smoke among the trees, farther north along the shore of the lake. It was a fair bet that it had been the stickies' camp and that they would have returned there with their prisoners.

Under Jehu's orders, the bucket chain had been quickly organized and was working well, water spraying onto the wood of the buildings that adjoined the heart of the fire, soaking the thatch and preserving it from the flying sparks. The timber walls, heated almost to the point where they would have spontaneously combusted, were literally steaming.

Michael appeared again from the crowd, this time without the blond woman on his arm. "They got Dean and Doc and Mildred," he said.

"Yeah. We heard a burst of shooting. But we don't see any bodies. They got every one of the little children from the place next along as well." Ryan looked at the teenager. "We're going to go after them before dawning. Want to come along?"

"Sure. Course I do." He hesitated. "You asked Moses for permission?"

"Permission?" Ryan shook his head. "We don't need his permission, Michael."

"You do if you want to take boats from the ville. Or use any of the brothers and sisters."

"Think he'd be able to stop us?"

Michael grinned, the first time since their arrival in the ville that he'd shown even a glimmer of his old self. "Guess not, Ryan."

THE WINDOW IN THE ROOF of Moses's dwelling was closed, and audience with the invisible ruler of Quindley was in the luxurious surroundings of his receiving room on the first floor. Jehu, pressed by Ryan, had led him there, accompanied by J.B. and Krysty.

The two-way mirror still concealed Moses from their sight, but his voice was calm and gentle, as though the disaster of the stickies' attack were the merest of flea bites.

"You wish to consult me, Ryan Cawdor."

"Muties took all of your littlest ones, and three of our friends."

"This is true. Sad, but true."

"Hour before first light I want to take as many boats as you can spare. Armed people. Land up the coast and hit the stickies in their camp. With any luck we can rescue a lot of your children as well as our companions."

"No," said the deep, gentle voice.

"No?"

"No."

Chapter Thirty-Three

Moses was utterly immovable.

"I hear all you say, outlander," he said calmly, "but you are deeply wrong."

"Wrong to save lives? Wrong to save the lives of children and friends?"

"To your way of thinking, I see why you cherish such beliefs, Ryan Cawdor. But what has happened was destined to happen. Our young ones will have a rebirthing and will rejoin us here in the ville of Quindley."

"That's total shit!" Krysty could no longer contain her anger, and she brushed away Jehu's restraining hand, striding forward to push her face within inches of the mirror. They all heard a rustle of sudden movement, as if Moses had been taken aback by her enraged approach.

"You are strangers here." There was an unmistakable note of tension in his voice. "Best that you leave us."

Ryan considered putting a dozen spaced rounds through the dark glass, in the hope of taking Moses out. But to do that—to assassinate their god—would bring a mob of armed men and women running for revenge.

J.B. rescued the moment of tension. "Sure, Moses," he said. "The fire's out now. I'd be grateful for a bed for a few hours. Then we'll quit your ville."

Moses had recovered his cool. "I had not looked for such wisdom from an oldie. Your thinking is correct, outlander Dix. You may be fed before departing. Jehu?"

"Master?"

"Arrange it."

"Yes, master."

Ryan stretched and yawned. "Guess I could do with some shut-eye as well."

"May your rest be gentle and filled only with dreams of light and hope."

"Thanks, Moses."

THEY PASSED THE REMAINS of the two murdered men, now just cooling ashes and tangled bones.

The ville was settling down after the horror of the sneak attack. The fires had been controlled. The only buildings destroyed were the living accommodation for visitors and the dormitory of the youngest children.

Fortunately none of Ryan's party had left any weapons or possessions in the rooms when they'd gone out to watch the sacrificial ceremony.

Jehu organized straw-filled mattresses for them in a storeroom that the ville used for late-summer fruit. It was lined with high shelves of planed elm, was pleasantly dry and smelled sweet and clean.

"Sleep well. There will be food in the morning. And we can give you something to ease your journeying. Some bread and apples, and flasks of water."

"Thanks," Ryan said. "Appreciate it."

Jehu paused in the doorway. He had brought them a pair of torches, sticking them into brackets in the wall. Their flickering light showed the struggle in his face. "Moses's rule runs only within the ville and its lands. If you wished to try to rescue your friends yourselves..."

"Appreciate that," Ryan replied. "You wouldn't know where Michael is?"

"No. He was walking with Dorothy out along the causeway after the fire was finished."

"Risky—" Krysty looked across the small room at Ryan"—isn't it, lover?"

"Not very, I guess." Ryan shook his head. "Stickies got what they wanted. Did it well. Good combat skills for them. Doubt there's any of them still around."

"I'll wish you a good sleep and a clean wakening." Jehu raised his hand in a sort of cautious wave, then left the building, pushing the door shut behind him.

Ryan waited a few seconds, listening to the sound of the young man's feet moving away from them. "Right," he said. "Let's get to some talking and then some doing."

RYAN WAS LOCKED into a bizarre dream. A young woman, naked and oiled, was leaning over him, scratching an intricate tattoo on his forehead with a bone needle, then rubbing a mixture of dark blue dye and spittle into the shallow cuts.

The point made a thin, tearing sound as it rubbed at the flesh above his good eye. Sometimes, in his dreams, Ryan found that he had both eyes. But not this time.

The strange rustling sound of the sharp point against his skin seemed louder.

Ryan blinked awake.

The small hut was almost totally dark, just tiny chinks of light between the feather-edge boarding. The albino teenager, Jak Lauren, had the best night sight of anyone Ryan had ever known. But his own vision was vastly better than average and he could make out a figure, black against the blackness, moving slowly toward him, feet making a rustling sound against the dusty wood of the floor.

Ryan drew the SIG-Sauer from by his head and leveled it at the intruder.

"One more step and you get to be dead," he said quietly.

"It's me, Ryan."

"Michael. What do you want?"

"To come with you."

Ryan was one of the most cautious men in all Deathlands. "When we leave the ville after first food?"

"No." There was something like a laugh in the young man's voice. "I've been with you long enough to know better than that, Ryan. I may be a stupe, but I'm not triple stupe."

"So?"

He knew that J.B. was awake and would be holding the Uzi ready to fire. And that Krysty, alongside him, was also alert, holding her own blaster.

"So, you're going to steal a boat and go after Dean and the others."

"Who says this?"

Michael squatted. "Don't waste time. I got the boat for you."

Ryan was taken by surprise. "Where?"

"Tied up by the burned-out portion of the ville. Smaller than the one we had the other day. Four oars."

Krysty spoke. "How about Dorothy, Michael?"

A long pause. "She doesn't know."

"If she finds out?"

"I don't know, Krysty. She's...real special. Like her a lot. Think she likes me. But she believes in everything that Moses says. Like they all do."

"You don't?" J.B. asked.

"No. Not now. When we got here, my head was fucked by what happened in the jumps and it seemed that Moses was the fountain of truth and wisdom. Sort of thing they tried to teach at Nil-Vanity. Then I saw the chillings and the way Moses treated the attack by the stickies. They got all those little children and he just doesn't..." His voice broke with his anguish. "He just doesn't seem to care at all!"

The room was silent.

Finally it was Ryan who spoke. "We go an hour before first light. Head north and land on this side of where we think the stickies have their camp. Mebbe be too late for... for some of the ones they took. Mutie bastards like the dark for their fires and their sporting. But they might hold them and have a real good time this coming night. Best we can hope for. Go in and hit them hard as we can."

"How you reckon to bring the children back here to the ville? They must have fifteen or twenty of them."

"Sure. Plan is to spring them safe. Point the kids this way and hope to chill enough of the stickies to slow them down in going after them."

"How about..." Michael hesitated.

"Go on." Ryan and the others waited for him to speak. Outside, far off, they all heard a coyote howling at the thin slice of silver moon.

"How about the ville? How about Quindley and everyone? Stickies could come here again."

"Trader used to say that you look after yourself and your friends. Anyone else you can help is just a bonus. But you never, *never* risk yourselves trying to help folk who won't get off their asses to help themselves."

THEY ALL DOZED FITFULLY for the remainder of the long night. Ryan had always been able to set himself a waking time and then rely on some mysterious element in his body and brain to pull him from sleep at the right moment.

He rolled over and picked up the Steyr. All of them had slept fully clothed, and it was only a handful of seconds before they were ready to move.

Ryan gathered the three close around him. "One thing," he whispered. "Anyone tries to stop us—anyone, Michael—then we have to take them out. Can't risk being stopped. Dean, Doc and Mildred are out there waiting and relying on us."

There was just the faint eastern glow of the false dawn, enough to make out the pale blur of Michael's face.

"You understand what Ryan's saying, don't you, Michael?" Krysty asked.

"Yeah. If Dorothy happened to come out and try to stop us leaving, then she gets chilled. Sure, Ryan. I understand."

THERE WAS NOBODY out there.

Despite the horror of the sneak attack from the stickies, Moses had ruled that there were to be no extra security precautions, no more than the usual couple of lookouts at the front, overlooking the causeway.

The rowboat was where Michael had tied it, the water of the lake lapping gently under its keel. The mirrored expanse of Shamplin stretched away from them, quiet and calm.

"Want to be on the way before the full dawn," Ryan said. "Be visible a long way off. Hoped there might have been a mist to cover us."

Krysty and J.B. took the bow pair of oars, settling them carefully into the oarlocks.

"Take that side, Michael," Ryan ordered. "Don't need anyone to steer. We can do it with the oars." The teenager stood still, hesitating. "What's wrong? Having second thoughts about coming with us?"

"No."

"Then we have to go."

"We coming back?"

"Here? Doubt it. You want to?"

"Maybe, Ryan."

"Then mebbe we can come back here. Have to see which way the knife lands."

"I hate having to make decisions. Doc said once that until you have to act, you still have a choice of an infinite number of possibilities. Once you actually do something, then you don't have any."

"Sounds like Doc," Krysty said.

Michael grinned, his teeth white in the dawn's gloom. "Yeah. It does."

He stepped down into the boat, balancing with an effortless grace. Ryan got in last, handing the rifle to the teenager, untying the painter from a wooden stake at the edge of the ville. One push of his oar and they began to drift silently out into the vast stillness of the lake.

"Try not to make any splashing until we're well away," J.B. whispered.

"How long will it take us?" Krysty asked.

"About an hour, I guess." Ryan gave the word for them to begin rowing, setting a steady rate. "Keep in close to the shore and the land when we get close enough to where we think their camp might be."

"Then what?" Michael asked.

"Then? Then we do what we can. Can't do any more than that. Nobody can."

Chapter Thirty-Four

Doc felt less than well. He had a bruise the size of a pigeon's egg just below and behind his right ear. His coat was torn. His beloved Le Mat was stuck in the belt of the tall mutie who appeared to be the leader of the stickie gang. There was a strip of skin peeled away from his right wrist by the vicious suckers of the first of the murderous attackers who'd suddenly loomed silently in at them, out of the blackness of the night.

His hands were tied behind him with thin cord, so painfully tight that he could feel his fingers swelling, blood seeping from beneath the nails.

Mildred lay on her side next to him, similarly bound, with young Dean a little farther along the line of prisoners. Three young girls from the ville were tied between him and Mildred. The remaining survivors of the raid were scattered around the clearing, all equally helpless.

It was well past midnight, and Doc guessed that the coolness in the air and the faintest pallor toward the east was a token of the coming dawn.

The fire at the center of the muties' camp still burned brightly, and there were piles of kindling all around the place. Most of their captors had slept at some point, simply pulling ragged blankets or piles of stinking furs over their bodies, leaving their prisoners to fend for themselves.

So far, they had only killed one of the children, a little boy of about six. The rest of the young ones from Quindley had begun to scream at the appalling horror of the scene, until the stickies had raged among them, beating them into silence with short-hafted clubs and whips.

Mildred opened one eye and looked around. "Actually managed to sleep a few minutes," she whispered. "Can't believe I did that. Soon be light."

"I believe so." Doc profoundly wished that he could have thought of something brave or witty to say, but he felt sick, old and terrified.

"Ryan'll be here soon," she said, seeing Dean's eyes on her, managing a wink to show him that she wasn't beaten yet. But with the stickies starting to rise and wander about, she didn't dare say more to reassure the boy.

Doc had been trying to count the number of muties in the camp. Not that he had any serious hope of escape, but it gave him something to occupy his mind. The trouble was that they kept moving around, and they all seemed to look the same. Lean, with stringy hair and dreadful complexions.

"Count the legs and divide by two," he'd breathed to himself. He made it around thirty or so. Two-thirds were male, though the women were difficult to tell apart. Most carried crude knives or axes, but several had blasters. It seemed as though they must have recently carried out a successful raid on a large ville or wag train. They had a stash of cans of lamp oil and tubs of pitch, which they'd used against Quindley.

Doc had learned a fair bit about the variety of human genetic mutations that had flowered across Deathlands since the long winters, and he knew that stickies were about as bad as they got. The only possible reason for taking prisoners was to torture and kill them with as much cruelty as possible. No ransom or trade would be taking place. Just some long, slow dying.

"How is your bruised head, my dear Mildred?"

"Like someone's been using it to line a parrot's cage. How about you?"

"Chipper and perky and ready to be up and doing. Soon as Ryan and the others get here."

"You sure they'll come, Doc?"

"Sure as I ever was about anything, madam. If they don't all arrive shortly, I shall, to put it mildly, be most frightfully disappointed."

IF IT HADN'T BEEN for the fact that they were on a desperate expedition to try to rescue their friends from the horror of the stickies, the boat trip across Shamplin Lake would have been surprisingly pleasant.

It was a calm, serene morning, the sun breaking through over the tops of the heavily wooded mountains to their right. There was absolutely no wind to ruffle the limitless expanse of black, mirrored water. Behind them, their vanishing wake stretched southward, creditably straight, arrowing toward the just visible bulk of the ville.

By the time there was enough light for them to have been seen, they were far enough away to be almost invisible to the naked eye. Ryan had deliberately steered them close to the eastern shore, in the shallows.

He set a good pace, trying to send the small boat darting northward at the best possible speed. There was no weak link among the four of them, and the oars rose and fell in graceful, unflagging unison.

Far over their heads, a lark soared and filled the morning sky with its piercing song. A hundred yards behind them a single fish leaped exultantly high from the water, its scales a dazzling rainbow of iridescence. It fell back into the lake with an audible plopping sound, leaving only a diminishing circle of ripples to mark where it had been.

Moments later it repeated its brave salute to the dawning. There was a humming of wings and a blur of movement as a falcon swooped on it, plucking it from the air in its cruel talons and bearing it off toward the shore.

"Should've kept its head down," J.B. grunted just behind Ryan.

MICHAEL HAD BEEN glancing back over his shoulder, disrupting the rhythm of the rowing. Ryan kept telling him to concentrate on his oar and not to worry about trying to spot any sign of the stickies' camp.

But it was the teenager who first saw the thin column of pale gray, almost white smoke, rising high above the dark mantle of conifers that shrouded the rolling hills to the east of the lake.

"Easy," Ryan cautioned, shipping his own oar, letting the boat coast silently forward under its own momentum. The only sound was the water dripping from the blades.

The camp was roughly where he'd remembered it from the previous day, looking to be about a half mile inland from the shore. He stared intently behind them, to the south, checking that there was no pursuit coming from Quindley that might hinder their rescue operation.

But the water was scraped clean of any life.

"Head in," he ordered.

"THINK THEY'LL FEED US, Mildred?"

"I somehow don't think so, Dean."

For a moment the prisoners were on their own, with the nearest of the muties fifty yards away. The little children from the ville all seemed to have subsided into a collective catatonic stupor. They wouldn't look up or move or respond to Mildred's and Doc's futile attempts to rouse them from their dismal apathy.

"Think Dad'll be here?"

Doc answered. "Does a dog piss in the sea? No, I fear that I have used the wrong phrase."

"You mean does a mutie shit in the woods, Doc."

"Indeed, I think it was something along those lines. But there is no scintilla of doubt that the inestimable Master Cawdor will be here with us in two shakes of a lamb's tail."

"They aiming to chill us all, Mildred?"

"Got to be their plan, son."

"You, as well?"

Mildred grinned, feeling the movement hurting where the corner of her mouth had been split by a savage punch. "Me, as well. Stickies aren't racially or sexually prejudiced when it comes to chilling, Dean."

THE KEEL OF THE BOAT kissed the soft shingle and came to a gentle stop.

"Tie it up?" Michael asked, leaping out, knee-deep in the cold water.

"Don't think this lake's tidal." Ryan glanced at J.B. for reassurance.

"Doubt it. Just pull it up." There was a bank of scrubby bushes nearby. "Put a bit of that over it, in case anyone passes by."

"We might need to get away fast." Krysty was sniffing the air like a hunting dog. "Bad taste to things, lover."

"Definitely the stickies?"

"For sure. Been some chilling already."

"Dean and the others?" Michael paused from putting armfuls of undergrowth over the boat.

"Can't tell. Have to wait for that."

Ryan stood back and looked at the concealed vessel. "That'll do it," he said. "Now, everyone knows where this is. Take a careful look around. Like Krysty says, we might be off and running good when we get back here. Won't be time to hunt around wondering where we hid it."

"What's the plan of attack, Ryan?" Michael was checking his Texas Longhorn Border Special, work-

ing the fluid action of the 6-round, centerfire .38 revolver, while the Armorer looked on approvingly.

"Tell you when we get there. Trader used to say that
it was hard to leave it too late to make a plan. But there
was a lot of good men six feet under because they tried
to make their combat plans too early."

Ryan had the Steyr slung over a shoulder, the SIG-
Sauer loose in its holster. The others all had their
weapons ready as they began the cautious walk
through the forbidding forest toward the stickies'
camp.

TWO MORE of the Quindley children had been killed,
butchered with a casual, brutish dispatch that brought
tears to Doc Tanner's rheumy old eyes. He managed
enough self-control to restrain himself from protest-
ing at the small massacre, knowing that to draw attention to himself was to insist on putting his signature
on his own death warrant.

One was a little boy who had started to snivel when
a passing mutie woman had kicked him in the ribs.
The second death that morning was a girl. Terrified
beyond all control, she had fouled herself, commit-
ting the unpardonable sin of drawing the stickies' attention to herself.

The golden sun was now well up, its fresh bright
light fingering between the branches of the tall, fra-
grant pines all around them.

Mildred wondered how long Ryan would be.

"I SMELL BURNED MEAT," Michael said, wrinkling his
nose in distaste.

"Probably not ordinary meat," Ryan replied quickly, instantly regretting his lack of thought.

"You mean they're setting fire to the kids? Or to..." Michael stopped walking and leaned a hand against the rough trunk of a towering ponderosa. "World'll be a cleaner place without those sicko bastards."

"Can't argue with that." Ryan looked around. "Must be getting close. Half mile or so. Better move to double-red. Stickies might be out hunting."

JEHU STOOD AND GLANCED at the painting of the animal's skull. He shuffled his feet and stared at his own reflection in the mirror, waiting to hear what Moses might say about the news of the outlanders escaping and stealing one of the ville's valuable boats.

"You believe that Sister Dorothy knew nothing of this, Jehu? You are sure?"

"Sure as I can be. She was really upset. She had formed close links with the outlander called Michael, and we believed that he was intending to stay here with us, though she knew nothing of your orders to have Ryan and the others executed while they ate their food this morning."

The calm voice sounded slightly bored with the whole business. "It matters not. If any of them return, then have them chilled immediately. Immediately."

"Yes, Moses. Immediately."

Chapter Thirty-Five

"Doesn't look to me like the stickies have been in these parts for very long."

J.B. thought about what Ryan had said, and nodded. "Must be right. No damage to the forest. No hacked trails. Usually leave a circle of devastation for a mile or more around one of their camps. Reckon they were moving through. That's why we found that body on the hillside before we got down into the ville."

They were sitting in a close circle behind a screen of wild cherries. An exquisite pentstemon was flowering just to the right of them. Krysty had picked one from a cluster of delicate pink blossoms, their heavy scent almost hiding the foul stench from the camp on the far side of the ridge.

"How we going to play this one, Ryan?" J. B. Dix was hunched over his Uzi, his glasses glinting in the bright sunlight. "A recce first?"

"Yeah. Don't know if they got huts or tents or anything. Where they got the prisoners. Tied up or not. How many of them. What kind of blasters."

"Shit lot that we don't know." Michael had been becoming visibly more tense ever since they landed the boat and began the trek through the woods.

Ryan nodded. "Yeah. Sure there is. But we know one thing the stickies don't."

"What?"

"We know that we're here."

RYAN CARRIED OUT the creepy-crawl himself, aware from endless experience that there was no substitute for personal appraisal of the scene for a potential firefight.

He counted around thirty stickies rather more than he'd anticipated, mostly men, and a few of them with blasters. He spotted one tall mutie sporting Doc's Le Mat in his belt and had no doubt that Mildred's Czech pistol and Dean's Browning were also somewhere in the crude camp.

He could see the prisoners easily enough.

With so many of the muties to watch the captives, there had been no effort made to chain or wire them together. As far as Ryan could make out, from behind the screen of some feathery tamarisks, Dean, Mildred and Doc were all alive and didn't show any obvious signs of serious injuries.

With the excellent Starlite scope on the rifle, it would have been easy for Ryan to have picked off at least half a dozen of the muties from where he was hiding. But that would still leave far too many to chill their prisoners before scuttling off into the woods around.

It needed some thinking.

THE SKINNY LEADER of the muties was interested in Doc and Mildred.

"What old fucks like you do in that young place? Huh?"

"I asked myself the same question, friend," Mildred replied. "A thousand times."

"So, what fucking answer?"

"Answer is that I don't know."

"Then you fucking stupe."

"Yeah."

The bulbous eyes with their oddly forked pupils turned toward Doc. "You oldest fuck I never saw. We heard that ville chills every fucker when they gets old."

Doc nodded. "You heard correctly."

"So why you alive?"

"Possibly my inherent charm. Perhaps my insistence on the most scrupulous standards of personal hygiene. That is the very best that I can offer by way of explanation."

The mutie looked at Doc for a long time, making the old man feel the sudden awful certainty of his now imminent death. Then the stickie smiled at him, oblivious of a thick thread of greenish spittle that was trailing down over its receding chin. "You funny fuck."

"Thank you."

"We give you fucking funny hot death, old fuck."

"MASSACRE THEM ALL?"

Michael sat with his head resting on his knees,

hands folded in front of him as though he'd been interrupted in midprayer.

"This a problem, Michael?"

The young man didn't answer Ryan. His eyes were closed, and his face had gone pale.

Krysty knelt by him. "Gaia, Michael! Don't come over all pious now."

"You're going to try and shoot down...how many? Twenty or thirty of God's creatures without a word of warning or a chance of survival."

J.B. spit in the dirt. His normally sallow cheeks were flushed with anger. "Tell you what. You go on down, Michael, and ask them to surrender."

"They wouldn't." He looked up at the Armorer.

"So, it's double stupe to suggest it, then?"

"Yeah. I know what. Can't we tell them they got no chance and let them go if they don't harm any of the children or Dean and the rest?"

"Dark night! Stickies aren't down-home folks, you shit-for-brains kid!"

Krysty stood up between the Armorer and the sitting teenager, holding out a hand. "Keep it down, both of you. Or we'll have muties all over us."

J.B. sighed. "Sure, sure. You're right, Krysty." He lowered his voice. "Michael, will you listen to me?"

"Sure. Look, I'm sorry about—"

J.B. put his hand on the young man's shoulder. "I know you weren't born in Deathlands. You see things like a..." He changed direction. "Stickies are't human beings, Michael. It would be like worrying about treading on a poisonous scorpion. If we don't go in against the sickhead bastards on full-auto, then there'll be deaths on our side. Might well be anyway. Nobody can ever predict where the cards are going to fall. But you have to plan it best you can."

It was an unusually long speech for the normally taciturn man, but Ryan couldn't find a word to disagree with.

Michael stood up, offered his hand and shook with J.B. "I see that now. I'm ready."

"Fine," Ryan said. "Then let's go."

A PAIR OF PLUMP-BREASTED pigeons fluttered noisily out of the forest, southwest of the muties' camp, circling three or four times, and then flying off toward the lake.

Dean sat up and stared at the birds, glancing sideways to see if any of the muties had noticed the brief disturbance. He glanced across at Doc and Mildred, but both of them were lying down, locked into their own thoughts.

The boy half smiled and lay down again, trying to exercise his tightly bound hands to keep them supple. Ready in case he needed to move fast.

THE MUTIE CAMP WAS SET in a large clearing, about a mile inland from the lake.

Ideally Ryan would have liked the chance to wait, then move in at the optimum time, perhaps a couple of hours after midnight, when most of the stickies would have collapsed into a drugged or drunken sleep.

But nighttime was when the perverted nuke mutations launched into their torturefests. To wait would almost certainly mean being too late.

Numbers were massively on the side of the stickies, but they seemed to be poorly armed. And there was no sign at all that they were worried about the possibility of anyone raiding them.

Which tipped the balance strongly in favor of the four attackers.

It was important to try to chill every one of the stickies. If a few escaped, then the retreat to the boat would be made that much more dangerous. The best way of ensuring that was for each of them to take a quadrant of the compass, and come in from four different directions to hit them hard and fast.

"Get the firstest with the mostest" had been Trader's basic ruling. When Ryan had once mentioned that to Doc, the old-timer had pointed out that it wasn't exactly original and had its origins with a commander in the ancient Civil War.

Before they separated, Ryan gave a last whispered warning to Michael and Krysty. There was no need to mention something so obvious to J.B.

"Danger is shooting each other. Aim low and keep a triple-red watch for the rest of us coming in."

There had been a momentary temptation to go opposite the Armorer, knowing that was safest. But he rejected the idea, choosing to go around to the north himself, leaving Michael to cover the south. Krysty took the lake side while J.B. circled to the east.

He and J.B. had chrons. The other two would have to rely on a measured count to make sure they were in position and ready to go in at the right moment.

Since there was no tearing hurry to initiate the attack, Ryan allowed a full half hour for everyone to get into position. At that point he would fire a single round in the air from the Steyr rifle.

"No questions?"

There were none. They'd agreed that they would set free the children if that proved possible, but only after they'd ensured the safety of Dean, Mildred and Doc.

As RYAN PICKED HIS WAY along the narrow trails between the tall trees, he heard a pair of pigeons rise noisily into the air, somewhere toward the lake, disturbed by Krysty's passing by. He hoped that none of the muties would have noticed it and made the connection.

When he was halfway around he wrinkled his nose at a bitter, acidic smell. He stopped in midstride and waited, listening intently. The path ahead was straight for fifty yards or so, and he could see a pile of fresh droppings, still steaming slightly in the cool morning air. Ryan had never been a great tracker, but he guessed that some large carnivore was nearby, possibly either a bear or a puma.

But the woods were brimming with a deep stillness, and he began to move on north, looping around the stickies' camp, not heading toward the scent of the smoke until he'd made sure there was no outer ring of sentries.

He checked his timing, the tiny digital numbers flicking over to show he'd been moving for just over sixteen minutes. Nearly a quarter of an hour remained before he'd fire the signal bullet and all hell would break loose in the serene New England forest.

Now he could smell the foul odors that he always associated with stickie camps—rotting food, burned meat, unwashed bodies and the peculiar decayed, fishlike stench that seemed to surround the creatures.

Most frontier villes would have any number of stray animals hanging around them, lean, slant-eyed mongrels and vicious feral cats. But there was something different about stickies. Even among their own mutie kind they were regarded as outcasts, and it was rare to find any sort of living creature within range of their malodorous camps.

Ryan picked his careful way closer.

"IF THIS RESCUE WERE to be done," Doc muttered, "then it were well that it were done quickly."

"Couldn't agree more," Mildred whispered. "Don't like the way they're collecting kindling and brushwood. Looks to me like they're planning a big blaze."

"With us as their center-ring, numero uno star attraction." Doc sniffed. "We shall this night, by God's grace, light such a candle, my good Dr. Wyeth, as shall never be extinguished in this fair land." He sniffed again. "My nose itches alarmingly. But I fear that it would be an ill thing to ask one of our captors to scratch it for me."

Mildred managed a weak smile. "Do that and the sons of bitches would just cut your nose off, Doc. And, probably, your chattering head with it."

One of the stickies walked by them, carrying an armful of loose branches. It heard them talking and glared in their direction, silencing them immediately.

RYAN WAS CLOSE ENOUGH to hear sounds from the camp, an occasional shout and once a cry of sudden pain.

Just ahead of him there was a tangle of fallen timber, piled almost shoulder-high. He began to pick his way around it when he heard the sound of feet, coming fast toward him.

The one-eyed man dropped to a crouch, easing the rifle onto the ground, holding the SIG-Sauer ready, hoping desperately that he wouldn't have to open fire and get their attack off to a messy and premature start.

He could catch the guttural, bubbling voices of stickies and risked a glance through the tangled branches, seeing that there were two of the muties. One carried a single-shot musket of immense age, while the other had only a short-handled ax tucked into its narrow string belt.

He caught the words "fire" and "wood" repeated several times as they drew closer. Now they'd stopped, only just the other side of the big deadfall.

Ryan waited.

Chapter Thirty-Six

Krysty had gone right to the shore of the sunlit lake before starting to work her way eastward again toward the stickies' camp. She had immediately found the boats that they'd used on the raid on Quindley the previous night, though "boats" wasn't the best word for a motley collection of rafts and crude canoes tugged up onto the pebbles.

From there the trail was easy to follow.

Bushes had been broken down and trees hacked with machetes. Barely concealed in the undergrowth, a quarter mile from Shamplin, Krysty saw a protruding pair of bare feet. Flies buzzed around the bloodied corpse, and her heart nearly stopped with the jolting fear that it might be Dean.

But it wasn't. It was a younger child, barely five years old, with its throat cut so savagely that the whiteness of the spine showed through the clotted blackness.

"Gaia!" Krysty drew her blaster and moved on a little faster, to be in position when Ryan fired the warning shot from his rifle. She had calculated that just over half of the time had gone.

RYAN DIDN'T HAVE a choice. The pair of stickies had started to strip away some of the dry wood from the deadfall, one of them walking straight to the side where he was crouched.

The SIG-Sauer P-226 was a fifteen-round, 9 mm automatic blaster. The four-and-a-half-inch barrel carried a built-in baffle silencer that had been developed during the middle and late 1990s. Like all silencers, prolonged firing greatly diminished its efficiency.

Ryan took a chance and jabbed the pistol into the skinny midriff of the surprised mutie, pulling the trigger twice. The explosions were doubly muffled, sounding no louder than a polite cough.

The stickie's mouth sagged open and it staggered a few clumsy steps backward, dropping the wood it had collected, tripping and landing on its back. The ax slipped from its belt. Its suckered hands opened and closed, reaching toward the two tiny black holes in its stomach.

Ryan didn't stop to watch something he'd already seen dozens of times in his life.

The body crashing to the ground had made enough noise to attract the attention of the other mutie, on the far side of the deadfall. "What happen, Jez?"

It was carrying the musket, and it immediately began to fumble with the grotesquely long blaster, struggling to get it cocked and aimed at the one-eyed norm who'd suddenly sprung from the forest's ferny floor.

Ryan didn't hesitate. He holstered the SIG-Sauer and stepped in close to the stickie.

He kicked it in the groin, the steel toe of the combat boot crushing the shrunken genitals up against the wedge of pubic bone. The mutie gave a squeak of agony, so feeble and high-pitched that it would hardly have disturbed a hunting bat. The old Kentucky long gun dropped silently to the dirt as the stickie started to double over. The breath seemed to have become trapped deep in its lungs by the shock of the attack. Blood was already trickling down its chin and chest from its open mouth where it had bitten the end off its tongue with its needle-filed teeth.

Ryan watched carefully, standing away until the thing was down on its knees, face pressed into the soft earth, rocking slowly back and forth. Then he stepped in, having checked all around him that the forest was deserted, pressed the barrel of the SIG-Sauer to the back of the stickie's neck and pulled the trigger for a third time.

This time the sound of the shot was a little louder, but he guessed that the light wind through the tall trees would probably have ridden over the noise.

The body of the mutie jerked once from the impact of the high-velocity bullet, then slid forward like a confident swimmer entering a deep pool, lying still. A river of blood began to leak from the massive exit wound at the base of the flattened nose.

Ryan looked around again, then picked up the rifle and slung it once more across his back. He checked his chron and saw that the chilling of the two stickies had taken him less than one hundred seconds from beginning to the ending.

It was now time for him to move in closer to the camp, ready to fire the signal round.

AT THE LAST MOMENT, Ryan had changed his mind and used the warning bullet to chill one of the stickies, putting the 7.62 mm round between the eyes of a white-haired mutie woman who was about to cut the throat of one of the Quindley children, two along from where Dean was tied.

It blew away most of the back of her angular skull, so that her brains exploded in a pink-gray mist, all over the row of young prisoners.

There was instant chaos and confusion—sound like ripping silk as J.B. walked calmly into the center of the camp, spraying lead from the Uzi, sending the stickies toppling like broken dolls; Krysty, hair like flame, came in from the direction of the lake, picking her shots with great care, very aware that her blaster held only five rounds; Michael, last of the four to appear, some seconds behind the other three, confronted several of the stickies who had already chosen the south side of their camp as the best line of escape from the murderous shooting that had erupted from the forest around them, shooting into them with the Texas Longhorn, his lips moving in what could have been either a prayer or a string of pattered curses.

The next two and a quarter minutes were a merciless massacre of blood and screams.

THEY'D AGREED IN ADVANCE that Krysty would be the one to head straight for the prisoners, using her knife to free Dean, Mildred and Doc. Michael would try to help her, while J.B. and Ryan, holding the serious firepower, would beat off any attacks on them from the stickies.

Like most plans, it didn't turn out quite like Ryan had expected.

The main difference was that their ambush of the camp was more shocking and successful than he could have hoped. In the first thirty seconds they managed to chill or mortally wound well over half of the stickies, while the rest of the muties screamed and ran around like headless chickens.

In the chaos and confusion, Ryan couldn't be certain, but his guess was that not a single shot was fired against them by the "defenders" of the camp. One woman threw a knife at him, and the hilt struck him a glancing blow in the small of the back. But he turned and shot her with the ninth of the ten rounds from the Steyr, the bullet sending her stumbling, her legs seeming like they wanted to move in five different directions. Until the wires went down and she slumped forward onto her face, with the loud crack of her nose splintering.

J.B. ran the Uzi in a careful, steady line, right to left, cutting down five stickies in that single burst. The bullets ripped them apart at waist-level, sending them rolling and weeping in a welter of their pale mutie blood.

Krysty would always remember the fourth of her five rounds. She had reached the line of prisoners, managing a reassuring grin for Dean. As she knelt, reaching for her knife, Doc barked out a warning of a stickie coming at her from behind, on hands and knees, trailing blood from a bullet that had smashed his left thigh apart.

She turned and snapped off the .38 at the crawling mutie. But one of the little girls from the ville, freaked into blind panic, jumped up at that moment and took the bullet through the throat. The heavy round nearly tore her head off her frail shoulders.

Krysty didn't flinch or hesitate, using the fifth and last bullet from her Smith & Wesson to chill the stickie, smack between the narrow, mad eyes.

She was never certain if anyone had seen the shot that killed the child and she never, ever mentioned it to a living soul.

Michael was ready to shoot, as some of the fleeing stickies raced toward him. But most turned at the moment he opened fire, scattering in all directions, to be gunned down by either Ryan or J.B. Michael was never sure that he actually shot anyone that ferocious, crazed morning among the pine-scented trees.

Mildred tried to keep track of the mutie that had taken away her beloved ZKR pistol, but she lost sight of his ragged pink shirt in the panic.

Doc sat up, his hands still bound behind him, ready to kick out if any of the stickies decided they they were going to try to take at least one of the norm prisoners with them into their arid shadowlands.

Dean whooped with an almost hysterical delight—
"Hot pipe, guys!"—every time one of their captors hit
the dirt and lay still.

Ryan dropped the empty rifle in the trampled earth
and stood stock-still, his feet spread, holding the SIG-
Sauer cocked. He moved it like the tongue of a rattler, tasting the dangers in the air, looking for a fresh
target.

But there wasn't one.

It was over.

The smoke from the stickies' fire drifted up se-
renely between the branches of the overhanging trees.
The children stopped their terrified keening, one by
one.

Nobody was shooting.

At a quick glance there were at least half a dozen of
the muties still alive, though all of them were sorely
wounded. J.B. had unslung the Smith & Wesson M-
4000 scattergun from his shoulders, the empty Uzi
dangling from a strap on his belt. But the lethal flé-
chettes weren't going to be needed.

Krysty was on her knees, cutting away with her slim
knife at the cords that tied Mildred's hands behind
her. Dean was already up, rubbing furiously at his
chafed wrists to try to restore the circulation to his
fingers. His eyes darted through the carnage as he
sought the mutie that had stolen his Browning Hi-
Power. Doc sat still, his head turning slowly from side
to side, as though he hadn't yet managed to take it all
in.

"That's it," Ryan said.

By the time everyone was untied, only three of the entire pack of stickies were still on this side of the dark river. Ryan went round with his flensing knife and opened up their carotid arteries.

And then there were none.

The children were sent packing, pointed in the southerly direction, assured that they were no longer in any danger. Most of them still seemed to be sunk in a trough of clinical shock, and they left without a word of thanks and without a backward glance.

Doc, Mildred and Dean recovered their blasters from the dead stickies, and the seven friends, safely reunited, set off through the forest to where they'd hidden the boat.

Chapter Thirty-Seven

"Simple choice, friends." Ryan sat in the stern of the crowded little boat, his hand on the tiller. "Jump straight away or stop off at Quindley and let Michael speak with Dorothy. Let's hear what anyone has to say."

They had made their way back to the concealed vessel without any trouble, pushing off and rowing a quarter mile out onto the still water of the lake, resting there, beyond the reach of any potential threat.

Michael put up a hand. "Can I go first, Ryan?"

"Course."

"The way I see it, we have to pass close by the ville anyway. We rescued their children, so Moses and the rest are going to be real glad to see us and hear the news."

Ryan nodded. "Probably right."

"Probably?"

"Not dealing with what you and I might think was a double-norm mind, Michael. Like watching a rabid fox and trying to decide who he's going to try and bite first. But I grant you that Quindley should be a touch grateful."

"So, we can go in?"

Ryan looked at the others. "Anyone have a problem with stopping off for a few minutes in Quindley?"

Dean raised a hand. "Why can't we row around the ville and then let Michael go in on his own? If he wants to see Dorothy another time that much."

"I don't mind," the teenager said.

"No." J.B. shook his head. He took off the fedora and wiped sweat from his temples. "We all go or none of us goes. Only safe way."

"Right." Ryan looked over his shoulder, toward the south and the ville. "We'll pull in on the lakeward side. Most of them'll be in the fields by now. Fair chance we can do this without shaking the trees."

IT WAS A PLEASANT and easy row back along the lake toward Quindley. Ryan steered them in a straight line, moving away from the shore.

"Nobody seen us yet," he said.

At a word, everyone shipped their oars, sliding them into the bottom of the boat. While it coasted gently forward, the ripple of water under the prow slowly diminished.

Dean was in the bow, ready to leap out and save it from jarring against the piling. He tied up the boat quickly.

The moments as they approached the ville from the water were the real danger. If there had been an ambush planned, that would have been the time and the place. Even with their superior firepower, they could have been blasted out of the lake by a dozen or so concealed rifles.

"Right. Triple red. Keep a skirmish line. Michael, where do you think Dorothy'll be now?"

"She said last night that it was her turn to be on duty in the temple, waiting on Moses. Guess I'll find her there."

"No. *We'll* find her there," Ryan said.

THE STREETS WERE DESERTED, so quiet that Ryan began to feel like they were walking into a trap. But the chances to coldcock them had already been there. Why wait?

He was out at point, with Krysty right behind him. The others were strung out, J.B. bringing up his usual rearguard position. The main gates were open, and they could see out along the causeway the neat allotments and tilled meadows. There was a scattering of the young people working there, but none of them noticed the intruders in their ville.

"Moses's place." Ryan held up a hand to stop them, looking all around. But there was still not a sniff of betrayal.

"Can I go first?" Michael asked. "I'd like to see her...sort of on my own. See if she still says she'll come... What she promised last night."

"What did she promise?" Mildred asked, but the young man turned away and ignored her question.

Ryan spit in the dirt. "We all go in together. J.B., you and Mildred wait out here and keep watch. Wouldn't want to find us trapped inside there."

"Sure."

"Let's go in."

It was cool as he pushed at the carved wooden door, feeling its ponderous weight as it swung silently open. The inner room was as luxurious and silent as ever, with torches blazing in iron sconces on the walls, their light dancing over the priceless old paintings that hung everywhere.

"I had not thought you would return."

The voice from behind the mirror was gentle and mildly amused, as though a bright little child had done something rather clever to entertain it.

"We set your babies free, Moses," Ryan said, looking at his own reflection in the mirror. "They're on their way back through the forest. Mebbe you should get Jehu to send a party out to bring them in."

"Perhaps. Perhaps not."

A maroon velvet curtain moved at the side of the large, dark mirror, and a hidden door opened and closed. Out came Jehu and Dorothy.

The blond youth had his hair loose. His deep blue eyes stared at Ryan. He was completely naked and his body was marked with crimson weals across his hairless chest, and down over his stomach and thighs.

Dorothy was partly dressed, but she, too, had whip marks across her bare breasts, and what looked like the jagged bites from sharp teeth disfigured her thighs. She held her head down and wouldn't look up at any of them. Not even Michael, who called to her.

"Dorothy! What the fuck's been happening?"

"Looks like Moses has been taking some sporting with his apostles," Ryan said, almost choking on his own bitter rage. "That why you keep them young and tender, Moses?"

"He's the lord, outlander," Dorothy said, trying to fasten a blouse across her nakedness, still not looking up.

"Some lord." Krysty glanced at Ryan. "We going to just leave this, lover?"

Moses laughed. "Such foolishness. All you oldies with your prim and prudish morality! Jehu!"

"Master?"

"Fetch the others and we will have a ceremony tonight that will long be spoken of, as we dispose of these interfering old, old outlanders. Go now."

"Yes, Master."

"Stay where you are, son," Doc said, the Le Mat pointing at the young man's chest.

"Do as I say, Jehu."

"Of course, Master."

Jehu turned, the golden down on his muscular buttocks gleaming in the light. Doc hesitated, unwilling to murder the naked young man by blowing him apart from behind. Jehu grabbed a torch and whirled it, so that flames streamed out, the fire hissing in the stillness.

"Mine," Ryan said.

The single bullet took Jehu below the breastbone, angling sideways and ripping out most of his lungs before tearing chunks of muscle from the pumping walls of his heart. His mouth opened in a gasp of shock and surprise, and his arms flew wide. The burning torch landed at the foot of a dusty tapestry, which immediately caught fire.

Jehu staggered a few clumsy steps, his eyes blank and blind, fingers clawing at the air. He slipped to his knees with blood frothing from his pale lips, dappling the wooden floor.

Dorothy looked up at the shot, blinking in horror. Michael ran the few steps to her side and put an arm around her. For a moment she resisted, trying to pull away, then she collapsed and started to weep.

"Good way to finish it," Krysty stated, not bothering to conceal her satisfaction.

"Put out the fire, children," Moses called, sounding amazingly unconcerned at the desperate threat to his home. The flames had reached the ceiling and were devouring slender beams, already lapping at some of the oil paintings.

"I have encountered varieties of evil and sickness in my long life," Doc said loud enough for the hidden godling to hear him. "But not, I think, anything to compare with the way you have corrupted and destroyed the innocents."

He leveled the gold-plated Le Mat and pulled the trigger. The single .65-caliber scattergun round shattered the ornate Gothic splendor of the mirror into ten thousand silvered shards of dark glass. As it collapsed into itself, it revealed the room beyond.

And it revealed Moses, lying on an antique sofa, its brocade material filthy and stained. He wore what looked like a bed sheet, which had once been virginal white and was now a disgusting mixture of different shades of dirt.

Moses was roughly four feet tall, and had to have weighed close to three hundred pounds. He had the soft, plump body of a child, but the seamed face and veiled eyes of an old man. His teeth as he smiled at the watchers were crooked and yellow, and his fingernails were grotesquely long, so jagged and distorted that they almost curled back on themselves.

"See my godhead," he giggled in that wonderful voice.

"See his boasted pomp and show," Doc shouted. "Your pleasure's faded, Moses. Reckoning time's here."

The fire was so hot that they all had to retreat toward the main entrance.

Moses sat up, the cloth falling away, revealing the folds and creases of his gross nakedness. "I have taken my sport where I found it," he said, smiling at them through the shimmering curtain of flames. "Founded this place and sucked it dry for so many, many years. Now I will pay for my sport. But it was so good, outlanders, so good!"

Moses disappeared behind the wall of fire, and they heard nothing more from him.

His temple had become an inferno.

"Nothing to keep us here," Ryan said, shouting to be heard above the noise of the fire. "Whole ville's likely to go."

Michael shepherded Dorothy out, his arm still tight around her. Dean followed, glancing back wonderingly at the cascade of multicolored fire that poured down the walls. Krysty and Doc followed, with Ryan last to leave the doomed building.

J.B. stood close by the door with Mildred, the Uzi in his hands. "You set the fire?" he asked Ryan. "Heard a couple of shots."

"Took out Jehu. He dropped the flaming torch and up it went. Doc blasted the mirror."

"Did you kill Moses?" Mildred asked.

"Tell you about it later." Ryan looked behind them. For a few moments there was no sign that the building was irredeemably ablaze. Then there was a whoosh of noise and heat, and part of the thatched roof exploded into smoky fire. Sparks and burning reeds were scattered over the roofs of the rest of the ville, most of which immediately caught fire.

Dorothy was sobbing noisily, her arms clasped around Michael. The rest of the young people of Quindley still hadn't noticed the fire, but it could only be a matter of seconds before they did and came running.

It was time to move on.

THE RAGING BLAZE, coupled with the death of their guru and leader, seemed to have totally destroyed the will of the young ones of the ville. Though they came dashing toward the column of smoke and flame, hesitating when they saw the heavily armed outlanders, not one of them made any attempt to stop Ryan and the others from leaving.

They parted like the Red Sea to let them pass along the causeway and out through the cultivated fields and orchards into the welcoming shadows of the forest around.

Dorothy paused at the fringe of the pines, dragging at Michael. "I can't leave like this," she said. "They need me at my home."

Mildred patted her on the shoulder. "Not really anything much left that looks like a home, girl."

The fire was unstoppable, leaping from wall to roof and back down to the next wall. One or two of the men and women were scooping up buckets of water from the lake, and throwing them at the ferocious wall of flame. But it was totally futile.

THEY REACHED the hidden redoubt without any further incident, Ryan leading them immediately through its deserted corridors and down into the mat-trans unit.

Dorothy shrank back as she saw the cold gleam of the light purple armaglass walls of the chamber.

"Be fine," Michael encouraged. "Trust me."

Chapter Thirty-Eight

It took the combined efforts of all of them to reassure the frightened young woman. Krysty stood behind her, stroking her long blond hair, trying to gentle her as though she were a terrified mare.

"Be all right. We've done it dozens and dozens of times," she said.

"But I can't leave my family and my brothers and all my sisters."

"You'll have me." Michael was also crying, great gobbets of tears running through the dirt on his cheeks. "And I need you, Dorothy."

There was no real hurry, but Ryan was beginning to lose patience with the tender scene. "Best get on with the jump," he said. "You and the girl can sort this out later, Michael. Right now I'd like to get away from here."

One by one they filed into the chamber, picking their places to sit down in a circle, backs against the walls. Michael led Dorothy, who seemed now to have recovered a little of her composure. Ryan waited, ready to close the armaglass door and trigger the mat-trans mechanism.

He was aware that all of them carried the scent of wood smoke clinging to their clothes.

"Everyone ready?" He looked around the circle.

Doc had been fumbling with the reloading of the Le Mat, assisted by J.B. Now he smiled up at Ryan, showing his wonderful set of gleaming teeth. "Ready as we'll ever be, my dear fellow. Shipshape and Bristol fashion."

J.B. simply nodded, allowing Mildred to take his hand. She also grinned at Ryan. "Ally ally oxen free," she said.

"Let's go, Dad." Dean sat with his knees drawn up to his chin, picking at a splinter in his thumb with the sharp point of his turquoise-hilted knife.

Krysty patted the space next to her. "Let's hope we have a better jump than the last time we tried."

"It'll be fine," Ryan said.

He looked last at Michael and Dorothy. "You two ready for this? It doesn't hurt, but it sort of scrambles your head and you kind of fall asleep for a few seconds. And you wake up somewhere else."

"And I'll be here for you." Michael looked unbelievably tense and worried, gripping the young woman by the wrist. "And you for me."

Dorothy said nothing. But she was trembling like an aspen in a hurricane, her teeth chattering, her eyes rolling in their sockets with fear.

Ryan closed the door and sat down by Krysty, laying the Steyr at his side, making himself comfortable. The wound in his neck gave a twinge of pain, and he touched it with the tip of a forefinger. The disks in the floor and ceiling were starting to glow, and the familiar mist was appearing.

He could hear a voice, a long way off, but he'd already closed his eye ready for the jump. It was a woman's, but Ryan didn't think that he recognized it.

The darkness was swimming around him.

"No... No... Can't..."

The voices merged.

Ryan reluctantly opened his eye again. Part of him saw what was happening, but a part of him was already slipping away on the jump.

Dorothy stood by the door, screaming, though she didn't seem to be making a sound.

Michael was on hands and knees, howling like a dog in pain, reaching out to her.

"No," Ryan said, struggling to move, but there was a massive weight settled across his limbs and he was paralyzed.

The door opened, and a vague figure stumbled through it—a woman, with hair like Kansas wheat.

"No."

Someone said it.

The shape disintegrated as it left the chamber, becoming transparent and without form.

The door closed again, and the blackness enclosed the gateway chamber and everyone inside it.

Chapter Thirty-Nine

The man astride the small black-and-white pony was lean and hard, with curling side whiskers.

He was reciting a monologue to himself, about the world being a stage and how everyone had to play a part. But that the fates had dealt him the hand of a lover, and that his girl had betrayed him, cheated him.

"But I'd rather carry on listenin' to those lies..."

The trail was narrow between the tall pines, and he'd heard talk at his previous night's lodgings of there being some big mutie critter in the woods. Half the trappers and hunters said it was a humpback grizzly sow. Others talked about a slewfoot cougar that already chilled a dozen settlers in that part of New England.

"They can bring down the curtain."

He reined in the pony and blew his nose on a torn cotton kerchief. Singing the old songs, best as he could recall them, of King Elvis always made Lonnie's eyes water. That was why he only ever gave voice when he was out on the trail, which was most of the time, selling his handmade blasters and rebuilds all across Deathlands.

His last trip had brought him the whole way from old Seattle in the west, into New Hampshire, alongside the great mirrored expanse of Shamplin Lake.

On previous trips, he'd been able to do some trading with the young folks at Quindley. They mostly used rifles and muskets. Lonnie generally didn't sell long guns. Too clumsy and too obvious. But the saddlebags that Lucifer carried were filled with the actions and locks for all blasters. Quindley—the ville that stuck out into the cold water like a diseased thumb, with that freak baron. Morgyn? Mordred?

"Moses," Lonnie said.

But the word of the gaudy where he'd stayed had told of some major disaster in the ville along the shore, a big fire that had filled the air for a hundred miles around with the heavy scent of wood smoke.

It had happened, so the scar-faced slut had told him, as they lay together on the unmade bed, about a week ago. The survivors had stumbled away as though they were in a daze, abandoning the place to nature.

"Lot starved," the woman had said. "Wandered around like they'd had their brains picked clean by crows. Didn't know what to do with themselves."

Lonnie figured that he was probably wasting his time by calling at the ruins, but you never knew. He'd once sold three-quarters of his stock to a white-haired granny near Duquesne, Missouri. She ran a traveling gaudy and needed some extra protection. Thrown in five freebies with her girls as part of the price.

He was nearing the end of his sweeping run from west to east. It had been an easy ride, with no serious

problems, apart from an earth slip in the Dakotas that
had delayed him for a couple of rainy days.

There was a sister who lived to the north east, on the
Lantic, with gray shores and thousands of hideous
spike-shelled crabs for company. New Haven. Lonnie
generally called in on her when he was in the area.

Now he was close to where Quindley had been.

He heeled Lucifer along, wary that the snaggle-
toothed brute might swing its head around to try to
take a chunk out of his thigh. It wouldn't have been
the first time.

Lonnie broke into his half-remembered version of
King Elvis's "Return to Sender," puzzling over the
line about her dress unsewn, as he always did.

Now he could smell the smoke, charred wood, still
hanging below the branches of the damp pines. Ahead
of him, as the trail opened out with a view north along
the lake, he saw that the stories had been right.

Quindley was gone.

A few blackened piles stuck up from the water, like
the remnants of trees when a forest fire's passed by.
The fields around still looked more or less the same,
though. As Lonnie drew closer, he could see that rank
weeds were already beginning to spring in among the
neat rows of crops.

He reined in Lucifer, right at the edge of the lake,
sighing to himself.

"Waste of time," he said. "Mission aborted."

He had a slight cold and reached inside his pocket
for a kerchief, his fingers encountering a folded piece

of paper. Lonnie knew what it was and took it out. He carefully opened the written message from those two cold-eyes up near Seattle. It was to be given to a one-eyed man traveling with a redhead, and a black woman and an old guy and some others that Lonnie couldn't quite remember.

The older of the pair had been a real triple-jack bastard. Eyes like obsidian chips washed in melt-water. He carried a battered Armalite like he knew how to use it. Other one was smaller. He'd done the writing, Lonnie recalled. They threatened him with what would happen if he didn't do his best to deliver the message.

"Well, I fucking tried. And enough is fucking enough."

He dropped the crumpled bit of paper into the lake and kicked Lucifer on again, northeast.

As it hit the water, the note unfolded like a moth leaving its cocoon, and for a few moments the words were legible before it became sodden and sank from view.

Success. Will stay round Seattle for three months. Come quick. Abe.

The sound of the pony's hooves faded into the distance.

Though the smell of wood smoke still lingered.

Join Mack Bolan's latest mission in

THE TERROR TRILOGY

Beginning in June 1994, Gold Eagle brings you another action-packed three-book in-line continuity, the Terror Trilogy. Featured are THE EXECUTIONER, ABLE TEAM and PHOENIX FORCE as they battle neo-Nazis and Arab terrorists to prevent war in the Middle East.

Be sure to catch all the action of this gripping trilogy, starting in June and continuing through to August.

Available at your favorite retail outlet, or order your copy now:

Book I:	JUNE	FIRE BURST (THE EXECUTIONER #186)	$3.50 U.S. $3.99 CAN.	☐
Book II:	JULY	CLEANSING FLAME (THE EXECUTIONER #187)	$3.50 U.S. $3.99 CAN.	☐
Book III:	AUGUST	INFERNO (352-page MACK BOLAN)	$4.99 U.S. $5.50 CAN.	☐

Total amount	$_____
Plus 75¢ postage ($1.00 in Canada)	$_____
Canadian residents add applicable federal and provincial taxes	
Total payable	$_____

To order, please send this form, along with your name, address, zip or postal code, and a check or money order for the total above, payable to Gold Eagle Books, to:

In the U.S.
Gold Eagle Books
3010 Walden Ave.
P. O. Box 9077
Buffalo, NY 14269-9077

In Canada
Gold Eagle Books
P. O. Box 636
Fort Erie, Ontario
L2A 5X3

TT94-2RR

A biochemical weapons conspiracy puts
America in the hot seat. Don't miss

STONY MAN™ 11

TARGET AMERICA

The Army of National Independence—ANI—is a
radical separatist group using terrorist activities
to "free" a captive Puerto Rico. When they plan a
master strike that will send shock waves through
the world, STONY MAN races to break the chain
of destruction.

Bolan targets a drug kingpin with a taste for
blood in

DON PENDLETON's

MACK BOLAN®

HELLGROUND

In the savage battlegrounds of the Tex-Mex netherworld,
Bolan and his allies orchestrate a search-and-destroy
mission—shaking up the hellgrounds to bring the enemy to
the front line.

GOLD
EAGLE ®

SB36